MIRRORS

MIRRORS

Naguib Mahfouz

illustrated by
Seif Wanli

translated by
Roger Allen

Zeitouna
The American University in Cairo Press

We are indebted to Christine Rousillon for reproductions of Seif Wanli's artwork.

First published in Egypt in 1999 by
The American University in Cairo Press
113 Kasr el Aini Street
Cairo, Egypt
http://aucpress.com

Dar el Kutub No. 14352/99
ISBN 977 424 560 1

Printed in Lebanon

NAGUIB MAHFOUZ was born in 1911 in the crowded Cairo district of Gamaliya, an area on which he has drawn heavily for the setting of many of his novels. At the age of twelve he moved with his family to the new suburb of Abbasiya. He worked in various government ministries until his retirement in 1971. He began writing at the age of seventeen, and his first novel, set in ancient Egypt, was published in 1939. Since then he has written over thirty novels and more than a hundred short stories, many of which have been made into successful films. He has also written many original screenplays, and he continues to write a weekly column in the Cairo daily al-Ahram. Today Naguib Mahfouz lives in the Cairo suburb of Agouza with his wife and two daughters.

The Swedish Academy of Letters in awarding Naguib Mahfouz the 1988 Nobel Prize for literature noted that Mahfouz "through works rich in nuance—now clear-sightedly realistic, now evocatively ambiguous—has formed an Arabic narrative art that applies to all mankind."

SEIF WANLI was born in 1906 in Alexandria to an old, aristocratic family. Although he first worked as a functionary in the Customs archives, art was his passion and, along with his younger brother Adham, he trained at the studio of the Italian artist Atorino Becchi in Alexandria. The brothers, inseparable until Adham's death in 1959, set up their own studio in downtown Alexandria, and when the Alexandria School of Fine Arts was established in 1957, they were appointed as teachers. When the Ministry of Culture was formed in 1959, they were awarded a life-time sabbatical.

Seif Wanli's prolific output is estimated at 3,000 oil paintings and more than 80,000 sketches; he also designed sets for theater and opera productions. He held or participated in at least twenty-one exhibits in Egypt and abroad. He died in 1979 in Stockholm, just before the start of a series of exhibitions of his work in Scandinavia.

ROGER ALLEN was born in England in 1942 and educated at Oxford University, where he obtained his doctorate in 1968 with a dissertation on the the early modern Egyptian writer Muhamad al-Muwaylihi, published as *A Period of Time*.

Since emigrating to the United States, he has specialized in Arabic literature and Arabic language pedagogy. His published works include *The Arabic Novel*, an anthology of critical writings *Modern Arabic Literature*, *The Arabic Literary Heritage*, and over forty articles on Arabic literature. In addition to *Mirrors*, he has translated Mahfouz's *Autumn Quail* (1985), Jabra Ibrahim Jabra *The Ship* (1985, with Adnan Haydar), Abdel Rahman Munif's *Endings* (1988), and a collection of short stories by Mahfouz and Yusuf Idris.

He currently teaches at the University of Pennsylvania. He is organist and choirmaster of St. Mary's Episcopal Church, Hamilton Village, Philadelphia.

Translator's Introduction

It was during a conversation with Naguib Mahfouz in the summer of 1971 that I first became acquainted with *Mirrors* (*al-Maraya*). We were discussing the series of lengthy, cyclical, and often cryptic stories that he had been writing for some time as a response to the events of the June War of 1967 and its aftermath. At the time I was in the process of producing an anthology of his short stories in English (published in 1973 as *God's World*), and I recollect observing to Mahfouz that the subtleties of language that were so much a part of these stories were extremely difficult to translate into another language. I inquired as to whether at some point he was planning to "emerge" from this cryptic mode and seek some other type of fictional discourse through which to express his artistry.

It was just then that he informed me that he was working on a completely new type of work, something that would attempt to move his writing in a different direction, a series of vignettes of Egyptian characters that would be published very soon. Mahfouz warned me to look for them in what was for him an unusual venue: the Egyptian television magazine. The reason, he noted with pleasure, was that a friend of his, the renowned artist, Seif Wanli, had done a portrait of each of the characters in his new work. The magazine had agreed to publish the portraits along with the text in serialized form.

My English translation of *al-Maraya* appeared in 1977; the economics of translated texts being what they are, the text appeared without the accompanying illustrations, but then so did the published Arabic version (1972). How great therefore has been my pleasure when some twenty years later I have been invited to republish my translation in reworked form with the portraits included. I can only hope that this edition of *Mirrors*, a realization of Mahfouz's original hopes and wishes—albeit in an English translation—will give him pleasure.

When the series of vignettes was first published, Mahfouz was quoted in the magazine as saying that he did not regard the work as a novel. At the time it certainly represented something new in his output, but developments in Arabic novel writing since the early 1970s, not to mention Mahfouz's own continuing experiments in fiction writing, have given us a longer temporal perspective through which to look back at this interesting work. What is clear is that it is certainly a product of its age, a process of surveying the past and even perhaps of "looking back in anger." Those with an intimate familiarity with the cultural life of Egypt during the course of this century have even been able (and willing) to identify certain of the vignettes in *Mirrors* as portraits of specific people. One might suggest that the often close proximity of fiction to biography (and indeed autobiography), something to which a number of literary critics have had occasion to refer, is very much a feature of this work of Mahfouz.

The narrator of *Mirrors* is born in the al-Husayniya quarter of Cairo, moves with his family to al-Abbasiya, is passionately fond of soccer, studies philosophy at university, works as a civil servant, and is also a writer. Since this "resume" is identical to that of Mahfouz himself, the suggestion of a close connection between author and narrator seems reasonable.

The narrator arranges his vignettes in Arabic alphabetical order, thus scrambling any other kind of presentational logic (such as that of time or gender). For example, the very last vignette is in fact chronologically the earliest: Yusriya Bashir, a girl with whom the seven-year-old narrator falls in love. Prominent participants in the narrator's life, and particularly his intellectual life, occur in many vignettes before they are finally presented in their own right. A figure like Professor Mahir Abd al-Karim, for example, is already a well-known and respected figure before the inexorable logic of the alphabet reaches the letter *mim*; the sculduggery of Eid Mansour is likewise familiar through several nefarious episodes before he is presented to the reader. What such a narrative arrangement indicates, of course, is something that we have come to expect from Mahfouz: the careful craftsmanship and organizational ability of a writer who plans his compositions down to the last detail—a long recognized feature of his masterly trio of novels, *The Trilogy*.

Mirrors serves as a fictional interpretation of the recent history of Egypt, its people, its politics, and its society. Political parties and movements and the politicians who lead them are all analyzed; major events like the Second World War and the conflicts with Israel impinge upon the lives of the narrator's friends and enemies alike; the consequences of wider educational opportunities are visited upon numerous households, and no more so than in the fraught realm of family authority and the emergence of women into the public domain. The narrator's acquaintances from childhood, schooldays, and civil service career take him from the lofty heights of intellectual salons to the seemy squalor of brothels and drug dens; from the dreams of youth and nationalistic ideals to the sobering realities of post-revolutionary society and clashing economic and political values. The technique that Mahfouz adopts in *Mirrors* allows his narrator to take a broad sweep (and, sometimes, a swipe) at Egyptian society; the vignettes are indeed 'mirrors,' reflectors of a process of rapid change that has radically transformed Mahfouz's homeland and its people, and not always to its advantage, during the course of this century.

Roger Allen
May 1999

MIRRORS

Ibrahim Aql

I first heard of Doctor Ibrahim Aql in an article by Ustaz Salim Gabr. I forget what it was about, but it described Aql as an outstanding intellect who could have revolutionized our culture if a cheap slander had not squashed him before he was established.

A scoundrel, claiming Aql defamed Islam in his doctoral thesis at the Sorbonne, had launched an attack in the press. The Doctor was accused of heresy, adopting missionary and orientalist views to obtain his degree at the expense of his religion and people—'they' demanded his expulsion from the university.

The Doctor was shaken. He was not a fighter, one to challenge public opinion, and he needed his post. He denied the accusation, pleading with people—among them his friend and colleague Doctor Mahir Abd al-Karim—to extinguish the fire and placate its instigators.

When I went to university in 1930, he was an associate professor. The ordeal had taught him to focus on teaching and withdraw from intellectual life. His spirit was encrusted in numb tedium and his classes—despite good health and the maturity of over forty years—were steeped in generalities. He soon became the laughing-stock of our circle.

Once during a lecture, I asked him, "Why haven't you written any books, Doctor?"

"Do you believe the world needs more books?" he replied in his thundering voice. Shaking his large head, he said contemptuously, "If we spread books over the earth, they would cover it twice, but if we counted the books with fresh thought, they wouldn't pave an alley!"

I often saw him at Doctor Mahir Abd al-Karim's salon at the mansion in al-Munira. How many thinkers did I meet in that salon? I still visit—time and place have changed, but memories of those meetings are lucidly recalled until today. Aql's imposing frame, natural dignity, and intelligent blue eyes blended well with the sumptuous classic room.

Unnaturally, the conversation turned to politics—normally avoided in respect for our host and his dislike of emotional outbursts. Family and upbringing had raised him in the National Party; all his students were Wafd youth. But the upheaval Ismail Sidqi had caused was hard to ignore. Students talked until Aql said, "Our constitution is a gain, but also a trap."

The young men prepared for battle.

"The national struggle has strayed from its goal. We're floundering in party squabbles. Every upheaval brings terrible repercussions to relationships and values; day by day, the legacy we inherited from the 1919 revolution crumbles," he continued.

"The people's legacy cannot crumble!" retorted a member of our young group.

Our professor, Mahir Abd al-Karim, smiled. "Our people are like the mythical beast that wakes up for a few days then sleeps for generations," he said in his gentle whispering voice.

"We'll never be harmed if we hold to the highest ideals," replied Aql.

As his blue eyes searched each face, he repeated rhythmically, "The highest ideals, the highest ideals..." He repeated it so often in his lectures on ethics that our friend Aglan Thabit, nicknamed him 'Doctor Highest Ideals.'

"I hope you don't consider ideals a product of religious faith," he added, in consideration perhaps of the agnostic wave sweeping through the college. "Regard them as the source of faith."

A shaykh from al-Azhar said, "Every day politics try us with a new ordeal."

"The highest ideals," Aql insisted, "if only they stayed with us."

"My dear Doctor," said Ustaz Salim Gabr, sinking his plump body in a soft armchair, "ethics are simply a matter of social relations. We must change society."

"Have you read Bergson's book on the origin of ethics and religion?" Aql asked.

"I read Bergson like a romantic poem," replied Salim Gabr derisively.

"You're dreaming of a revolution like the one in Russia fourteen years ago. But it shows serious complications daily," Mahir Abd al-Karim said.

"We only learn about Russia from what we read in Western books and newspapers," replied Salim Gabr angrily.

A truce reigned while we sipped our cups of cinnamon, savoring the hazelnuts, almonds, and walnuts inside. A young man broke it. "The only solution is to eliminate minority parties hankering for power."

"That's a weak interpretation of class struggle," Gabr commented.

"The prime minister claims he's seeking independence," said Aql. "Allow him to try."

"Even if it forces us to accept a treaty like the February 28th Declaration?"

"Genuine independence is in the highest ideals and Banque Misr," the Doctor retorted.

I was often troubled by the contradiction in political awareness between the popular classes and the intelligentsia. There, it's a burning emotion rapidly leading to bloodshed; here, it's rhetorical debates that blunt spirits and thwart hopes. I thought about it again as we made our way back from al-Munira.

We exchanged opinions feverishly.

"There must be a revolution!"

"Is a strike enough to start one?"

"They say that's how the 1919 revolution started."

"How did it start?"

"So near, yet so far."

That summer, I met Aql with his family—his wife and two boys—at Casino Anfushi in Alexandria. I would sit there after my morning swim with coffee and newspapers, watching rehearsals for the evening show despite my dislike for European singing. He introduced me to his wife, an inspector at the Ministry of Education. I was delighted to see how he adored his sons and his playfulness, although his wife disapproved of his pampering. He won me over with his paternal feelings. I had little respect for his refusal to write and disinterest in his work, but I admired his appearance, humor, and philosophical sarcasm.

"Do you usually swim here at Anfushi?" he asked me.

"The waves are much gentler than at Shatbi," I replied.

"Alexandria will be completely changed when the corniche is completed."

I agreed. "But you hate Ismail Sidqi," he said with a smile.

"A human being cannot survive on the corniche," I replied, suppressing the bitterness aroused by that name.

"There's nothing like politics to pervert human thought," he laughed. Pointing to his wife, he said, "Her mother, my mother-in-law, is in the Wafd women's committee."

I gave her a grateful look in respect for her mother.

At the beginning of the new academic year, Aql was appointed to an important university post, sacrificing all his highest ideals.

Cries against the Palace rang throughout the Valley. *The Times* said demonstrators in Aswan called Mustafa al-Nahhas president of the republic. A country divided—a minority supported the king and a hostile majority hardly concealed its true enmity. Then, there was Doctor Ibrahim Aql publishing an article in *al-Ahram*, asking for loyalty to the crown and praising the royal family's efforts for the nation's renaissance. It was a crisis—ethics sank to the abyss, men lost all dignity. The innocent watched the farce red-eyed but their ranks were not entirely free of corruption. A time of earthquakes and volcanoes; shattered dreams resurrected the twin demons, opportunism and crime. An era of martyrs from all classes.

The Doctor strutted in our midst, affecting steadiness and courage, his challenging glares hiding defeat and guilt. We greeted him with the respect his position demanded, but regarded him with disdain. Yes, a scornful disdain. Not hatred or the desire to kill that we felt toward many politicians—his character did not arouse it: with his humour and acrobatic capers, he appeared a clown or an imposter, not a scoundrel, blood-spiller, or enemy of the people.

It was the last day of classes. We were leaving for a short break before final exams. He invited us to meet in his office. We were ten men, the graduating class in the department he chaired in addition to his important post.

He sat us in front of his desk. Silently, his blue eyes traveled across our faces. Then he smiled, and with his contemptuous shake of the head said, "We're about to separate, and farewells require a word. I've often guessed your feelings, but it's not as you imagine."

Finally after a long silence, he was broaching the subject. But we had to maintain decorum and caution; there was an oral and written exam for every subject and the department council could adjust final results regardless of grades. This put us at his mercy, with no appeal.

"I found some people making speeches and others working. I chose to join the workers. Ultimately, we're all Egyptians."

We remained silent.

Then, one bravely responded, "One standing for independence and the constitution is better than one who builds a corniche and sheds blood."

His name was Ishaq Boqtor, the only rich boy among us. After exams, he was leaving for his plantation on the outskirts of Cairo to grow flowers.

Aql didn't get angry. Smiling, he said sadly, "There's nothing like politics to corrupt the mind." Then in a hopeful tone added, "Truth, worship truth! Nothing in existence is more valuable or noble. Worship it and reject anything that might corrupt it."

Silently, we remembered the oral exam and the department council.

"I shan't argue with Boqtor," he continued. "I shan't utter a word of politics. I've invited you to look together at the future."

Relief spread like light; we were rescued from the perils of politics, and he was opening the door to the future that we'd been watching with gloom since cabinet decrees froze appointments and promotions indefinitely. What hope was left for us?

"This is a time of crisis, a crisis devastating the entire world, not just your country as some people claim. What are you going to do?" he asked.

He paused for a moment. "You won't find a position as quickly as you would like, or start a family in the near future. Some may have better luck than others."

He received our sullen glances with a smile.

"Even the few opportunities open to doctors, engineers, and lawyers won't come your way. But something important remains for you, a jewel no one is used to wearing yet."

Our eyes shone with interest.

"Ahead of you lies the path of truth and values!"

Each recalled his family, his beloved, the dreams built on the expected job.

"Rid yourselves of extravagant worldly ambition and be content with what the world provides. But don't put a limit to the yearning for truth."

Had he called us in to torture and humiliate us?

"Sitting under a tree on a clear day is better than owning an estate."

You say that, you who sold all values for . . .

"The wisdom of life is the most valuable prize of our numbered days."

Barely past the college gates, we burst into laughter from the violent contrariety and from despair, competing in foul descriptions—the bastard, the clown, the impostor.

After graduation, he disappeared from my mind except on rare occasions. He avoided Doctor Mahir Abd al-Karim's salon after his leap to high office, afraid of attack by extremists, only meeting his old friend in private.

Thirteen years passed without seeing him until a tragic event occurred. He lost both sons in the 1947 cholera epidemic. I was shocked when I heard, remembering Casino Anfushi as he played with the two boys. I went to Giza for the funeral. It was a moving procession. The man walked behind the two coffins, his tall figure a portrait of blind despair. I don't think he recognized me when I offered my condolences. He looked at nobody and noticed nothing. But when Doctor Mahir Abd al-Karim went to offer his condolences, he blinked to stifle a tear despite the determined front. At midnight, Abd al-Karim invited me to ride back in his car.

"God be with him," he whispered. "It's an unbearable calamity."

I agreed, deeply moved.

"Something he said worried me."

I asked what it was.

"He said death was beautiful but maligned; without it, life would have no value!"

He was silent. "God be with him," he said at last.

Once again, Doctor Ibrahim Aql disappeared from sight, although his tragedy lingered with me for a long time. At al-Munira salon, I followed his news in the years after the incident. He was often seen in al-Husayn mosque, sitting for hours in front of the mausoleum; he had become a dervish, surrendering unconditionally to faith. His behavior prompted debate about faith in general, faith by upbringing, faith by conviction, faith by disaster, philosophers' faith, old people's faith. Mahir Abd al-Karim refuted any argument in which he detected the slightest attack on his old friend.

In 1950, Aql reached retirement age and devoted himself to dervish life. One day in 1953, I met him at Bab al-Akhdar in al-Husayn. His dignified appearance, enhanced by grey hair, drew me. I approached, holding out my hand. He shook my hand, not appearing to know me. When I reminded him, he cried out, "You! How are you? What are you doing?"

When I replied, he said, "Please forgive me, I don't read."

We walked to his car at al-Azhar. "What's happening in the world?" he asked.

I recounted what I thought worth mentioning, alluding to the new revolution.

Ibrahim Aql

"Up-down, death-resurrection, civilian-soldier, let the world carry on. I'm preparing for another journey," he said.

Again I lost track of him until I read his obituary in 1957. I heard his nephew had found a manuscript, a beautiful, undated translation of Baudelaire's *Fleurs du mal*. The nephew was his only heir (his wife had died the year before), and allowed its publication. His name in Arabic literature is now linked with Baudelaire and *Fleurs du mal*.

There is no disagreement among Doctor Ibrahim Aql's students—with no exception, they considered him a clown. But an important thinker like Ustaz Salim Gabr considered him the victim of a corrupt society, although he could not forgive him his defeatism.

One day my professor, Mahir Abd al-Karim, told me in his whispering voice, "You are all unfair to Ibrahim Aql."

I said nothing out of respect for his feelings toward his friend.

"He was a rare intellect. He dazzled us with his intelligence at the Sorbonne."

"But no one benefited."

He ignored my comment. "He was the only one in Egypt with a philosophical mind, a comprehensive vision. He wasn't a writer, but certainly a gifted talker, a Socrates who singled out his closest friends with the cream of his thoughts, offering what came easy to other people."

"Maybe he needs a new Plato to redeem him," I suggested.

But he had vanished. All that remains is a tragedy and a rare translation of *Fleurs du mal*.

Ahmad Qadri

His name recalls honey pastries, the cinema, and an unforgettable event. A relative from the provinces who stayed with us in Cairo during festivals, his visits were spent playing in the quiet streets of Abbasiya, amid fields and gardens. I was nine or ten, he was five years older, an only child and a devil. One day he suggested a trip; as proof of its innocence, he asked my father if I could go along. So off I went, in my short suit.

On our way to the tram stop, he said, "I'll buy you biscuits on one condition."

"What?" I asked.

"You memorize what I'll tell you and repeat it when we return."

I asked what I had to memorize.

"We went to the Olympia and saw a Charlie Chaplin movie."

I made the promise and received the biscuits. We got off the tram at a street I'd never seen before. He led me from one alley to another through an exciting, new world, finally dragging me to the entrance of a strange-looking house. Three women sat in the hallway, colorfully made-up and dressed, unconcerned about revealing parts of their bodies above the leg and below the neck. One rose, and he seated me in her place.

"Don't move until I return," he said.

He asked the two other women to watch me and went inside with his friend. I fixed my gaze on the floor tiles, sensing that a serious offense was being committed nearby. One sang, "The day the bite bit me"; the other, leaning toward me asked, "Do you have half a riyal?"

"No," I replied.

"How much have you got?"

"A shilling," I answered, polite but fearful.

"Fine. Would you like to see something nice you've never seen before?"

"But he said not to move."

"It'll only take a minute in that room."

"No!"

"Don't be afraid. What are you afraid of?"

She led me by the hand to the room and closed the door.

"Give me the shilling," she said.

I surrendered it with no hesitation.

"Take off your suit," she said, caressing me with her eyes.

"No!" I said in a panic.

She took off her dress. I saw a naked woman for the first time. The aggressive, brazen gesture filled me with fear, the stolen look even more. Trembling, I retreated toward the door, opened it, and rushed outside, her rippling laughter a snake in pursuit. The other woman received me with a cackle, pointing to the chair for me to sit down. But I stood in the hallway, not wanting to touch or be touched. Loafers outside the house stared in amazement, spitting dirty jokes in my face. The agony I suffered until Ahmad returned.

"Why are you standing there like a sentry?" he asked.

I clung to his arm as he led me outside. The journey home wasn't as simple—we encountered a huge demonstration, so he made his way through side alleys with bullets whizzing through the air. Sitting in the tram, he cross-examined me.

"Where were we, champ?" he asked.

"At the Olympia cinema," I answered with a dry mouth.

"What did we see?"

"Charlie Chaplin."

"Great. Why are you looking so glum?"

"Nothing."

"Did the two women bother you?"

"No."

He watched me anxiously. "What is it?" he asked.

Sadness overcame me and I almost burst into tears.

"What is it?"

"Nothing," I answered bitterly. "Dora isn't as beautiful as I had imagined!"

"Dora? Who's Dora?"

"Dan's sweetheart."

"Who's Dan?"

"The adventure hero. Don't you read *Boys' Magazine*?"

"*Boys!* What are you hallucinating about? We're not going home until you're normal."

He didn't know how I adored Dora, imagining her body was pure diamond.

But generally, his days in Cairo were among my happiest. He taught me football, boxing, and weightlifting, and entertained me with his comic anecdotes. He copied Charlie Chaplin's walk, sang famous skits, and imitated the village headman and the chief watchman. Then his parents moved to Abdin and his visits became less frequent. He stumbled in secondary school and joined the police academy. After graduation, his high grades posted him in Cairo. Busy with his new life, he no longer visited and we became almost strangers. During his first assignment in Cairo, I saw him once by accident, sneaking out of Isam Bey's mansion after an amorous adventure. His parents died and I almost forgot him, until events during and after the Second World War summoned him back, when he was appointed to the political police.

Ahmad Qadri was not the Ahmad Qadri I had known—now a terrifying figure surrounded by horror stories, a torture whip in the hands of tyrants inflaming nation and nationalists. I listened, amazed. How could the saucy prankster change into a satanic torturer? How could he mutilate young patriots, flog them, extinguish cigarettes on their eyelids, pull out their nails?

I followed discussions about him by Reda Hamada, Salim Gabr, and other intellectuals and patriots. As the revolution has not taken place, they said, at least form secret societies for political assassination to defend the unarmed people. Then there was an assassination attempt against him in front of Club Muhammad Ali, but he miraculously escaped from the fugitive criminals, as they were then called.

After the 1952 revolution, he was investigated but was only sent into retirement. For me, he dissolved into oblivion until the autumn of 1967 when I was called to the Anglo-American Hospital. He'd had a heart attack. I didn't recognize him; he was over sixty, reminding me of his father in his last days.

"I'm sorry to bother you," he said.

I tried to comfort him.

"You're the only person I have left," he whispered, "To bury me if it's over."

I encouraged him again. His doctor assured me that he was no longer in danger and his recovery depended entirely on him.

"I have more than one ailment," he said, in response to the news.

Behind his remark, I detected alcohol, women, and gambling.

"Avoid excitement to prevent another attack."

"It's coming for sure," he said scornfully.

In vain, I searched his invalid face for signs of the savage beast who had spread terror, or the young, lovable clown. A sense of duty was all I felt toward him. I learned he was living in a small apartment in Zamalek. Of course, he had never married. His only friends were a group of old Greeks addicted to the horse tracks.

"It seems that I'm finished—just like them."

I understood whom he meant. The bitterness of the June war still hung on our lips. I realized the rancor he'd felt since his retirement, but I resisted discussing his resentment aggravated by illness, as it challenged my own feelings. In any case, his black prophecy about his life and that of the revolution did not come to pass.

Three weeks later, he left the hospital and visited me at home to express gratitude. He seemed reasonably well, flirting with memories of the past generation. I felt an irresistible urge to dig into his strange past. Opportunity presented itself.

"I couldn't believe what they said about you."

He completely ignored my remark; I thought I'd made a mistake. Then, as if stating an unrelated fact, he said, "Sometimes a car knocks down a pedestrian and kills him." Defying his

Ahmad Qadri

doctor's advice, he lit a cigarette. "It's wrong to blame the car. It's either the driver's fault, or the road, or the manufacturer, or even the victim. The car is blameless.

"Why didn't we torture people during Wafd regimes? There are two types of government: one, brought by the people, gives man his right to human dignity, even at the state's expense; the other, brought by the state, reveres the state at the expense of the individual.

"We didn't torture people the way you think. We tortured like you fill out a form or write a report to the minister—only a job with its scale of excellence in performing public duties. A zealot amongst us executing his work with secret or obvious relish is no different from one of your people being excessively devoted to his job to hide a failing or a persistent misery."

As he was talking, his gaze fell on a photograph on the table.

"Isn't that Doctor Ibrahim Aql?" he asked.

"Yes, with some old friends and professors. Did you know Doctor Aql?"

"No, but circumstances required me to track his photographs in the press."

"What circumstances?"

He reflected for long time. "Do you recall the death of his sons?"

"Certainly," I replied. "They died in the cholera epidemic."

He laughed. "It seems, God knows, that cholera wasn't the culprit."

"What are you saying?" I asked in bewilderment.

"My chief—God rest his soul—whispered to me that they had been murdered."

"Murdered?!"

"Control yourself. It's past history now."

"But how were they murdered? Who did it?"

"Nothing is confirmed, believe me, nothing. Even my chief heard only a whisper about the love affair of an important woman and one of the king's men and murder in a secluded house on the desert road."

"Tell me more."

"I know no more. Nothing is confirmed. Believe me, nothing is confirmed."

He insisted and I saw no reason to disbelieve him. I told Doctor Mahir Abd al-Karim the story. His quiet face showed more amazement than I'd ever seen before.

"I refuse to believe the late Ibrahim Aql kept a secret from me," he said.

"Maybe the palace connection forced his silence," I suggested.

He shook his head in doubt and disbelief. I decided to forget the matter.

Ahmad Qadri disappeared from my life again. I'd spot him at the Phoenix Café with a group of old foreigners. Early in 1970, I saw him walking across Talaat Harb Square; from the sagging cheeks, I surmised he'd had his teeth removed, but his health looked better than expected.

Amani Muhammad

We met over the telephone. She began with the usual greetings. Could she ask me about debates she was following on television? She appeared interested in the arts, was searching for references, and was keen to meet me.

I invited her to my office, but she said she abhorred office atmosphere and suggested a rendezvous outdoors. We met at the Pyramids rest-house toward the end of spring in 1965.

I expected a student or recent graduate. The woman who approached was a mature forty, with a voluptuous body and light-colored eyes, straddling the thin line between a liberated, modern woman and the flashy prostitute. I had the provocative sensation that art would not be our only companion. Swayed by neither acceptance nor rejection, I surrendered to circumstance. We sat in the garden overlooking the city; our glances reflecting coy anticipation.

"Excuse my forwardness." Her tongue turned the *r* into *gh*. "I had to meet you."

I assured her that I was delighted.

"The vacuum in my life can only be filled by art. Fortunately, I have the aptitude."

"Madam is in the civil service?"

"No, I don't even have a college degree, only the secondary certificate. But I'm an excellent reader and I've written several radio plays."

"I wasn't fortunate enough to hear them."

"That's not surprising."

She showered me with compliments and I thanked her for her appreciation.

"I need some historical references to continue writing."

"A simple request."

"I want to write about famous women of the East who played great roles in love."

"Exciting topics."

She smiled gently. "I hope you'll collaborate?"

"I'm very busy with other projects," excusing myself without hesitation.

She ignored my objection, looking at the treetops below. "We'll work in gardens. Unless…" she paused, "you honor my house."

The new foray succeeded in overcoming my hesitancy.

"Your house?"

"I haven't explained my social situation. I'm divorced. I live with my old aunt. My son and daughter live with their father."

"But your aunt?"

"There's nothing wrong with work."

Staring into the distance, she said, "A working atmosphere could be arranged."

"But…"

"But?"

"Frankly, it seems a pity that a woman like you could not enjoy her marital life."

"It wasn't successful, not a single day," she said angrily.

"Incredible."

"He taught me to hate him, and I didn't love him before."

"Then why did you agree to marry him?"

"I was forced. I was sixteen, utterly immature, and my opinion carried no weight."

"Many happy marriages start that way."

"He's a selfish, brutal monster."

As she didn't go into details, my interest waned. It seemed an old memory that had receded forever. Now, even art retreated to the margin. With an unexpected move, her soft hand crept and rested on mine.

Amani Muhammad

"I need a man I can trust."

Despite the exaggerations and lies, I felt sorry for her.

"Are you that interested in art?" I teased.

"Art and life!" she replied with a laugh.

Art and history were forgotten as we wandered around the desert by the Pyramids. Our attention focused on contemporary reality; reality of the house to be precise, her aunt in particular—her old age, her heavy sleeping, her diminished senses.

"Unless you'd rather meet in another house."

Sinking into the conspiracy, desire flooded me. "Let's do it today."

"Let me prepare the atmosphere," she said with guileless delight.

When we met in the room, my senses were intoxicated with scents of perfume and alcohol wafting on waves of a pale red light, returning to distant memories I never expected to retrieve. I found myself once more fettered in silk, succumbing to drunken desire with no real love. Amani was diligent in her care, finding a port after stumbling in darkness, an unlimited yearning for love and tenderness, fired by a heart deprived of love, motherhood, and confidence.

She confided her secrets during our successive meetings.

"My financial situation is good, I have nothing to complain about . . .

"God forgive my father and have mercy on him! He was the cause . . .

"Young men these days can't be trusted. God protect my daughter . . ."

My heightened sense of responsibility expanded even more whenever I remembered that our life together had no common foundation, that it couldn't continue indefinitely, that affection and sex were not enough to secure our one-winged family.

That same year, either the end of summer or beginning of fall, Ustaz Abduh al-Basyuni came to my office. I recognized him immediately, despite the incredible change. I greeted him warmly, as though it was not a quarter of a century since we had last met. What could have changed him so much? He was only a few years older than me.

"What are you doing now?" I asked.

He ignored my question. "You're probably wondering why I'm calling on you after such a long time."

"I hope it's something good, old friend."

"I'm here as Amani Muhammad's husband," he said quietly.

A second passed before it exploded. Consciousness faded, place and time vanished. All I could see was Abduh al-Basyuni's dark, round face, a statue placed in front of my desk before time began. I said nothing and had no idea what showed on my face.

Shaking his head gently, he said tamely, "Don't be alarmed." Some sort of smile. "You know nothing about it." Then reassuringly, "I didn't come for vengeance."

I found my chair, my room—my world about to disintegrate.

"Fortunately, my days in Paris were not wasted!" I heard him say.

"Perhaps it's another woman," I said, surrendering to fate.

"I mean the woman you were with yesterday."

"But she's divorced!"

"She's my wife, I'm her husband!"

"What a disaster," I muttered.

"I didn't come out of anger or vengeance."

"But I'm dying of remorse and sadness."

"It's not your fault, you're just her latest catch."

"What?"

"Time and again. Each time I intervene to save her, save my children's future."

"What a life! Why do you put up with it?"

"No escape. I refuse to divorce her, even though she's asked."

"Why?"

"She's the mother of my adolescent son and daughter. Divorce would mean her prostitution!"

"She might remarry."

"She's no longer fit for that."

"A difficult and tragic situation."

"That's why I'm determined to get her back and save what can be saved. Fortunately, my life in Paris wasn't wasted."

"Life is horrible if it's corrupt," I said sadly.

"Yes. Maybe she talked about me. I too have things to say, but I'm determined to salvage as much as possible."

"I never imagined I'd be facing you in such a situation," I said apologetically.

This time, he disregarded my regrets. He lit a cigarette, smoking pensively, a broken pyramid. "Do you remember my past life?"

I recalled our days at university, his leaving to study in Paris at his expense and returning two or three years later empty-handed, his election to parliament, the prestige of family, the party, and a seat in parliament. "Of course I remember."

"In the July revolution, I saw no contradiction between its ideas and my free thinking."

"That's reasonable."

"I worked sincerely with it, but I was falsely accused of a party conspiracy. I was arrested and my property confiscated."

Shocked, I found nothing to say.

"I found myself a beggar in the street."

"But your wife has money."

"She's poorer than poverty," he said with a laugh. "She has a rich aunt who has another heir. She probably lied about that too."

For a while we said nothing.

"Is that what ruined your marriage?" I asked.

"No. I worked earnestly, devoting all my time to translation and adaptation. Old classmates working in the press helped me publish. But the ordeal changed my personality. There was constant conflict between us."

"But these are circumstances that can be healed."

"It had already gone bad."

"A terrible loss. Can nothing be done?"

"She's a fool, not worth keeping if it weren't for the children."

26

He was silent for a moment. "I hit her once. I was insanely angry. She's never forgiven me."

"I'm sorry about all the bad luck you've had."

"I'm asking you to break off your relationship with her ..."

"Of course!" I replied, hardly believing my easy escape.

"... and try to convince her to return home."

"I'll do everything I can."

"Enough talk about this ugly subject," he said with a decisive wave.

I let out a deep breath. He reminisced about the old days, about Doctor Ibrahim Aql and our professor, Mahir Abd al-Karim. "I haven't been to his salon since I left for Paris but I've visited him several times. I'm thinking of returning to the salon meetings." Shaking his head, he said, "He lost his land to the agricultural reform, sold al-Munira mansion, and bought a villa in Heliopolis, where his salon meets now."

"I know. I've been attending the salon regularly since 1930."

Congratulating me on my success, he said, "I'm striving to keep my dignity."

"You're a fine example."

"I've got numerous translation projects, books, plays, screenplays."

"Excellent."

"But I need contracts with cultural organizations."

"Submit what you've got."

He was silent for a moment. "I was told submitting was not enough."

"What do you mean?" I asked, feigning ignorance.

"They say you need money, but I haven't got any."

"Don't believe everything they say."

"Or write favorable critiques of prominent figures in the organizations."

"I said don't believe everything you hear!"

"I'm prepared to swear that any mule among them is greater than Ahmad Shawqi. But competition among fawning critics has left no room for an unknown like myself. I'm not in radio or television, so I can't invite them to shows to present their work. I can only follow the natural path, which, as you know, is unnatural."

He laughed for the first time. I felt safer. I tried to dispel his doubts and encourage him. He rose, reminding me of his request. I said I would exert superhuman effort.

I kept my promise. I had barely broached the subject when Amani, eyes blazing with anger, shouted, "The monster got to you!" I reminded her of her duty. "You don't know him!"

"I've known him for a long time. He's not as bad as you imagine. He's better than many."

"No, you don't know him."

I persisted.

"Enough, " she screamed. "Don't abuse me."

"How could you hide your marital situation, knowing he wanted you back?"

"He is not at all jealous."

"He loves his children."

"He loves himself!"

"The issue ..."

"The issue is that you don't love me. Love in this world died a long time ago," she said, drying her eyes. "You never once told me you loved me, but I don't blame you."

"You deserve to be loved, but I'm not worthy of it."

"Talk, talk, talk."

"You'll find what's more important at home."

I left feeling liberated, safe, and full of remorse. Then I was overwhelmed by profound sadness, pity for my old friend Abduh al-Basyuni and his wife Amani Muhammad. I expected him to call, but he didn't. I wanted to call her, but there was no opportunity. I met him occasionally, sensing that he was progressing along his charted course with determination.

In 1968 or '69, walking in Ramses Street in front of the Telephone Building, I saw Amani coming toward me. Instinctively, I held out my hand. She shook it with embarrassment. I felt I'd made a mistake. "I hope you're well," I said, apologizing in a whisper.

"God be praised," she replied, moving on.

She was overweight and composed. Her embarrassment convinced me that she suffered the responsibility of a conservative woman who had been forced by circumstance to shake the hand of a 'strange' man.

Anwar al-Halawani

His name recalls an entire world. Bait al-Qadi Square between al-Gamaliya, Khan Gaafar, and al-Nahhasin, walnut trees laden with sparrows' nests, the old police station, in the center the water trough for donkeys and mules, the kiosk for the public water tap. This was my childhood playground.

I looked out for Anwar al-Halawani as he left his house next to ours and when he came home. An unusual young man, among the first in the neighborhood to receive an education, a student in law school. Perhaps I admired his incredibly tall fez, his thick, twisted mustache, his handsome suit. He walked with a poise beyond his years. I imitated him when I could.

I remember drinking sherbet to celebrate his success in the Baccalaureate. His mother gave it to me herself; she was from the provinces—I imitated her accent.

Events were secretly unfolding around me as I played under the walnut trees.

I awoke one morning to screams from our neighbors' house. Our house was in chaos. I scrutinized the agitated men and women. I discovered that our young neighbor, Anwar al-Halawani, had been killed by a bullet during a demonstration, shot by an English soldier. For the first time, I learned the meaning of the word 'kill' in real life, not in a folk tale; and I heard, for the first time, about the 'bullet,' my first aural connection with this product of civilization. There was another new word, 'demonstration,' which needed much explanation. It may also have been the first time I heard of a new species of human beings in my young life, 'the English.'

Conversation flew around the house and the square echoed the words; others were added, 'revolution,' 'the people,' 'Saad Zaghloul.' Words poured until I drowned. I let out an insistent barrage of questions. What did 'killed' mean? Where had Anwar gone? What was waiting for him in the world he had gone to? Who was 'the English'? Why had he killed him? What was a 'revolution'? 'Saad Zaghloul'? Soon, the frenzied events spilled into the square outside.

I squatted by the window, my bulging eyes staring at the surging mass of people in suits and gallabiyas, even women in carriages and carts, carrying flags and shouting. I heard the

Anwar al-Halawani

whine of bullets—yes, for the first time—coming from trucks and horseback. I saw the English with their tall helmets, their bristling mustaches, and alien faces. I saw dozens of corpses scattered around the square, and I saw human blood staining clothes and the earth. And I heard voices crying, "Long live the nation!" and "We die, long live Saad!"

Badr al-Ziyadi

A classmate in secondary school, fat and spirited, Badr al-Ziyadi loved food, play, girls, and the nation. His father was the school prefect; we knew him two years before he was accused of insulting the royal persona, was tried, found guilty, and sentenced to six months in prison. The sentence was suspended, but he was fired from his job. Badr boasted of his father's courage and nationalism and we played along; insulting the royal persona was not a bad level in the struggle, assuring its owner a place among fighters for the cause.

Badr was an ordinary student in class, even indolent. His real glory was in the schoolyard, a magnet attracting students from every class. As the center, his talents ignited, reciting patriotic poetry, recounting funny anecdotes, or initiating strange challenges. Once he asked about the best place to make love. Each made some reply, he shook his head contemptuously until our ideas were exhausted.

"The cemetery!" he answered.

Astonished, we laughed at what we thought a joke.

"During festivals, people sleep in cemetery yards, men and women. Women usually far outnumber men. In the dark, there are untold opportunities!"

"But the occasion isn't conducive to love."

"Love doesn't select occasions. It's always appropriate!" he said with conviction, recounting how he'd pounced upon a servant girl with his aunt's corpse laid out for burial and women wailing in the courtyard.

He had an inexhaustible supply of strange stories. But his brilliance shone on the soccer field. He was the striker of the school team, famed for speed and deftness—his impelling force and contradictory corpulence aroused gales of laughter—an amazing skill at swerving, dribbling, and drawing the ball to his feet, a feint that toppled opponents to the ground, and powerful shots. He was preparing to play for clubs and dreamed of the Olympics. Mr. Simpson, chief trainer of the Ministry of Education, liked him. After a school competition, he advised him to lose weight; Badr responded by consuming an entire cake and a large number of sandwiches and pastries at the tea party that followed the game.

One morning, Badr al-Ziyadi bellowed—with all others—for the 1923 constitution and the fall of dictatorship. King Fuad had dissolved the Nahhas cabinet and appointed Muhammad Mahmoud prime minister, who suspended the constitution for three years. Schools went on strike, ours included. But the police surrounded us and we could not leave. To arm for battle, we tore down trees, windows, and doors, invaded the school cafeteria, and commandeered trays, pots, ladles, knives, and forks. Our angry cries attacked every quarter, even the king's. Then the soldiers attacked, beating us with long sticks, while English constables fired in the air to scare us. It was an uneven fight; none escaped unscathed, many were wounded, a student and a janitor were killed. The student was Badr al-Ziyadi, felled by a blow on the back of his head.

Badr al-Ziyadi

Next day, the entire school decided to attend his funeral, but the police had cordoned off Qasr al-Aini hospital, full of dead students. The corpses, guarded by the police, were carried straight to the cemeteries. Individually, we went to our old school prefect's house to pay our respects.

The old man is still alive, probably about seventy-five. I see him, when I visit Abbasiya, at a small café near his house, broken by age and poverty, hardly the image of the freedom fighter who had faced life with courage, losing his job and his son. From his secluded spot, he watches cars rush by, ferrying successful members of society, proud of life's prosperity, never touched by its fire. What goes through his mind as he observes this strange, impetuous flow? Or have old age and time inured him to all but the transitory moment?

As for Badr, a photograph of the soccer team still holds us together—he in the middle, the ball between his feet, eyeing the camera, happy and self-confident.

Bilal Abduh al-Basyuni

It was a chance meeting at Gad Abu al-Ela's villa, early in 1970, and although we never became friends—in fact we never met again—he left an indelible mark.

When I arrived at the villa that evening, there was nobody in the reception hall except Ustaz Gad Abu al-Ela, my old classmate Abduh al-Basyuni, and a handsome young man who resembled him. He introduced him as "My son, Doctor Bilal."

I remembered the son and daughter, topic of a sad conversation between Abduh and myself, then between me and Amani Muhammad, five years earlier.

I joined the aimless conversation as I felt my old guilt return. Then Abduh, pointing to his son, said, "The doctor's thinking of emigrating."

Intrigued, I looked at the young man with curiosity. 'Emigration' was a new term in our vocabulary that provoked our wonder—us, the older generation. Here was one of its knights, an inviting opportunity.

"He's being considered for a study mission to the United States, but he plans to emigrate," Abduh continued.

"And what's your opinion?" asked Gad Abu al-Ela.

"What's the value of my opinion or my wishes?" Abduh replied with a laugh.

"Out of interest."

"I don't agree."

"And Amani Hanem?"

My confusion mounted at the mention of her name. I learned, for the first time, that she had returned to her family, and was surprised to hear Gad refer to her with familiarity.

"She welcomes the idea, thinking she can visit the United States whenever she wishes."

Our host laughed. "There's a brilliant future awaiting you here."

"I'm looking for a healthy scientific environment," Bilal replied.

"The emigration of his friend, Doctor Yusri, has gone to his head," Abduh said. "But Yusri is anomalous and not a good example. He was a successful doctor, but his anger never subsided, a constant bitter criticism brewing with hatred for the country and everyone in it. He seized the opportunity of a scholarship and stayed there."

"And succeeded brilliantly, both in his work and his research," interjected Bilal.

Bilal Abduh al-Basyuni

"He was also successful here, so what's the point of emigrating?"

"The scientific environment, father!" Bilal replied. "Look at the deputy of my hospital department. He earned his doctorate with high honors; awaiting recognition, he was attacked and denied the position he deserved. So he emigrated. When he presented his research in the United States, he received several offers from universities and hospitals."

He spoke with exasperation, almost anger.

"There may be faults, but not enough to force successful people to emigrate," I commented.

"The entire situation is lamentable," he insisted without changing his tone.

"It's good that you feel that way, but who else will bring reform?"

"I won't bother with that."

"But your homeland's value can't be denied or ignored."

"My first homeland is science!" He hesitated as if taking himself to account. "The homeland ... socialism ... Arab nationalism, what can I say? Don't think I'm frivolous, but what's left after the 5th of June?"

"The years that have passed since the debacle are enough to make it a lesson."

"No use, it's a generation that only accepts what's in its head," Abduh said.

"That's all right," said Gad Abu al-Ela. "But one shouldn't forget one's homeland."

"Science is our only savior," Bilal replied. "Not nationalism or socialism—science alone can face the problems impeding humanity's progress. Nationalism, socialism, and capitalism create problems every day with their selfish shortsightedness. Then they devise solutions that in the end exacerbate the problems."

"What keeps you from research and science in your country?" I asked.

"A primitive research environment, a stifling atmosphere for thought, justice, recognition. So I think of emigration. I'll be more useful to my country in America. Science is for mankind—except for the science of war and destruction, science is for mankind," he replied.

"What about his sister?" Gad asked Abduh.

"She gets her degree in pharmacy at the end of the year and is even keener to emigrate."

Gad laughed. "What about the man of her dreams? Hasn't she thought of that?"

"What we consider a problem is a game to them."

"Art has yet to provide a model of this generation," said Gad. "I wish I could be the first!"

"It's there in flesh and blood on the stage of our miserable life," I commented.

"You dream of escape as the ship faces the storm," Abduh told his son.

I felt Abduh was not serious in his opposition; he could hardly hide his admiration for his son. Bilal shrugged his shoulders disdainfully. He represented a new stand in patriotism, that old trust that had exhausted our generation.

"The truth is I dream of a scientific institution that would rule the world for the world's own good," he said with a laugh that reminded me of his mother.

"And what about values?" I asked. "Science doesn't deal with them, and man needs them no less than he needs facts."

He looked at me helplessly. "It shouldn't mean a desperate adherence to worn-out values," he replied. "You cling to them, fearing the adventure of seeking others. Science doesn't provide values, but it sets an example for courage. When classical determinism flagged, science adapted itself to probability, proceeding without looking back."

34

"It's absurd to argue with people when there is no common language," said Gad.

I shook with anger. "You want to emigrate to civilization instead of developing one at home."

"Man is originally a migrating creature," he retorted furiously. "Homeland is the place that affords you happiness and prosperity. That's why only the elite emigrate. Backward people ..."

"Backward people should be eliminated!" I concluded.

His anger subsided. "If population growth continues at this rate, there'll be no means to feed it. It may be in civilization's interest to eliminate entire species," he replied with a laugh.

"Enough!" his father cried.

"How happy Israel would be with you!" said Gad.

Angry again, he said, "I challenge Israel to do to us what we've done to ourselves!"

I passed the night recalling his words. I concluded there was no survival for the human race except by eliminating the forces that exploit man's thought to enslave him, contriving conflicts that consume his potential—a first step to gather the world in a union based on wisdom and science, to re-educate the human being as a citizen of one world that provides him with security, and unleashes his creative powers to fulfill himself, shape his values, and proceed with courage toward the heart of truth concealed in this dazzling, mysterious universe. That, or a future that made me grateful for being of a generation about to complete its journey through this extraordinary life, circling—with its good and evil—the brink of a volcano.

I met Abduh al-Basyuni some months later at Doctor Mahir Abd al-Karim's salon, and immediately asked about his son. He told me he had left.

"His sister will be joining him soon. I often feel a painful twinge, but my time has taught me to submit to fate," he confessed. "I don't deny that I'm convinced of their decision. Why didn't our sterile education prepare us for emigration?!"

"Science is a world language, our profession deals with local riddles," I replied.

I told him of the thoughts that had overcome me after listening to his son. He laughed.

"We old men have simple needs. My daily happiness is complete with a cup of coffee with milk and two biscuits."

Soraya Raafat

I met her as I started my civil service career, in 1935. She came to visit her uncle at the ministry. He introduced us. She was a student at the Higher Institute for Education, about to become a teacher, moderately beautiful with an exquisite body and eyes that shone with intelligence and personality.

Ustaz Abbas Fawzi, chief of the secretariat, noticed my admiration. One day after she had left, he said as he signed documents, "Time you settled down and started a family."

I realized I'd been caught. "Do you think so?" I asked.

"Your net salary is eight pounds. That's enough to marry two women."

I laughed. "Do you favor marriage to a working woman?" voicing our generation's concerns.

"Just as one can find a deviant housewife, there's an honorable working woman," he replied.

In his twisted way, he was warning me, but her sexual attraction was beyond cautioning. I prepared to move closer. As a student, she enjoyed a degree of freedom—that should have aroused my doubts, and the look in her hot, fearless eyes, their disquieting responsiveness, should have held me back. Instead it seduced me. I waited for her outside, motivated by good intentions and the promise of adventure. Shaking her hand, I walked by her side. "Can we sit together for a while?"

"Why?" she asked pretending surprise.

"To get better acquainted."

"Not today."

She wanted to say goodbye. "But you didn't decide on another day," I insisted.

She slowed down as though lost. "Monday morning then, at ten in the zoo."

Although her acceptance fulfilled my heart's desire, it confirmed my misgivings about her freedom—adventure gained over good intentions. We met in front of the zoo, strolled and chatted. I declared my admiration. The conversation drifted to details of our lives and our future. My suppressed emotions were torturing me, and I was confident she would respond as she had to the rendezvous. The first opportunity we were alone, I tried to kiss her. She avoided me. She must have read in my eyes a discomforting meaning. "What's wrong with you?" she demanded angrily.

I pointed to a thicket. "Let's sit there."

She stiffened. "It seems you've misjudged me."

"No!" A cold wave swept over me.

"Or I misjudged you."

"Neither, please," I replied with a warmth fueled by regret.

The storm subsided. We sat and resumed our comfortable conversation, parting with the promise of another meeting. I was strongly attracted; even marriage seemed appealing. At our following meeting, she gave me an ivory pen. The gift enchanted me.

"I hesitated for a long time, I thought of not seeing you," she said.

"Why?" I asked in alarm.

"I'm afraid of disappointment."

I pressed her hand affectionately. "You know full well that I love you," I said.

We continued to meet, considering the practical steps that normally precede an engagement. Her older, married sister accompanied her once and we discussed whether she would keep her job or devote herself to her home.

"How will the home function properly if you keep your job?" I asked innocently.

"Then what was the use of her studies and hard work?" her sister asked.

"With my salary, we can do without her job, and she can devote her effort to our home."

"For all your education, you're still old-fashioned," her sister laughed.

Soraya interrupted, "No one has asked my opinion."

"You're participating with your silence," I said.

"No!"

"What's your opinion, my dear?"

"I'll work at what I was trained for until the end."

On our last meeting before the date set to bring the families together, she was unusually nervous and distracted.

Soraya Raafat

"Something's bothering you," I said.

"Yes!" she replied simply.

"What is it?"

"It can't be delayed any longer, I was wrong to wait until now. We must be honest."

"Haven't we been honest already?"

"No! Love demands the truth."

"Of course," I said anxiously.

"Then I must tell you," she said closing her eyes.

She confessed tearfully that someone had deceived her at a tender age. I didn't understand, it sounded like a joke. Fatalism swept me—everything was tolerable, I was nothing—before I slid down an abyss of paralyzed submission, into a winter ditch covered with ashes.

Peering through her tearful lashes, she whispered in despair, "Didn't I tell you?"

"Huh?" I muttered like an imbecile.

"You don't love me."

"Me! Don't say that."

"You'll never forgive me."

"Who was it?" I asked, disentangling myself from her flow of thought.

"It doesn't matter."

"Who was it?" I asked emphatically.

"A bastard!"

"But who?"

"Don't torture me!" She picked up her handbag. "Goodbye."

"Don't leave," I said mechanically.

Standing up, she said, "You've given me your answer without saying a word."

"But I didn't speak!"

"I refuse anything less than complete trust."

Finding comfort in her leaving, I said, "I need a few minutes to think."

"Goodbye," she said again, walking away proudly.

The problem seemed a Gordian knot. My love revealed a violent passion, nothing more, as though my old love for Safaa had exhausted my capacity for real love. In those days, such a slip was unforgivable. We were battling dense layers from a distant past—whenever a layer was erased, another surfaced, demanding pain and effort to vanquish it. We had to cover five or six centuries in a quarter of a century.

Sad and disappointed, I had no doubt that Soraya had left my life forever. She no longer came to visit her uncle. I didn't see her until 1939, at the Agriculture and Industry Exhibition that was held just before the outbreak of the Second World War. I was walking around with Eid Mansour, my childhood friend. Suddenly there was Soraya with her older sister and her children. She didn't see me, but I saw her, so did my friend. He whispered, "Look at that girl."

"What about her?" I asked.

"She's from Sakakini, she's my aunt's neighbor."

He laughed coarsely, making a rude gesture with his hand. I realized he was the one who had assaulted her.

"You bastard!" I said with a disgust he could not comprehend.

He laughed. "Even so, I heard she's engaged and getting married this year!"

Many years passed without seeing or hearing of Soraya, until I visited Salim Gabr after the defeat of 1967. I found her with others in his study. Those days, I sought out gatherings of colleagues and friends as a burning man looks for anything—cover, dirt, water—to put out the fire on his clothes. I found Gad Abu al-Ela, Reda Hamada, Azmi Shaker, Kamil Ramzi, and a dignified woman in her fifties that I recognized as Soraya Raafat. Waving a general greeting, I sat down. My hand didn't touch hers, but I felt she had remembered me. The conversation revolved around the defeat: defining its dimensions, analyzing the causes, foretelling its future …

As they left, Soraya shook Salim's hand, "Our appointment is for Monday," she said.

He confirmed the date as he accompanied her to the door. "She came to invite me to a patriotic debate at the Teachers' Union," he said.

"Who is she?" I asked, feigning ignorance.

"Doctora Soraya Raafat, a senior education inspector. Her husband is an eminent scholar, devoted to his research. She's a major figure in our feminist movement, worthy of the respect of her sex and her country. Its rare to find a woman of her personality, learning, and morality."

I remembered Eid Mansour; my weakness and defeat; childhood friends like Khalil Zaki and Sayyid Shouayr; Ahmad Qadri, the relative I hadn't seen in ages. I remembered dozens with whom I'd knocked around in the course of life. Their faces emerged amid a cloud of putrid dust, like insects emerging after the collapse of a derelict house.

Gad Abu al-Ela

He exists and does not exist. We met in 1960. He telephoned at my office requesting a meeting. I welcomed him, impressed by his fame in the literary world. He had written five novels, maybe more. Publicity for his novels filled the front pages, and publication was followed by streams of adulatory reviews; they had been translated into French and English, the foreign reviews translated and published in our press. Such success could only come to a serious and important writer. I made several attempts to read his works, but could not finish one. I felt no need to read attentively, amazed to find no talent, not even of local interest. All his works were made into radio shows and films; none succeeded, yet they forged their way ahead with the pride of rare jewels.

When he came to visit, I found him pleasant and polite, a suave talker who quickly made you feel like an old friend with no room for formality. He announced his desire to befriend me and invited me to his literary salon in his elegant home in Dokki. I've been a frequent visitor since, meeting him alone or among colleagues. Abduh al-Basyuni may have been the last to join us, some two years after our unforgettable meeting.

He revealed his history at my first visit. Pointing to a photograph in a gilded frame, he said, "My father—God rest his soul—was an antique dealer in Khan al-Khalili. If matters had followed their natural course, I'd be only a dealer and be spared the split personality."

I asked what he meant by split personality.

"Early on, I sensed the gift of talent. I pressed my father until he agreed to send me to France after secondary school. I didn't believe in structured study. I joined an institute to learn French, then directed my energy to the real sources of art, the museums, theaters, concert halls, and books. I was forced to end my study three years later when my father died. As the eldest son, I returned to manage the store." He talked of being divided between commerce and literature, of his difficult path to fulfilling his talent by using every spare moment of his scarce time.

His words and conversations over the years did not inspire my confidence. He was cheerful, average in intelligence, close to superficial, with a thin veneer of culture. This and my earlier readings of his novels, inclined me to believe the gossip in intellectual circles. It was said that his three years in France were spent fooling around. They testified to a skill in business that earned him a huge fortune, which continues to grow. All could see that he was a lover of art and, perhaps even more, of fame, but alas, he had no talent. He succumbed to a path fraught with mishaps, insisting on being a litterateur and supplementing the lack of talent with money. He wrote his experiences then showed them to an intimate circle of writers and critics. Upon their advice, he rewrote the work—sometimes whole chapters were written for him. Then it went to the language experts—lavishly rewarded, of course—for polish and corrections. The handsome edition, printed at his expense, emerged from the printshop looking—as some have declared—like a bride. His attention then went to the critics as reviews filled the literary pages. And he spent double that on translation. Thus he imposed himself on the literary world. In the same fashion, he conquered radio, television, and cinema, not concerned to make a penny, spending more if necessary. He disdains the mercantile class, his source of wealth and power, where he is a respected star, and plants himself satanically in the cultural community that rejects him and where he is a despised stranger.

Once as we talked about him, I asked Doctor Zuhayr Kamil, "What pleasure does he derive from his wasted effort, when he's the first to know his falseness?"

"You're wrong. He might believe himself," he replied.

"I doubt it."

"Maybe he believes his experience—which he thinks is the foundation of his work—is everything. Structure, style, and craft are secondary and insignificant, the work of hired slaves."

"There's no end to human arrogance," said Reda Hamada in support.

"Falseness in life is the secret that makes man's inner self a rare truth; it hides from him although it's obvious to all," laughed Zuhayr. "I now believe that people are bastards with no ethics. It would be better for them to admit it and build their communal life on that admission. The new ethical issue becomes how to maintain public welfare and human happiness in a society of bastards and scum."

Abduh al-Basyuni appeared late in Abu al-Ela's salon, in 1968 or even later. I hadn't seen him since our terrible meeting. Gad has found a valuable catch, I thought.

We shook hands warmly, like the old school days, as if the sin had never been. I suppressed a powerful desire to ask about his wife, whether she had returned to him. He made no mention.

"The caravan continues, difficulties are overcome. My son Bilal is in his final year of medicine. He's a promising genius. His sister is no less intelligent: she's at the pharmaceutical college. Soon, I'll reach financial and emotional stability."

I congratulated him. "It seems you met Gad Abu al-Ela only recently?"

"Two years ago," he whispered. "I've only come to his salon a few times and you weren't here. I've written most of his radio and television series."

We laughed.

Gad Abu al-Ela

"Until now, I haven't been able to sell one serial that carries my name."

Aglan Thabit visited me when Ustaz Gad Abu al-Ela was awarded the State Prize. "Have they no fear of God?" he laughed sarcastically. As we chatted, Abduh al-Basyuni was mentioned. "You probably didn't know his wife was Gad's mistress."

A tremor ran through me that Aglan neither noticed nor suspected.

"Fear God yourself," I said.

"Believe me, I'm a specialist in this sort of news. Abduh al-Basyuni knows it too. He caught them in a villa by the Pyramids. He was satisfied with breaking up the affair and accepting delivery of his wife. A close friendship between husband and former lover ensued."

"When was that?" I asked, trying hard to control myself.

"A few years ago; three, four, maybe five. What a phony!"

"Abduh al-Basyuni?"

"No, he's a miserable ass. I mean the great prize winner."

"Yes."

"It's incredible how his heroes are models of honesty, generosity, and virtue!"

"Yes."

"A curse on all of us until Judgment Day!" he laughed.

Gaafar Khalil

His memory recalls Abbasiya, our neighborhood in the twenties—quietness, open fields, and lush gardens. To the east were fortress-like mansions and almost deserted streets enveloped in dignified silence. To the west, single houses, with small back gardens—enlivened by a vine, a guava tree, sage, roses, carnation plots—and surrounded by fields; at their edge, a waterwheel turned by thickets of henna trees, the soil scented with mountain crest and tomatoes, a few palm trees scattered around. Beyond the house fences extended a forest of prickly pear bushes. Nothing but the rumbling tram car penetrated the neighborhood's daytime silence, and at night only the watchman's cry echoed in its corners. Nightfall wrapped it in pitch darkness relieved by radiant lanterns dangling from the front doors.

The day we moved from the old neighborhood, while porters hauled furniture inside the new home, youngsters close to my age gathered in the street to scout. I came out and found Gaafar Khalil, Surour Abd al-Baqi, Sayyid Shouayr, Eid Mansour, Reda Hamada, Khalil Zaki, and Shaarawi al-Fahham in front of me.

We exchanged glances, until Khalil Zaki asked, "Will you play with us?"

I hesitated. Surour Abd al-Baqi asked, "Where are you from?"

"Al-Husayn," I replied, prompted by my good manners.

"Do you play soccer?" asked Gaafar Khalil.

"No."

"Learn. When do you start elementary school?"

"After vacation."

"We'll all start at the same time."

"Did you see any demonstrations on the way here?" Reda Hamada asked.

"We came through al-Husayniya. All the shops and cafés were closed in full strike."

Gaafar Khalil

"Did you meet any English?"

"Just one patrol. Do you see them around here?"

Gaafar Khalil laughed and gestured. "Their barracks are over there, in the heart of Abbasiya. You'll see them wherever you go."

"Did you finish pre-school?" Surour asked.

"I was there for two years and at the Koranic school for two years before that."

"There are no Koranic schools here."

I said nothing, watching uneasily, but our friendship had started, and has not been interrupted, except by two deaths. Gaafar Khalil was my classmate through elementary and secondary school and college. He was light-spirited and humorous, outstanding in both work and play. He invited me to watch a soccer game at al-Ahli Club. When I inquired about expenses, he replied, "Not a millieme."

We went on foot in gallabiyas and sandals, through al-Dahir, Faggala, Station Square, Abbas, Khedive Ismail Square, and across Qasr al-Nil bridge until we reached the club. The group climbed up a tall tree, taking their seats on the branches; I could only do the same. I watched my first soccer game, and I saw players who have not left me: Husayn Higazi and Marei. I saw the English play—I had assumed they only killed—and was amazed to watch Ali al-Husni knocking them to the ground without a bloody battle ensuing. I was pleased and happy, beginning a passionate love for a new hobby. I believed the English could be beaten, if only on the Ahli field. But we were late getting home and I paid dearly.

I joined their club, Lion Heart, and we played soccer games among the prickly pears. I competed with Gaafar and even Eid Mansour, who imagined himself a future professional.

Gaafar Khalil had a fine voice: he sang the songs of Sayyid Darwish, Munira al-Mahdiya, and Abd al-Latif al-Banna. In time, he wrote *zagal* poetry; he even turned film scenes into *zagal* shows and directed and performed them in the prickly pear forest. I never knew him to have a love affair, although I caught him once teaching a Jewish girl from the neighborhood to ride a bicycle. As we grew closer, I learned that he was truly poor; probably the poorest of the group. His father, despite his lengthy service, had remained a minor official. Yet Gaafar was fun-loving and commanding. His many interests in sports and art did not include politics—patriotism, as it was known then—and he maintained this passivity through university and after graduation.

I told him one day, "It's amazing that you're not interested in what's smoldering in us."

"Patriotism has its men. I'm not one—still I wish them success."

"But every citizen is its man."

"I find my happiness among artists."

In secondary school, with his forward nature, he frequented the musicians' guild and attended their free concerts and the *zagal* gatherings at the Khedivial Café. Through the late Kamal Selim, he found his way to cinema, playing extras in films, writing film treatments while still at university, then co-writing a screenplay after graduation in 1934. He was appointed to teach English; in his school, he was known for sports and the drama club. He bewitched people with his engaging personality.

"Civil service is just a step, I know my goal," he told me.

It was hard to know his goal. Was he *zagal* poet, actor, singer, or screenplay writer?

"What's your goal, O king of goals?"

"Cinema."

"Cinema?"

"Yes. It's the league of all arts, the world of magic, luxury, and beauty. I'll have a field day with acting, writing, and singing." He laughed. "My appearance is acceptable. Don't judge me by my past; poverty didn't provide enough food. Judge with your eyes when my body profits from the meat I was deprived of unfairly."

Between his graduation and the Second World War, he progressed steadily in his film career. He adapted four stories, wrote six screenplays, played supporting roles in ten films, and wrote dozens of songs. His finances improved considerably. He was loyal to his poor family, moving them to a new building on the main street. He lived with them, but kept a private apartment on Champollion Street for his work—or rather, work and pleasure—and preserved old relationships with his neighborhood and friends.

One year after the war, he was selected for a scholarship to the United States, unexpectedly made possible by a friend in the art world on good terms with the minister of education. During his absence, his letters never ceased: he was preparing a doctorate on art in Arab society and intended to study screenwriting in Los Angeles; others said he earned good money writing for magazines, that he was trying his luck at writing for radio, that he would return with a fair amount of American dollars.

He returned to Egypt in 1950. I visited him the following day at the family home where now only the mother lived. We embraced warmly. I found many of his artist friends and all our childhood friends, except Shaarawi al-Fahham who had been killed in a raid during the war. He was asked whether he would keep his old job or resign to concentrate on his art. "I'll stay on until I've met the time requirement of the scholarship, which is five years," he replied.

"American life is strange and great. The American has qualities that should not be underestimated, but I was revolted and depressed after the Hiroshima bomb. It seems they are becoming unusually interested in the Middle East—we should take that into account." Enthusiastically he added, "I have ideas to develop the film industry in Egypt."

Gaiety overtook the gathering and the room filled with laughter, especially after we were joined by the late Shaykh Zakariya Ahmad. I left that evening after Gaafar had asked me to meet him Friday morning in his Champollion flat.

Next morning, I read his obituary in *al-Ahram*. Yes, his obituary. As he left the house at eight that evening, his foot slipped on a banana skin. He lost his balance and fell, hitting his head against the pavement. He died seconds later, in front of the entrance to the building.

Hanan Mustafa

A voice called. I turned around; a woman in her sixties looked at me with smiling blue eyes. I searched her face, then remembrance rushed like a waft of scented flowers.

"Hanan!" I shouted.

"Yes, Hanan. How are you?" she replied with what seemed like gratitude.

We shook hands warmly. "I remembered you easily, you haven't changed much. I was afraid you wouldn't remember me but it seems I haven't changed hopelessly. What brings you to Gleem in May? Do you live here in Alexandria?"

"No, I've come to rent an apartment for the summer. What about you?"

"The same. Are you alone?"

"Yes."

"So am I."

We inquired about each other's family, learned who was gone and who remained. I told her about my life.

"I have have four married daughters. I've been a grandmother for some time. My husband died two years ago," she informed me.

We strolled along the corniche. "When did you last see me?" she asked.

I thought carefully. "Forty-four years?"

"A scandal!" she laughed. "Still, I recognized you at first glance."

"As I recognized you."

"You hesitated a little."

"From surprise."

"Do you remember the old love?" she asked.

Her words were effusive, punctuated with loud intermittent laughter, reminding me of the gossip about her mother's lunacy. We walked for a few minutes, then went our ways.

I returned to the Abbasiya of fields, gardens, and tranquility. The Mustafa house rose in my memory, the father, mother, son, and Hanan—a house that impressed our imagination with its special magic. In the afternoon, the father rocked his chair in the reception room overlooking the street, a table by his side—with a bottle, an ice bucket, a glass, and a tray of mezze. A portly man of medium height, red-faced, bald, contemptuously challenging tradition. First he would be silent, sedate, even haughty and introverted, but as he expanded with intoxication, he obliged the street and passers-by with humanitarian glances. Thereafter, he deigned to address street vendors—of sweet potatoes, salep, or ice cream, according to the season. He might even joke with them or ask them to repeat the jingle with which they advertised their wares.

We stood close by to listen, watch, and participate in the fun, our remarks mostly derisive—except Gaafar Khalil, who admired him, considering him a spectacle no less entertaining than the cinema or circus.

During this daily session, the mistress of the house would appear, tall and thin, leaning on a stick with a slight limp, casting a haughty, disdainful glance. Woe to us if she spotted us watching and laughing! She would berate us with abuse and damnation, cursing our families who hadn't raised us properly, then disappear from the room, insulting people and country. She was considered abnormal, like her husband, and was often seen arguing with vendors and servants. It was said that she was ten years older than him, that she was wealthy, with land and money, whereas he owned only part of an endowment, and that she had married him, despite his lack of education and occupation, for his ancestry.

Among the regular passers-by on the street was a gypsy woman who tended sheep, barefoot, in a black gown gathered at the waist with a belt, and covered with a black shawl under which a black veil hid her face and revealed only the eyes.

We had an ongoing feud. Whenever she approached with her sheep, we shouted in unison, "Gypsy woman, undo your belt!" She would pelt us with whatever stones lay within her reach.

Hanan Mustafa

Mustafa Bey became concerned, scolding us in her defense. One day, Sayyid Shouayr, the first in sexual awareness, said, "Don't you see what's between the ram and the ewe?"

This was followed by a violent quarrel between the bey and his wife that shattered the walls of the house and invaded the quiet street, until the jalousies crowded with outlines of women. The man left the house and was never seen again. It was rumored in the neighborhood that he married the gypsy and lived with her in Darb al-Ahmar.

Finding herself with no man, the wife assumed both roles. She was truly strange—she allowed Hanan to play with her peers but prevented her elder brother, Sulayman, from leaving the house except in her company. He was a handsome, nimble boy; we saw him playing in the garden alone or with a servant, gentle and refined, even gentler than his sister. We exchanged glances, wishing he would play with us, and he wished to play with us, but we remained strangers until he and his family left the neighborhood.

My heart clung to Hanan before I had reached adolescence. She was fair, blue-eyed, and soft-voiced. Ramadan nights were a happy occasion for children of both sexes to meet in the street, to see each other in the light of the lanterns they waved. We sang Ramadan songs and exchanged latent love, our innocent feelings satisfied with glances, demonstrating elegance in running and singing, or secret smiles.

When she reached twelve, she was forbidden both street and school. Her home didn't believe in education or work, considering them the necessities of poor people. Even Sulayman abandoned elementary school.

With my sweetheart's disappearance from the street, my passion increased and she became my only concern. She let me see her stealthily from a window, or we would express our sentiments by lighting matches in the dark on the roof. Then we went a step further, and her servant shuttled secretly between us carrying greetings and flowers. It made me happy, indescribably happy. I craved more but didn't know how; a mysterious anxiety sneaked into my soul, yanked at by forces of joy and depression.

Then her mother called on us—she who rarely visited or was visited. With a bluntness only a woman like her could show, she suggested we get married.

The proposal came as a shock for my parents.

"It's a great honor, but they're not yet thirteen," they replied.

She hit the ground with her stick. "Marriages are arranged between children in diapers."

"But he hasn't finished elementary school and still has a long way to go," they said.

"My daughter is rich, he won't need a degree or a job," she said haughtily.

"But education is necessary, and so is a job."

"Nonsense…"

"He owns nothing nor will he own anything, and he will not accept to be just the husband of a rich wife."

"What's to be done?" she asked sharply.

"Wait until he finishes his education. He can marry then …"

"And how long is the wait?"

"Ten years, at least."

"You are refusing a blessing," she shouted.

She rose, angry, and repeated in a sharper tone, "You are refusing a blessing."

She left scowling and haughty. I was cross-examined to reveal the reasons behind the strange visit. No doubt the crazy mother, discovering her daughter's secret, had condescended to propose the happy solution (as she imagined), confident of acceptance. I was deeply affected and wished to apologize to Hanan but was perturbed when she no longer waved from her window and her servant stopped coming. I returned one afternoon from school to learn that the Mustafa family had left the house and the neighborhood for an unknown place. For the first time in my life, I suffered the torment of deprivation and abandonment. But it didn't kill or overwhelm me—it gripped me for a while, then faded into an unexciting memory.

I didn't set eyes on Hanan until I met her in Gleem in May 1969, nearing sixty. As for her brother, Sulayman, I had news of him from the late Gaafar Khalil when he was involved in cinema. He met him at Studio Misr, a dancer in a troupe brought in for a musical.

"I greeted him and reminded him who I was," Gaafar said. "He remembered me. He said he had become fascinated by dance and had devoted his life to it."

I was astonished by the unexpected ending, but Gaafar, with his big laugh, said, "It seems he's pursuing his passion and his life in absolute freedom."

During the Gleem encounter, Hanan told me her father had died following an appendectomy the year they had moved from Abbasiya. Her mother had died only two years ago; Sulayman had completely cut himself off—she learned his news from show magazines.

Khalil Zaki

Among Abbasiya friends, evil and aggression were named after him. Proximity imposed him; disagreement meant battle and none escaped. Until today, there's a scar on my forehead left by his clog—we disagreed over Husayn Higazi and Mahmoud Mukhtar, who was a better soccer player? I said Higazi, he said Mukhtar, then came the blow with the clog, blood spilled down my face and gallabiya. He quarreled with Gaafar Khalil over Charlie Chaplin and Max Lander, he fought with Eid Mansour when he borrowed a piaster and put off payment. His only match was Sayyid Shouayr; when they fought, we saw the first fair fight: blood gushed from both noses, both gallabiyas were ripped—imagining what awaited him at home with his torn gallabiya doubled our pleasure.

Boycott was useless. He'd soon forget and return, calling it quits—accept him or a fight would erupt. He was not without use, our leader in fights with kids from other neighborhoods, especially after soccer games. His father, a spice merchant in Bayn al-Ganayin, treated him with proverbial cruelty, often brutally beating him in the street in front of his friends with no mercy. Khalil hated him, dreaming night and day of his death. The father was an opium addict—Khalil divulged his secret and slandered him everywhere—and the worst model for the head of a family, but he singled out Khalil for his hatred and cruelty. We followed this relationship with incredulity and alarm—Surour Abd al-Baqi interpreted it religiously: "God imposed his father on him as He imposed the flood on Noah's people."

After repeated failures in elementary school, his father put him to work in the store. We sighed with relief, imagining we were rid of his evil, but he wasn't gone a month.

"All's well?" we said, hiding our disappointment.

"The son of a crazy woman threw me out!"

"Of the store?"

"And the house!"

Sayyid Shouayr brought us the news—his father was a merchant and a friend of Khalil's father. He had assaulted a customer and had repeatedly stolen money from the store; the man was forced to throw him out.

We were sullen—he would be free to hound us with his overbearing stubbornness. We bore his expenses in cafés and on trips; otherwise we had no idea where he spent his time, where he slept, or how he ate. We were now in secondary school; Gaafar Khalil entered the world of cinema and dragged him along to work as an extra, which gave him a little money. There he met Sulayman Mustafa, the dancer, buzzing around him with opportunistic instincts. Soon, a strange friendship developed as he joined his entourage and profited from his money. Gaafar Khalil laughingly recounted his adventures. One day, he said, "Our friend went too far as usual. Sulayman got fed up and threw him out."

"He threw him out?" we cried, expecting the worst.

"Now he's threatening him."

"The poor man has fallen in the trap of his misdeeds."

"But Sulayman has friends in high places. Our friend Khalil found himself dragged to the police station and whipped until his voice was hoarse from screaming. He was released after signing a restraining order."

Khalil returned to loitering, then vanished and we heard nothing. Eid Mansour brought the first news, from a brothel in Sakakini. "I saw him sitting with the Madam like a partner!"

Gaafar Khalil—his favorite, who had opened the door to a livelihood—brought us the real story. He would visit a brothel as a customer. When he'd taken his pleasure and was asked for payment, he'd threaten to call the police. If they called in the bouncer, he'd tear him apart. He soon imposed himself as bouncer of the establishment. Before long, his protection covered every brothel in Sakakini. His affairs prospered, he discovered luxury. It was a dangerous life, but it suited him as he suited it. He climbed to the top until he leapt to the exclusive brothels downtown. Luck smiled when he did an important doctor an 'amorous' favor; it smiled again when the doctor was appointed dean of the Medical School—he was rewarded with an administrative post in Qasr al-Aini Hospital. Khalil Zaki found himself a functionary in an important hospital, protégé of the dean—the pay was small but the profits unimaginable. He returned to visit us at the café, with the air of affluence, ordering a narghile and green tea, eyeing us from on high as befitted a functionary in the company of schoolchildren.

"What about the other profession?" I asked Gaafar Khalil once.

"It seems you know nothing about the hospital's profits," he laughed.

"He severed relations with the brothels?"

"Of course, except for the select few, the very excellent ones, from a distance for rare favors to the elite."

He knew a rich butcher—a drug addict—and asked for his daughter's hand. She was the man's only child after her two brothers were killed in the demonstrations that racked the country at the start of Ismail Sidqi's regime. Khalil married a girl with a promised inheritance of four buildings on Farouq Street and plenty of cash. One year after the marriage, the rich butcher was arrested while taking drugs and was sentenced to a year in prison. His health

Khalil Zaki

could not stand it and he died in the prison hospital. Administering the estate fell to Khalil Zaki. When the news arrived, none of us doubted that Khalil had betrayed his father-in-law; the idea prevailed to the point of conviction.

"A historic deal," said Eid Mansour, almost with envy.

"God recompense him for the four buildings," laughed Gaafar Khalil.

"Poor woman, we'll see her begging in the street soon," said Reda Hamada.

The war came and went but I saw him rarely; not after Gaafar Khalil's funeral in 1950, nor did he cross my mind until 1970. It was early autumn. I was at the Trianon; a black Buick pulled up and a face peered through its window. He approached laughing, we greeted each other, and he sat down. Despite his age, his short body appeared clearly sculpted and strongly built, his savage, vicious visage elevated only a fraction by the sharkskin suit. He had kept his fez to hide a baldness scarred with stitches, remains of his battles. We talked of friends.

"Perhaps you don't know that I've become an Alexandrian," he said.

"Really?"

"My youngest daughter is a literature student; she didn't find an opening in Cairo, so I moved to Alexandria and bought a villa in Lauren. You'll see it for yourself!"

I thanked him. "And your job?" I asked.

"Two years ago, I got angina and retired," he said.

"Your health..." I offered politely.

"My health is fine but I don't follow medical advice." He laughed, revealing his stained teeth. "In addition to the daughter I told you about, I have three engineers and a doctor."

I expressed appreciation and admiration. Dissolving in laughter, he said, "I knew how to be a father!" Then, in a tone of regret, "I wish they were like me, only interested in themselves and their future, but they've made me dizzy with their political debates."

I stole inquiring glances. Would he still leap to aggression if conditions were appropriate? To what extent had he really changed? How did he see his past? What image did he portray in front of his children? Could he bear someone telling his story? Weren't three engineers and a doctor sufficient penance for a black past? What was better: escaping the law despite his crimes to offer the country four scholars; or arrest so that justice could rest on its throne?

I recalled Zuhayr Kamil's words: "I now believe that people are bastards with no ethics. It would be better for them to admit it and build their communal life on that admission. The new ethical issue becomes how to maintain public welfare and human happiness in a society of bastards and scum."

Durriya Salim

"Allow me to say hello..."

The shadow of a smile appeared on her lips. Encouraged, I said, "It's impossible not to exchange greetings after what happened..."

She broke her silence. "After what happened?"

"After what happened between our eyes."

She laughed innocently. "I accept the greeting," she said.

"That's the first step."

Durriya Salim

"Are there others?"

She came with three children to Montaza, they swam in the sea while she sat alone in the casino, watching them from the window. My attention was attracted to a smiling face and a body bursting with feminine maturity. I was enamored by an affectionate look in her eyes, made to receive and welcome. I soon felt a gentle invitation like a delicate flower; ignoring it was beyond human power. We exchanged passing words, agreeing to meet in the Swan Garden. On my way there, I was convinced she was a special type of woman, a widow or divorced.

But she simply said, "I'm married!"

Taken aback, I said, "But I always see you alone."

"He's on a short scholarship abroad that ends this year."

I was dumbfounded.

"Are you afraid of married women?" she asked with a laugh.

"I'm thinking..."

"Think about preparing a safe place to meet in Cairo," she interrupted.

"Agreed," I replied enthusiastically.

"And don't misunderstand me."

"How, and why?"

"Maybe you wonder what's behind a woman who responded to your first gesture?"

Those were my thoughts, but I said, "I was no less responsive and I was the initiator."

"We have a right to be candid," she replied gently.

I contemplated the affair with the sobriety of one who hadn't fallen under a mad urge. I told myself that I liked this woman and desired her but would not love her. A place was found on the Saqqara road. I had imagined a flaming episode, but when I had closed the door, I found myself in the presence of a new woman. Relaxed on the sofa, not even removing the silk scarf around her neck, she was calm, surrendering, peering at me with affectionate eyes. I caressed her and kissed her lips. She responded to my emotions with a contented, loving smile. When I offered her a drink, she refused; when I invited her to bed, she whispered in my ear, "I wish we could spend our time in quiet, innocent happiness."

"I don't believe it."

She rose. "Don't consider it an end in itself."

Despite the attraction, I believe it was quite possible for her to spend the time in "quiet, innocent happiness"—a great contradiction between the easy woman responding to the first gesture and this gentle, ascetic woman.

"You're a strange character," I said.

"Really. Why?"

When I hesitated, she asked, "Do you value my company?"

"Certainly."

"That's what interests me."

The weekly meetings continued—with no real love on my side and no infidelity on hers. When the curtain of formality was removed, I said, "I confess I thought you playful, in Montaza."

"What do you mean?" she asked with interest.

"An innocent meaning."

"God forgive you."

I held her hand. "I wonder what drives you to another man's arms?"

"Another?!"

"I mean other than your husband?"

A tear fluttered in her lashes. "People hate being cross-examined."

After consistent meetings, and tamed by habit, she surrendered her memories.

"I was married after a profound love story."

She was a nurse and he an intern.

"We shared a beautiful love. Frankly I submitted to him on our first meeting."

"And he married you?"

"He was gallant, a true lover."

"How beautiful!"

"We lived for a long time as happy as could be, and I bore him three children."

She stopped. "Then what?" I asked.

"Nothing," she replied, as one awakening from a sweet dream.

"How are things today?"

"As usual."

"What do you mean?"

"All this time lost at the expense of our love," she said laughing.

"Can we continue to meet when he returns?"

"Why not?"

My attachment was courtesy, then habit. Her gentleness, care, and affection grew, until one day she said, "I can't imagine my life without you."

I found the safest answer was a long kiss but she demanded stubbornly, "And you?"

"Like you and more."

"You never told me that you loved me."

"But I really do love you, and that's more important," I replied.

Doctor Sadiq Abd al-Hamid returned from his scholarship. She talked about him objectively, as if he were a phenomenon that she was not strongly related to, but with a respect that could not be surpassed. At that time, I had started visiting Gad Abu al-Ela's salon, and there I met Doctor Sadiq Abd al-Hamid! Gad Abu al-Ela told us how he had visited the doctor for a medical consultation and how their relationship had become close. A rare spiritual friendship developed between us, and in turn, I introduced him to the Salim Gabr and Zuhayr Kamil meetings and to Doctor Mahir Abd al-Karim's salon. I was amazed to see a man of Durriya's age, perhaps a few years younger, handsome, intelligent, with unlimited spiritual aspiration. And so our friendship began four months after my affair with his wife! It upset me to the point of torture. Durriya, not expecting it, was shocked. She noticed my agitation and the gloom that hung over our meetings, strangling them—it seemed the current of life was flowing toward a blocked corner to pronounce its death.

"Forget he's my husband. I need never have mentioned a word about his identity or name," she pleaded.

"It's useless to imagine unrealistic possibilities," I replied in confusion.

"We must preserve our relationship—it's more important than everything else."

"I'm in torment," I said, truly sad.

"Maybe if he knew about our relationship, he wouldn't care," she said with unusual passion. I looked at her shocked, not believing what she was saying.

"He doesn't love me—hasn't loved me for three years or more, believe me."

"I believe you and I'm sorry."

"He's seeing another woman. If he weren't so devoted to his children, he'd have left us and married her!"

"Durriya, I'm sorry."

"What do you mean, sorry?"

"Sorry about your situation. And mine is not enviable."

"If you loved me, you wouldn't feel sorry at all!"

"The fact is, I can't bear this situation."

She turned her red-eyed face away. "You hardly know him. Does friendship grow from nothing? Love is stronger than friendship. But the truth is that you don't love me."

I had nothing to say, so I remained silent. And with silence, the curtain came down on our sad, contrived affair. When we left our nest, I observed her mature person, suffering life's most difficult stage under the weight of abandonment and disappointment. My heart shriveled in pain and sorrow. Outside, a cold wind lashed at us like a whip in the dark night.

Reda Hamada

He relates to the Abbasiya of fields and gardens, like Gaafar Khalil, Khalil Zaki, and Hanan Mustafa; and to values and principles, to the violent waves of life, to human will when it mobilizes for struggle and transcends despair and grief. He is tall—like our friend Surour Abd al-Baqi—a giant even as boys playing in the prickly pear forest, among the few to face Khalil Zaki's aggression with courage.

From primary school, he was known for intense patriotism. He talked of Saad Zaghloul more than Husayn Higazi, Charlie Chaplin, or Abd al-Halim al-Masri, the wrestler. He must have inherited it from his family, famous on our street for patriotism and learning. His father was director of the Fever Hospital in Abbasiya, and his mother a teacher, among the first educated women and a pioneer feminist, his sister a science prodigy sent to study in England, and his brother had done well in law school. The family was also known for calamities. The mother died when he was a baby, the father was fired for serving the Wafd when it was founded, his sister died in England, and his brother was killed during the 1919 revolution.

Reda's frequent boasting about his brother and his martyrdom, intelligence, and industry, angered Khalil Zaki. "Why did that lunatic get himself killed?" he asked me.

"For independence," I replied innocently.

"Were the English living on his chest?" he asked sarcastically.

When I met Reda, he lived with his father and an old servant. He hated the house—a prison with no bars—and was terrorized by his father. The father secluded himself at home after his dismissal, leaving only when called for a private consultation. Shaping Reda to compensate for his losses, he severely taxed him, demanding excellence in education, ethics, and patriotism, observing him relentlessly with no tolerance. Reda grew up puritanical, ascetic, industrious, well-informed, ambitious, but he always wanted for tenderness. He would often say, "Tell me

Reda Hamada

about your mother, how you love her and how she loves you," and in a tremulous voice chant, "Your mother entrusted me her yearning, when she bade me farewell, and a letter to carry its words heals the sick."

Once his father humiliated him in the street for some oversight. Gravely affected, he was silent as we walked until we stopped at the public water fountain, our habit every afternoon during the holidays. Nobody noticed when he left for a while then returned. Suddenly he bent over, clutching his stomach with frantic hands and screaming. He fell to the ground under a tree, shaking convulsively in the dust, biting at the tree roots in pain. Alarmed, we gathered and a crowd formed. The police and an ambulance arrived, and he was taken to Qasr al-Aini hospital where he was treated for the carbolic acid he had drunk to commit suicide.

The event shook me. "How could you?" I asked him later.

He smiled sadly. "Didn't you see how he humiliated me in front of you?"

This inauspicious attempt changed his father's treatment. His excellence in school won him respect, but did not stop his involvement in politics—now less intense as the wave of revolt retreated. We had reached our first degree of awareness after the bloody revolution had been transformed into an other-worldly sacred myth; of its souvenirs each retained a fleeting scene, memories of a martyr, a slogan, nothing more. We both joined the demonstration led by Nadir Burhan in support of Saad Zaghloul in his constitutional row with King Fuad. His relationship with Badr al-Ziyadi grew stronger in secondary school, as their outlooks were similar.

When Muhammad Mahmoud came to power, Badr said, "Our enemy was the English . . ."

"And the king," replied Reda Hamada.

"They're one and the same."

"I agree."

"There's a new enemy on the scene," Badr said.

When Badr was killed, Reda was grief-stricken. "Badr died while Khalil Zaki lives."

"And Muhammad Mahmoud lives too," I said sadly.

Reda's political work increased. He sat with Mustafa al-Nahhas among the student delegates, he was arrested during the Muhammad Mahmoud era, was almost killed under Sidqi, a student leader in Law School—I listened to his fiery speeches on campus. The model wafdist—faith in independence, the constitution, and democracy.

In his angry observation of politics, an idea sprouted in which he eventually believed. "The Wafd—or the people—lost its force the day leaders of the Black Hand Society were arrested."

"But the Wafd advocates legitimate struggle," I said innocently.

He laughed. "Forget what they say. Our only hope is to demolish the palace and minority parties, then face the English as a single body!"

He loved Soraya Raafat and wanted to ask for her hand when he was in Law School. He didn't tell me, nor did I reveal my relationship with her, but I learned the story after the defeat of 1967. Reda was present at Salim Gabr's office when Soraya appeared. When we later met at his house in Heliopolis, he asked me, "Do you remember the lady in Salim Gabr's office?"

"Soraya Raafat?" I asked with interest.

He laughed. "She was from Sakakini, I was in love with her when I was a law student and decided to get engaged to her, except . . ."

"Except?"

"I saw her with our friend Eid Mansour!"

Then I told him of my story with her.

Reda graduated from Law School in 1934 and worked as a lawyer. His father died, leaving him a decent fortune. He shone as a political writer, established himself in law and was elected representative of our constituency in the 1942 elections.

The 4th of February affair shocked me, precipitating a crisis in my wafdism that I confessed.

"I believe Mustafa al-Nahhas has saved the nation and the throne," he replied.

"Imagine British tanks making the national leader prime minister," I said.

"The English were our enemy, but today they're fighting on the side we wish to win."

"A dreadful mistake is burning my soul like poison."

"Do you want fascism to win, like those around the king?" he asked.

"Of course not."

"Then look at the 4th of February in that light."

He was elected again in 1950. Sadness filled him as he felt the Wafd deteriorating; a cancer had sneaked to its will and integrity, and people's enthusiasm had waned. He quivered with joy when Mustafa al-Nahhas abrogated the treaty and proclaimed resistance, the day a scent of 1919 spread through the valley. Disappointments followed like blows until the July 1952 revolution.

He was excited. "The Wafd will return unchallenged," he told me.

As the revolution followed its charted course, he hoped it would make the Wafd's supporters its base but was crushed when political parties were dissolved.

"We're embarking into military rule, only God knows its extent," he said.

"Retire from politics," I said sincerely, "and focus on your profession."

"No choice," he replied with a laugh.

But loyalty to his leader and colleagues made him suspect. He was arrested more than once. He had married in 1940; his wife bore him one son before an ailment made her barren. I often admired his son's intelligence and vivacity. When Reda was arrested, he was subjected to a campaign of defamation. The son, tortured by schoolmates, suffered a nervous breakdown. He locked himself up at home, going from bad to worse until his father had to commit him to a mental institution. His mother could not take the shock, was paralyzed, and died the same year. Reda found himself a lonely, old man, drowning in sorrows. His family curse had snared him.

"Reda Hamada is finished," I said to myself.

But he was not. He moved to Heliopolis and devoted himself to his profession and his books. The last ten years have been his most successful. Today, he is one of the most distinguished lawyers, and assiduously applies himself to writing what he has entitled the "Encyclopedia of Criminal Sciences"—its introduction covers philosophical views and psychological insights that testify to his encyclopedic knowledge and immense abilities.

This is not new to me: I've heard him debate with Doctor Mahir Abd al-Karim, Salim Gabr, Zuhayr Kamil as if he were an encyclopedia of philosophy, politics, and literature. In law, he is unquestionably an authority. But my primary admiration is for his ethical personality, very few of those I've known can equal that. It's not strange that I should be taken by constructive ethics—as a witness of moral collapse, I saw myself living in a large whorehouse, not a society.

In Reda Hamada, I found a man of pure intentions, guiltless, sincere, faithful to principles—freedom, democracy, culture, a⁰ religious creed purged of fanaticism and superstition.

Yes, he rejected leftist views and could not grow with the times. I knew him as the model young revolutionary, then, in old age, a stubborn conservative—although he never admitted it—always repeating that liberalism was the last word in man's political history. His ethical personality supported him through the tragedies that dogged his life, its magic backing him as the values and people he worshiped disappear—freedom, democracy, Mustafa al-Nahhas, his wife and son. As everything beautiful left his life, he didn't crumble but persevered in work, facing life with a steely will, on good terms with friends and salons. Whenever he approaches with his tall frame and white hair or he delights me with his conversation, a joyful vigor is sparked in my soul, and I renew my admiration for him and the blessed life that created him.

Zahran Hassouna

Some friends are of a special type, friends of a place they never transgress; there was a time I called them 'café friends.' In the café, we'd exchange warm greetings, chat, then go our ways. One might enjoy a quality worthy of consideration that left its imprint before dissolving in forgetfulness—such is Zahran Hassouna. I knew him at Café Rex during the Second World War where I occasionally went with Gaafar Khalil, Reda Hamada, Shaarawi al-Fahham, and Eid Mansour. He came with a group of friends on Sundays; stocky, of medium height, with a large head that seemed deformed. We were introduced through backgammon, then became friends.

Introducing himself, he said, "I was employed in the Ministry of Commerce and Industry but resigned to work in commerce."

At prayer times, he and his friends retreated to a corner behind the bar to pray together. He led the prayers, being the only one to have performed the pilgrimage. Religion occupied considerable space in their conversation, revealing a simple, sincere faith, a mesh of belief and fantastic, popular legends—yet undoubtedly sincere. Their company was enjoyable, sporting the generosity and gallantry of local townfolks. One day Eid Mansour said, "I have news about Hagg Zahran Hassouna. He was forced to resign because of disreputable behavior."

"Which sort of disreputable behavior?"

"Bribery!"

Eid Mansour delighted in proving people had no decency—like himself. "I'm skeptical of everyone, particularly the religious," he said with a laugh.

"But not every religious person is a hypocrite," retorted Reda Hamada.

"Zahran Hassouna doesn't rise to the level of hypocrisy," said Eid Mansour, laughing more.

We laughed as he explained, "Hypocrisy conceals disbelief while proclaiming belief, but he's too stupid to be a disbeliever. I don't doubt his faith."

"Maybe he was involved in bribery under compelling circumstances."

"Perhaps."

We noticed that Zahran Hassouna worked energetically in the black market, trading matches and whisky, then food supplies. He didn't hide it, even offering us his services, so I couldn't resist asking, "Hagg, doesn't the black market conflict with your piety?"

Zahran Hassouna

"The world has one method, the afterlife another," he replied with confidence.

"But God cannot approve of starving the poor."

"I atone with prayer, fasting, and alms, what else do you want?" he replied tranquilly.

I told my friends, "The man sins knowingly, not through ignorance or hypocrisy."

"He amasses wealth, turns to religion for atonement, and his thefts are transformed into legitimate profit. Religion for Zahran is encouragement to sin. He steals food from the poor while his face glows with faith and tranquility," laughed Eid Mansour.

I watched with contemplative, scornful eyes as they prayed in the café—bending and prostrating, lowering their eyelids in submission—they were thieving bastards with no right to remain on earth a single hour. I saw no use in arguing with him; he always seemed tranquil and self-confident, believing in evil as he did in good, obeying Satan as he obeyed God, oscillating between them like a clever merchant in an open market and careful that, in the end, his revenue would exceed his expense. I found excuses for bastards like Khalil Zaki and Sayyid Shouayr, even Eid Mansour, who never dealt with religion seriously; rushing into life instinctively with their dry, practical minds in an atmosphere of tense struggle. Then I went into a grim spiritual depression, almost rejecting the entire human experience. The issue became the centerpiece of endless conversations among us.

"It seems there is no honest merchant," said Reda Hamada.

"There's no honest person," said Eid Mansour.

"What's the role of religion then?" I asked.

"Why should we hold to ethics if they only lead to failure?" asked Eid Mansour.

It lingered for years until I discussed it at Doctor Mahir Abd al-Karim's salon—from a critique of Egyptian reality to the philosophical apotheosis of good and evil, recalling Doctor Ibrahim Aql, his philosophy of highest ideals, and contradictory conduct. I remember Ustaz Salim Gabr's dictum: "No matter what, the stages mankind traversed from the jungle to the moon cannot be ignored"; or Reda Hamada saying: "Valuable instincts, worthy of rejuvenating confidence, exist—man's devotion to serving his family, brilliant intelligence devoted to truth, instances of rare heroics"; and: "Don't be excessively idealistic or you'll die of disgust!"

Zahran Hassouna amassed a fortune during the war, rising to the status of millionaire. In 1945, he founded a contracting company. I chose not to expose him when his son, an engineering student, was killed in the Battle of the Canal after the 1936 treaty was abrogated. The man walked behind the coffin, clutching the arms of two friends, red-eyed, soul lost. Our relationship was confined to exchanging pleasantries on social occasions. But Eid Mansour, the closest to him because of his commercial activities, assured me he continued to collect money and perform prayers. As he continued to flourish, he moved to a mansion in Maadi. At fifty, he married a twenty-year-old with the excuse that his first wife refused him marital pleasure after the death of her son. The pilgrimage remained his annual spiritual excursion. His activities increased after the revolution. He wasn't a landowner, but his company was nationalized during the 1961 nationalizations—the towering building, whose stones he had carved with intelligence, fraud, will, opportunism, faith, and debauchery, collapsed.

Reda Hamada responded with anger, reaffirming his position on the revolution.

"But you know the man," I said.

"It's a matter of principle," he replied.

"It isn't a matter of principle or a man, it's about a regime that blessed it all," I replied.

"Wait until you discover the new regime. Zahran Hassouna started as an employee, like those who pounced on his company to manage it," he said bitterly.

When Hagg Zahran recovered from the shock, he sold his mansion and opened a café in Heliopolis, insuring a decent living. He always puts on a courageous, steadfast front with us, commenting on all matters in phrases with religious undertones like *al-hamdulillah* and 'It's God's will,' or 'There is no power or strength save in God.' Occasionally, caution makes him praise the decree that stripped him of his fortune. "Justice we must accept willingly," he says.

But he exposes himself by ill-concealed flashes of joy over calamities like the economic crisis, the Yemen fiasco, and finally the 5th of June defeat, when his head spun with the intoxication of victory! That cursed day, I was struck by opposing currents, almost losing my mind. My respect for Reda Hamada grew when the tragedy broke his back as it had broken ours—that day, he forgot everything except love for his homeland.

Zuhayr Kamil

When we started university, he was an assistant in the Arabic Language Department expecting a scholarship to study in France. He was praised by Doctors Mahir Abd al-Karim and Ibrahim Aql. The latter said, "He is a model of the genius peasant."

Reda Hamada told me, "I met him in Saad Zaghloul's house during student meetings; he's from Samanud and knows Mustafa al-Nahhas personally."

He left on his scholarship in 1932, returned a professor in 1938 or 1939, and was appointed to the university faculty. Between his appointment and 1950, his intellectual activity centered on the university and writing, publishing his well-known books on criticism, western and eastern critics, and studies of Shakespeare, Racine, Baudelaire, Eliot, and the Andalusian poets. He attended Doctor Mahir Abd al-Karim's salon—a strong friendship grew between us.

During the war, he married a Greek girl, who worked at the Venus and bore him two sons and a daughter. Literally a university professor, he devoted his life to academic research and talked of nothing else. I never knew him to have another interest. Occasionally, I tried without success to detect the old Wafd student. Unlike most people, he wished victory for the Allies, out of love for democracy as he said, siding with his wife, or his fanatical worship of France.

In 1950, he gave us an unexpected surprise—he ran as a Wafd candidate in Cairo, winning with an overwhelming majority. His conduct raised many questions.

"A regrettable decision," said Mahir Abd al-Karim despite his extreme reserve.

"Maybe he's dreaming of becoming Minister of Education," Reda Hamada told me.

It could be a while before the dream came true. Meanwhile, how was he to cope on a small pension and a parliamentarian's stipend of no more than fifty pounds?

"Time will tell!" said Reda Hamada.

It did, sooner than expected. His political articles appeared in the Wafd press—he emerged as a first class political writer—and pieces of criticism in the weeklies. Zahran Hassouna had contracts with the government that required a contact for safe passage. He asked us to introduce him to our friend, the deputy, and a strong relationship ensued. Whispers traveled concerning Doctor Zuhayr Kamil's strange, even suspicious actions.

I asked Reda Hamada. "What do you think of what's being said about Zuhayr Kamil?"

"It's said he's become a job broker," he replied in a rage. "It's said he does Zahran Hassouna favors for generous rewards," he added, shaking his head sadly.

"Is it true?"

"Yes. I sometimes wonder if there is a difference between the Wafd and other parties."

"Can you imagine Zuhayr Kamil forsaking professorship to practice graft and corruption?"

"He was always a bastard, waiting for an opportunity for his talent. He found it in politics."

We bemoaned our genius friend and our stolid party.

When the Wafd government was dismissed after the Cairo fire, Zuhayr tried returning to the university but failed. He continued as a political writer and critic, peering anxiously into the future now that he had acquired a taste for fine living.

We met one day at Salim Gabr's house. He was agitated. "What's happening? The king has gone mad, everything is falling apart. Our political situation resembles Doctor Ibrahim Aql; he began as a brilliant scholar and finished a dervish."

"The Wafd is like its leader, a kind old man besieged by senility and deterioration," said Reda.

"It can't continue this way," Salim Gabr said. "What about tomorrow?"

"The Wafd is still the best of the lot. The king will have to recall it to avoid a full-scale revolution," replied Zuhayr Kamil.

"A revolution is better than the Wafd," said Salim Gabr.

"The Muslim Brothers and the communists are waiting," said Reda Hamada.

"Neither has a majority," Zuhayr Kamil retorted sharply.

"The nation is not ready for communism, and no faith can absorb the young people torn between revolution and profligacy," Salim Gabr said.

The July revolution defied every conjecture. Zuhayr Kamil found himself in a corner—with doors closed to politics and the university, he puzzled over what to do and what to write. As intentions veered toward liquidating political parties that now bore the weight of attack, particularly the Wafd, the professor hit us with the second surprise: fiery articles blitzed the Wafd, behind every corruption gnawing at the bones of the nation. The articles provoked a storm of suppressed anger in wafdist hearts, but no one could downplay their seriousness, coming from a man with a respected university background who had served in the Wafd's last parliament. He was appointed to a major newspaper—his pen now belonged to the revolution—to edit its literary section, becoming the leading critic of contemporary literature.

Due to his new responsibilities, or perhaps ashamed of his sudden about-face, he avoided Doctor Mahir Abd al-Karim's salon.

"Would it not have been better for him to remain at the university?" Doctor Mahir asked.

"Did you see what the bastard did to himself?" remarked Reda Hamada.

"His excuse may be that he's sided with a force whose nationalism is unquestionable," I said.

He reappeared at his favorite meeting places—Doctor Mahir Abd al-Karim's salon and Salim Gabr's office. We returned to meeting regularly, and I to observing his inner self.

"There was no use resisting, so why should I?" he said. "I was almost bankrupt, but money wasn't the only motive. My conscience is clear."

"Then you believe in the July Revolution?" I ventured.

Zuhayr Kamil

Examining me with his intelligent eyes, he said, "A blessed movement. Its momentum prevented the explosion of a revolution that loomed on the horizon."

"What an idea!"

"I confess I'm not a revolutionary. I approve of neither the reactionary Muslim Brothers nor the revolutionary communists. I believe in the steady reform that we're following. It's the way of the Wafd if its young faction had won."

But with observation, I noticed his emotions were uneasy with his thoughts—his apparent enthusiasm to justify his own coup d'état. Over time, he was forced to confess a little.

"Wouldn't it have been better at the hands of a popular uprising led by Wafd youth?"

"The important thing is that it happened," I replied.

"But a human being cannot relinquish his personal mentality, so bid farewell to freedom."

Reda Hamada was imprisoned at the time. When his name came up, Zuhayr said, "God be with him."

"I'm sure of his innocence," I said confidently.

"Why?"

"I know better than anyone that he is an honorable man."

Did my comment annoy him? At any rate, he said, "That generation of politicians should take our old professor, Ibrahim Aql, as an example."

I was stunned. "Ibrahim Aql suffers from total dervish syndrome. I saw it myself when I ran into him in al-Husayn."

"Exactly. Becoming a dervish is a way of confronting the cholera that destroyed his sons."

"What do you mean?"

"I mean if you face an insurmountable disaster, become a dervish, any kind of dervish. Useless resistance will land you in jail."

At about the same time, Zuhayr Kamil the critic staged another kind of coup. He peddled his criticism, disdainfully accepting gifts and money, and evaluating art and artists accordingly. As theater and cinema flourished and his profits doubled, he built an elegant villa in Dokki and bought a Mercedes. Abandoning moderation in food and drink, he gained weight until he was unrecognizable. Of his old qualities, only his broad culture and trained taste in art survived. Despite the revolutionism he had adopted as a career, longing gleamed in his eyes if the Wafd was mentioned—I even learned that a friend had taken a message to Mustafa al-Nahhas, apologizing for his actions and explaining the circumstances that forced his decision.

When the July Revolution announced its socialist policy, with his usual zeal he studied socialism to offer knowledgeable support and maintain his position as one of its foremost writers. Within a few years he had translated four books on socialism then published his own work, *This Nation's Socialism*. At this point, he despaired of convincing me of his sincerity—I had always known him as a liberal democrat.

"How did you turn socialist with such manic speed?" I asked him laughing.

He laughed. "People adopt the religion of the land," he replied.

"Do you think they believe you?"

"Nobody believes anybody anymore. What's important is what you say and do."

He was overcome with laughter. "They often wonder about the secret of the flourishing of the theater. Do you know the secret? We've all become actors."

"And yet, this regime has brought more prosperity than any other," I responded.

"Everything now has its value except human beings," he said with a sigh.

"When did a human being have value in our country?" I asked bitterly. "At least today he is free of economic, class, and racial slavery. The individual's turn will come when he deserves it!"

He reached the climax of his literary fall when he wrote an essay on the literature of Gad Abu al-Ela. Gad had tried to make his acquaintance around 1960, the same year he met me. The essay was a surprise. No matter what the price was—rumored to be a set of antique arabesques and one thousand pounds—it proved my friend had stooped low and lost all sense of shame. Abduh al-Basyuni spoke the truth when he said, "A book only a prostitute would dare write!"

Twice, Zuhayr Kamil almost declared apostasy—the 1956 Suez war and the 1967 debacle. Each time he assumed the revolution had been annihilated and prepared for his future anew; and I realized the degree of his opportunism—he owed the revolution his power and wealth.

I compared him to Reda Hamada—both were deeply cultured, both belonged to the former political generation aborted by the revolution, both believed in an anti-socialist ideology; the inner self of one was so rotten it disgusted insects, while a noble spirit rested in the other, making him worthy of sanctity and worship.

The year following the 1967 defeat, events struck at the heart of his family. His two sons insisted on emigrating to Canada. He could not dissuade them, and their mother encouraged them. They left Zuhayr heartbroken.

"I'm a peasant," he told me. "It's the peasant's nature to love keeping his sons close."

I asked him what led them to emigrate.

"Hope in a better future." Shrugging his shoulders sadly, he said, "The nation no longer has any value. Unconcerned or in despair, they have forsaken it in mid-crisis to chase a seductive dream." He was overtaken by sudden anger. "My mind is with them, but my heart is aching."

His daughter fell in love with a Greek when she visited Greece with her mother and married him, sneering at tradition. His wife commuted between Cairo and Athens, settling in her native land before the year was out. Zuhayr Kamil found himself alone at sixty, ailing with diabetes and high blood pressure—not unlike Reda Hamada who created his own finale by transcending his grief, Zuhayr suffered the bitterness of loneliness, disgust, and abandonment.

One day Abduh al-Basyuni asked me at Gad Abu al-Ela's salon, "Do you know Nimat Arif?"

When I replied that I didn't, he said, "She's a trainee journalist."

"And how does that concern me?"

He laughed. "She's Zuhayr Kamil's mistress."

"Zuhayr Kamil! He's an old man, well over sixty."

"You'll hear of their marriage soon."

I did. And I met the bride, a beautiful girl in her twenties. In her company, the professor turned to pleasure and comfort, picking up a pen only to write his weekly column on general daily topics and dispensing with books and reference works. But his illness set in, confining him terminally to bed and extinguishing the only bright wick in his darkened life—his mind. We still visit him from time to time, holding our discussions in his bedroom. He participates with his ear or some brief phrases that have lost their intelligent allusions and suggestive ideas, a reminder of how everything comes to an end.

Saba Ramzi

Saba Ramzi

A classmate in secondary school—two years, then he vanished. Although this is going back to 1925, I still remember his bright, sharp, almond eyes and his pitifully short height. An excellent athlete in the special section and in soccer, he was Badr al-Ziyadi's right wing: when the ball passed between them it spelled danger for any team we played. Thus he acquired fame and respect at school despite his shortness. In our leisure time, we read al-Manfaluti, memorizing his musical phrases. When I once mentioned the novels of Michel Zévaco, his face darkened. "Did you believe how his novels described the popes?" he asked me.

"Why shouldn't I?" I asked innocently.

"He's an enemy of Catholicism, and is bent on slandering the Pope," he replied.

I learned of new words like Catholic, Protestant, and Orthodox. I was confused until our classmate Nagi Murqus explained that the Egyptian Christian faith was Orthodox, and that missionaries had corrupted some Copts and converted them to Catholicism or Protestantism.

Gaafar Khalil teased Saba. "Now we know you're a corrupt Copt!"

Gaafar Khalil gave away his secret. "Can you keep a secret?" he asked us one day.

Our eyes inquired eagerly. "The right wing, Saba Ramzi, is in love with a teacher at the Abbasiya girls' school!"

We watched him after school as he followed her to the outskirts of Bab al-Shaariya. One day as we took turns reading from *Magdoline*, his voice trembled until he stopped reading. He felt my eyes staring at his closed eyelids.

"I saw you following me," he muttered. "I love her like the Stephen in this book, even more."

He found moral support: I was in love too.

"I'll love her whatever the price!"

"But she's a teacher, and you're still a pupil," I said sympathetically.

"Love is stronger than everything," he insisted. "I try to speak to her but she ignores me. They say it's a way of coquetry, what do you think?"

"I don't know."

"How do I know if she loves me or not?"

"I don't know."

"Shall we ask Gaafar Khalil and Badr al-Ziyadi?"

"No. They love a joke and they'll make one of you!" I warned.

His daily pursuit of the teacher continued fruitlessly. His self-confidence grew feeble and he was overcome by sadness. One afternoon we witnessed a scene difficult to erase. We saw him brazenly block the teacher's path.

"Please. . ." he said.

She stepped aside and continued. He followed.

"Just a word. . ."

"I can't put up with you forever," she shouted angrily.

"Listen to a courteous word. . ."

"Leave me alone or I'll call the police."

She moved away in quick, angry steps. He watched her bewildered. In a flash, he thrust his hand into his pocket, pulled out a revolver, aimed it at her, and fired! The girl screamed, her face turned to the sky in a convulsed movement, then she fell on her back. Saba stared at her, arm

69

Salim Gabr

dangling by his side clutching the revolver, frozen until he was arrested. The girl was dead before the ambulance arrived. Later we learned that Saba had stolen the revolver from his officer brother to commit his crime in desperation. We heard nothing more of him and never saw him again. He marked us with an indelible impression, then left.

Salim Gabr

I knew of Salim Gabr as a columnist at *Kawkab al-Sharq* in 1926. Badr al-Ziyadi, the first to praise him, described his articles as eloquent and useful. An enthusiastic advocate of modern civilization, economic independence, the liberation of women, and the hat instead of the fez, he was a law graduate who never practiced and almost every year went on a cultural tour of England and France. During the 1919 revolution, he marched with law students, taking a bullet in the shoulder the day al-Azhar was attacked. Later he worked in the Wafd press, continuing in journalism until today.

His politics changed when Saad Zaghloul became prime minister in 1924. When we became close friends, he shed light on that period of his life.

"Saad Zaghloul shouldn't have accepted the cabinet. With the Wafd behind him, he should have stayed in the popular arena until the Wafd had completed its mission," he said.

"Was that when you left the Wafd?"

"No. But my real interest changed to another direction."

It changed to communism, and has thus remained. But he never forgot he was a journalist in the Wafd press and avoided topics that might embarrass the leader—he developed a line to vent his new beliefs indirectly without conflicting outwardly with Wafd policy, advocating women's liberation, science, and industry. Taking a step further, he wrote a treatise on economic doctrines and included the history of socialism. About 1930, he published a second treatise on Karl Marx that was quickly confiscated by the authorities, and he was subjected to a fierce attack from conservatives who accused him of heresy and anarchy.

We met while I was at university at the Munira salon; meeting often there or in his office at the newspaper. I introduced him to Reda Hamada and Gaafar Khalil; we discussed politics and socialism but were not open to his class warfare and dictatorship of the proletariat.

"Socialism arriving through parliament, that's my dream!" I said.

"I'm an enemy of the Wafd," he replied, challenging my thoughts.

"How can you say that?!"

"And I support the king and minority parties."

I laughed in disbelief.

"The Wafd is the opium of the people!" His fist pounded the table. "The Wafd is responsible for the people's surrender to dreams that will never materialize and will always be incapable of doing them any real service. But if the king and his parties are in control, and corruption sets in and spreads, people will lose hope and prepare for a real revolution!"

"What's the point, when the English suffocate us?" I asked.

"Expect miracles with desperation."

Doctor Ibrahim Aql noticed my tendency to repeat the views of Salim Gabr.

"Beware of Salim Gabr's false philosophy!" he warned me.

I took Gabr's side. "I first heard of you in an article he wrote in your defense."

"It was no defense, it was an embarrassment. He does not accept a thinker unless he proclaims his heresy or anarchy," he replied sarcastically.

Abbas Fawzi was present and sided with the stronger as usual. "He's an immoral man," he said. "The proof is he doesn't believe in marriage."

"But he is married," I replied. "He introduced me to his wife in the Orman garden!"

"His mistress, a French widow, you didn't know?" Abbas said with a laugh.

She was indeed his mistress; he remained faithful to her until her death in 1960. Abd al-Rahman Shaaban the translator told me their story. She'd been the wife of an engineer for the Electric Company and had fallen in love with Salim Gabr while her husband was still alive. When he died, they lived together without marriage. She was a liberated woman, a communist. She owned property in Egypt but traveled often to France and hated the idea of having children.

Before the Second World War, Salim Gabr wrote an objective book on comparative religion. It caused an uproar. The author was accused of defaming Islam and was taken to court. The court acquitted him but banned the book. During the war, he launched attacks against Nazism and Fascism that were favorably received at the British Ambassador's residence. He was invited to give weekly talks on the radio.

"They say you've become a friend of the British Embassy," I said.

"Neither enmity nor friendship last," he replied. "In this war, I'm an English ally!"

"Their star seems to be on the wane!" I said.

"There's no fear of a Nazi victory. Even if it won, history has laws more powerful than war or victory," he retorted sharply.

When the Wafd returned to power, he worked with it, as he had done before Saad Zaghloul's cabinet; and when Rommel's armies marched toward the Egyptian border, he fled with the others to the Sudan, returning when the scales were tipped to resume his journalistic crusade.

He sat between me and Reda Hamada at Gaafar Khalil's funeral in 1950 and talked of the nation's joy for the Wafd's return. But added, "No party, no matter how popular, can cope with the situation any more." He spoke of the United States as the spirit of evil in the world. "There's no rescue for the world except world communism."

When he left, Reda said, "There's no one like this man, all agree in hating him."

"But he's a man of conviction, with no ulterior motives," I replied sincerely.

With the July 1952 revolution, the harmonious logical structure revealed strange, fantastic contradictions. On the surface he played the anticipated role—an intellectual reality clear to friend and foe. He worked for the revolution's newspaper, placing his pen at its service, but to his intimate circle, he was an unidentifiable bundle of contradictions.

His enthusiasm for abolishing the monarchy was unsurpassable; he considered the revolution a miracle but whispered tepidly, "The king is gone, replaced by countless kings."

He was overjoyed with the destruction of feudalism and the limit on land ownership, but said, "It's either ownership or no ownership. Distributing land to the peasants will reinforce the ownership instinct inherited from the dark ages."

When the political parties he had so often attacked were disbanded, he grieved for the

Wafd. "How can the country carry on without a popular base?"

And he said, "The temporary sacrifice of freedom for communism is reasonable, but we're moving with neither freedom nor communism!"

When the regime waged war against communists and Muslim Brothers, he said, "They're destroying the positive forces. No communism, no Muslim Brothers, no parties—who will execute their policies? Only mercenary bureaucrats are left, they're building on a straw foundation."

Communists were no better; they only earned his sympathy when they were detained or imprisoned; he accused them of degeneration and fall. I concluded that he was a strange person born to protest for the love of opposition. If the regime was feudalist, he was a communist; if it was leftist, he was a conservative—yes, a conservative! When the Soviet Union supported the revolution in war and peace, I heard what I had never expected.

"Communism is a great system," he said with burning anger, "but what's a communist? A machine not a human being!"

"Why do people want to emigrate to the United States?" he once asked me unabashed.

"Because they find bread and freedom there!" I replied sarcastically.

"Life has no value without freedom, so don't be fanatical," he retorted angrily.

"You're the one who taught me," I said with a laugh.

"We're dead, dead! When will we be resurrected?"

"Sometimes, I don't understand you," I said frankly.

"I'm as clear as the sun," he replied sharply. "You've become used to long explanations, commentaries, and commentaries on commentaries."

I heard at the Anglo Bar of his French mistress's death. I went to his home on Qasr al-Nil Street but it was locked and there was no reply; nor did I find him at his newspaper office. It seems that after her burial he had gone to Aswan for a month of solitude. When we met, he had his usual energy, but a sadness had been imprinted on his face and accompanied him for a long time. He disliked discussing his private affairs, never speaking a word about his love, family, or childhood, as though he were only a public figure, public inside and out.

"Don't you ever regret not marrying and having children?" I asked him.

"Regret is a silly religious habit," he replied sarcastically.

Yet I felt—rightly or perhaps it was a fancy—that he suffered bitter loneliness in old age. That period of his life thrived with fierce arguments, often reaching painful candor with friends.

"Admit that you're a reactionary time has left behind," he once told Reda Hamada.

Another time, he said to Doctor Zuhayr Kamil, "You don't critique, you destroy values!"

Gad Abu al-Ela asked him what he thought of his literary works.

"It would be better to save your time for the antique trade," Salim replied.

He was among those secretly delighted with the disaster that struck the country on the 5th of June 1967—a strange position adopted by all enemies of the revolution, joined by this deviant man, born to oppose the regime, at all times its gadfly.

"What's the point of being free of a class only to fall into the clutches of a regime of steel? The regime is more oppressive than class, than Satan himself!" he said, venting his anger.

But the revolution did not disintegrate, it healed its wounds, rejuvenated, and prepared for a new battle. His resentment—torn between contradictions—continued. On the surface, he maintained his public persona since 1924, remaining the revolution's loyal writer. Although now seventy, solitary, with no sense of humor, he is still in good health. He may well be the only Egyptian I know whom I've never heard joke, with no artistic interests that I know about—he doesn't even appreciate music. The little literature he reads, he interprets politically, as though he was born deviant, cut off from all enjoyment and beauty. Recently he has focused on belief in science, cloning his old belief in ideology.

"When will science rule? When will scientists rule?" he often asks—his last slogan, to satisfy his eternal opposition to all regimes.

"He's crazy and that's the truth," Reda Hamada said.

"There's another truth," I added. "His words have left their mark on generations."

Surour Abd al-Baqi

An Abbasiya friend. His father was a famous, rich lawyer, his mother a forceful character who ran her household with an iron hand. Father, son, and both daughters submitted. She was a miser, who haggled mercilessly with street vendors, calling off a deal for a single millieme, and weighed her purchases on a pair of scales she'd bought for the purpose. It showed in Surour's conduct among us—refined, well-mannered, and frugal; it was a special relationship—he was never apart but never assimilated, refraining from our unrestrained humor and dirty jokes. One day we were discussing a new singer—Umm Kulthum.

"I heard her at a wedding. Her voice is better than Munira al-Mahdiya," Surour said.

That was too much for us.

"Munira's voice rises, and none rises above it," Gaafar Khalil replied.

Khalil Zaki, who wasn't even interested in singing, attacked Surour with his usual impertinence. "Don't repeat your mother's views among us!"

Surour became angry and shouted, "My mother is none of your business."

The reply arrived in a punch. They fought until we separated them.

He was a hardworking student, but his success never measured up to his industry. Actually, we never thought he was intelligent. He almost split us when he demanded proper manners.

"Dirty words should not be uttered among us, we must act with respect," he said.

Khalil Zaki and Sayyid Shouayr both snorted at the same time.

"Or else I'll have to boycott you!" Surour continued.

"Suggest what you like, but no boycott!" I replied in alarm, as I was fond of him.

"His words are worthy of respect," said Reda Hamada.

"Foul language is like spice on food," Gaafar Khalil replied.

"I can't mention your fathers or mothers without the appropriate insult," said Eid Mansour.

"If our meetings are devoid of insults, that'll be their end," warned Shaarawi al-Fahham.

We debated the issue seriously, agreeing to continue our liberal conduct with the exception of Surour Abd al-Baqi, who would receive special, polite treatment.

His attitude toward politics was similar: he avoided it and showed no interest. He would not even join the peaceful demonstration to Abdin Square in support of Saad Zaghloul for prime minister. The day of the strike when Badr al-Ziyadi was killed, Surour stayed at home.

Surour Abd al-Baqi

Despite his good looks, he avoided girls and never flirted. He always felt his mother's eyes were watching him. Our reading time he spent in his garden, tending to flowers and lifting weights. He showed an early interest in studying medicine, but his baccalaureate grades were not high enough. So, he persuaded his parents to let him enroll at the College of Medicine in London. An Egyptian college would accept a student if he passed two years successfully in England. He returned to Cairo after two years, and joined the College of Medicine. We discussed the matter.

"He isn't stupid as we thought, or he wouldn't have succeeded in England," said Reda.

"And the admission system at the Egyptian College of Medicine isn't as flawless as people imagine," said Eid Mansour.

"And opportunities are not equal between rich and poor!" added Gaafar Khalil.

Surour Abd al-Baqi graduated in 1936; four years later, he married a girl from an influential family. He advanced until he became one of the most important surgeons in Egypt. With his fortune, he constructed a large building downtown and a beautiful villa in Maadi.

He was known for his ethics, humanity, and professional skill. An exemplary doctor, compassionate with patients, never greedy or exploiting, loved by his students, he often battled the college council for his uncompromising idealism. Still, he remained naive in matters of culture and politics, without a broad view of the society where he shone as one of its stars.

Major events passed him, until the July revolution, with its social impact, forced him out of his haven for the first time. He took an interest in this revolution that affected livelihood and changed conditions; an anxiety he had never known now crept over him. Agricultural reform had hit his wife—with the stroke of a pen, five hundred feddans flew out of his family's hand. The man, accustomed to the sanctity of money and property, was aghast, his family burned with enmity, he was implicitly an enemy. He was passed for deanship although he rightfully deserved it. He became bitter and sad.

"I thought of resigning, to focus on my private practice. But I don't like to shirk my academic responsibilities," he told me with sincerity.

From that moment, he took an interest in public life, especially politics—avoided all his life, it had now raided his home. We met infrequently at the Maadi Club when his schedule allowed. Reda Hamada and I stayed in touch with him, and Khalil Zaki because of his job at Qasr al-Aini. But he remembered everyone with affection. He was saddened by the deaths of Shaarawi al-Fahham and Gaafar Khalil, and Sayyid Shouayr's fall. Whenever Eid Mansour was mentioned, he'd say laughingly, "Shylock! Damn him!"

At the time, Reda Hamada, struck by the misfortune of his wife and son, grew closer to Surour—a similar burden despite its variance. The famous arms deal with Czechoslovakia alarmed Doctor Surour Abd al-Baqi. "It's the first step towards communism," he said.

In the Suez war and subsequent withdrawal of the invaders, he searched for consolation. "But for the United States, we'd have been finished," he commented.

"No, it was the Russian ultimatum," I said.

He objected violently. "We should never neglect American friendship again."

When the socialist laws were announced, dread overcame him, falling into a depression.

"You have a profession, you'll never know poverty," I told him.

"Nothing has value anymore," he said. "My wife advises me to emigrate."

"There's no need for that," Reda Hamada told him.

"Socialism is an expression of envy against the successful," he replied. "Our rulers usurped power with guns, not knowledge."

"What about poverty in Egypt?" Reda asked him.

"One's position is decided according to ability. That's God's wisdom!" he replied naively.

I realized that despite a person's learning or ethics, there was no substitute for cultural awareness, which of course included politics. No matter how brilliant or useful, he will not realize his human potential until he can see himself, not as an independent individual, but as a cell that had life only through cooperative existence in the human body. Doctor Surour, with his strong body, handsome face, and scientific skill, staggered because a hand took from the surplus of those who owned everything to heal the hungry millions. I was overwrought to hear vindictiveness in his tone after the June 1967 defeat, when he couldn't hide his joy at what he thought to be salvation. I discussed it with my friend Kamil Ramzi.

"Don't be surprised or shocked, better know the truth, however strange or cruel," he said. "Two sides are wrestling relentlessly. On one side are the Russians, the Arab socialists, and the people who have found in socialism their promised Eden; on the other are the Americans, the Israelis, and those who see socialism as an obstacle to their ambition and greed."

"And the nation and nationalism?" I asked him.

"The meaning of nationhood has changed," he replied. "It's no longer a land with borders, it's a spiritual environment defined by opinions and beliefs."

Suad Wahbi

She graced our college for one year, but dazzled our imagination for a long time. In 1930, there were ten female students; they carried a harem aura about them—modest dress, no make-up or jewelry, alone in the front row of the lecture hall as if they were in the harem section of a tram car. No greetings were exchanged; if it was necessary to ask a question or borrow a notebook, caution and coyness were employed, still it never passed peacefully, attracting attention, small talk, and a torrent of remarks.

In this conservative, frustrated atmosphere, Suad Wahbi sparkled like a star descending upon us from space. She was the most beautiful of all the girls, the tallest, with the most mature feminine figure. Not satisfied, she added color to her cheeks and lips, tightened her dress until it screamed, and walked with a swing. She'd enter the lecture hall late on purpose—after we had taken our places and the professor was about to start—rushing in, as if apologetic; her full breasts quivered, seducing the rows of students buzzing like bees. Her name became famous, adjectives were specially coined, she was 'Mistress Suad,' 'College Suad,' and 'Suad Afar.' Unlike the other girls, she was fearless, facing us with confidence, never concealing her self-admiration, discussing with professors in a voice everyone could hear. In a word, time and space both spoke.

"She's a whore not a student," said Mahmoud Darwish.

"What was she like in secondary school? We missed half our lives," said Gaafar Khalil.

"She's only in college to catch a husband," I replied.

"Or a lover!"

Suad Wahbi

Stories were spun; I've no idea if they were based on reality or imagination.

"It seems she's from the Jewish quarter, raised in an atmosphere of absolute sexual freedom!"

"And her family is loose, father, mother, and sisters."

"She's not a virgin, and she's initiated to night life, drunkenness, and debauchery!"

Encouraged, Gaafar Khalil tried to start an affair but was rejected and failed. Others were rejected and failed. Yet she never withheld her friendship from a male student who maintained propriety. Her fame rose to university heights—students from law school came to inspect. In English literature class, she sometimes read parts of Othello in a gentle, theatrical recital that bewitched minds. Even the English professor was impressed and gave her special treatment. Upright students—especially those from the provinces—debated the Suad phenomenon, inquiring about its undesirable consequences. The epidemic of their concern reached Doctor Ibrahim Aql, whose tall stature exerted paternal care over students and the highest ideals. He seized the opportunity of an uproar in the lecture hall over the quivering full breasts, and aimed the magic of his blue eyes on everyone until they sobered to maturity and peace.

"There must be some difference between the lecture hall in our university and Badia's nightclub," he said.

The hall shook with inappropriate laughter.

Shaking his head with his tall tarboosh, he added, "Remember that all of us, men and women, are scrutinized under the critics' microscope. A large number of them have not yet accepted the idea of co-education at university, or even higher education for women at all."

At the end of the lecture, he summoned Suad Wahbi to his office. We guessed the topic of conversation and predicted its inevitable outcome. Many were already sorry at their imminent loss of daily seductive excitement. Suad Wahbi left the Doctor's office scowling. When she saw the crowds waiting outside, she said sharply in a loud, challenging voice, "I will not permit anybody to remove my personal liberty!"

She insisted on enjoying her liberty, until we were surprised by her expulsion. Some were delighted, others felt a passing regret, but there was unanimous agreement to resist the reactionary political power that had suppressed the nation's freedom.

Suad's father came to see the dean; the expulsion was rescinded, after he assured him that his demands would be met.

The amazing part about Suad's return came from Gaafar Khalil. He asked me with a grin, "Have you heard the secret behind Suad's return?"

"What secret?"

"They say the Minister of Education commended her to the dean."

"But the minister is a reactionary, always babbling about respecting tradition."

"They also say he's having an affair with the girl."

In any case, Suad returned. When she appeared, we welcomed her with a round of applause. We saw her natural face for the first time—which was just as beautiful—her dress was more conservative in length and width; as for her breasts, her father's assurance could not change their position or seductiveness, and they remained firm, challenging dean and tradition.

One day, a student said, "I saw her with the Englishman in the Japanese garden at Helwan."

The news spread around the college. A friend asked her about it. She said she'd met him there by chance, so they walked around chatting. The story was now confirmed and reached college officials, impertinently challenging all. No action could be taken against the English teacher for fear of angering the High Commissioner, and it was not possible to punish the student for fear of angering the teacher! We appreciated all the political and psychological ramifications of the situation.

"England has added to the 28th of February declaration a special clause for Suad Wahbi," said Gaafar Khalil with his usual sarcasm.

"The British fleet threatens to occupy the customs house if Suad Wahbi is subjected to any pressure," added another.

Poetry was written and recited about the affair, sarcastic remarks were exchanged in the dean's hearing. But at the beginning of the next academic year, the situation had changed. The English teacher chose not to renew his contract, and Suad did not return to college. Where did she go? It is said she left with the English teacher; it is said that she got married; and it is said she became a prostitute on Alfi Street. Despite my many ramblings around Cairo, I have never set eyes on her since that far-off date.

Sayyid Shouayr

He was the real leader of the Abbasiya friends. True, Khalil Zaki was as strong, maybe stronger, but leadership doesn't depend on strength alone, not without love. Sayyid Shouayr was loved, he was generous, a clown in play and a star on Ramadan nights; comparing him to Khalil Zaki was always inevitable—both were strong and quick to aggression, Khalil departing from criminal fierceness, Sayyid from brazen recklessness. Both failed in primary school and were employed in their fathers' stores, both were exiled from their fathers' care—Khalil for his viciousness, Sayyid for his conduct with female customers.

From the corner of his sly eye, he spotted my love for Hanan, playfully ridiculing my hesitation. "Your love is nonsense," he told me. I didn't enjoy my love being another object of his ridicule, but he said, "Take my advice and meet her in the prickly pear forest."

Wednesday evenings during the annual vacation, he invited us to a sufi dhikr in the courtyard of his home, at the end of our street in Bayn al-Ganayin. We sat on two adjacent sofas, following the chants and watching the movements, sipping cinnamon and tea. Whenever his father moved away, he'd recount another episode from his obscene repertoire on sufis. His family was as religious as he was profane. I failed to understand him.

When he despaired of primary school, he went to work at his father's store in al-Ghuriya. We'd visit him after sunset during vacations. After closing, he took us around al-Husayn, from alley to alley, café to café. Under his guidance, we knew the madmen of Bab al-Akhdar, al-Fishawi, al-Midaq, and Khan al-Khalili; Ali Mahmoud's call to prayer; and the *mawawil* songs of al-Arabi. He taught us—in our first year of secondary school—to smoke the *goza*, the *buri*, and the narghile, and to play backgammon and dominoes. Those were his happiest days. He lived in his father's home, spent his wages on pleasures, imitating men when he was fourteen.

He flirted once with a woman customer while her husband stood outside the store, and a fight ensued. His father broke it up, then beat his son in front of the crowd. Sayyid lost his

Sayyid Shouayr

mind and poured his wrath on the merchandise, the glass and metal containers, the bottles of perfume .... His father threw him out—out of his store, out of his house—and relations were severed forever. We suggested our fathers mediate, but Sayyid refused proudly. "The prison of home no longer suits me, God's world is wide," he said.

We thought it a tantrum, but time proved he was truly a man of the wide world, with a strange capacity to sever family ties, discarding them like garbage. I couldn't reason it at the time, but later realized he'd been an outcast adolescent among three successful brothers; one worked with the father after finishing commercial school, the others continued their education with considerable success.

"Any merchant in the neighborhood would love to hire me!" he told me proudly.

"But this women business is dangerous," I replied.

"A woman loiters from store to store in search of a wink or a sweet word. Buying and selling only happen on holidays!"

He did work in many stores until the economic crisis strangled commerce. He was laid off and found himself alone, with no resources, family, or hope. Being students, we couldn't help, but he knew a café owner in Margush who sold drugs wholesale. He suggested Sayyid distribute on commission and he accepted, telling us with childish boastfulness. We were alarmed.

"You're crazy!" said Surour Abd al-Baqi.

"Impossible!" Reda Hamada told him.

He mocked our panic and begged us not to tell Khalil Zaki, whom he hated. He plunged recklessly, and extricated himself from hunger. His next step led to the prostitution neighborhoods—not an amateur, but a pro living with a woman in her house. He invited us to tour his new kingdom. Surour Abd al-Baqi declined. We went, drawn by curiosity, frustrated lust, and the magic of adventure. I recalled my experience with Ahmad Qadri and found the house, amazed by its new faces. Sayyid Shouayr led us through these paths as he had done in al-Husayn, teaching us the customs and secrets. We partied at lively cafés and assemblies of madams, thugs, and addicts, until the lewd songs, mocking lyrics, dirty jokes, and naked dances resonated in our heads like black magic, filling our hearts with joy and sorrow.

By the power of the Almighty, he joined the class of businessmen, opening a café in Wagh al-Birka—elegant, with cheap liquor, and a musician who enchanted the drunk and stoned clientele. He ran it with a thug's firmness and the smile of a merchant, sporting an effendi's suit, proof of his respectable roots, unlike other café owners who were drug addicts of low origin.

With the Second World War, his profits doubled, but his woman deserted him, joining the troop of beautiful prostitutes who preferred the night clubs with British soldiers. Only withered old hags remained in the old neighborhood, which deteriorated and was no longer fit for effendis. We saw Sayyid sporadically. Shaarawi al-Fahham's funeral reunited us. Once again, in a corner of the funeral tent, Gaafar Khalil, Khalil Zaki, Reda Hamada, Doctor Surour Abd al-Baqi, Eid Mansour, Sayyid Shouayr, and I came together.

The life-long friends met after losing one—in their prime, between thirty and thirty-five years old, each had found his path: the teacher, the civil servant, the lawyer, the doctor, the merchant, the pimp, the addict, and the drug dealer. We lamented our deceased friend.

"He left a vacuum that cannot be filled ..."

"What beautiful memories he leaves..."

"He lived and died laughing..."

"All his life, he bet on a dream that wouldn't materialize."

Sayyid rebuked us for not visiting him. We apologized, saying the old neighborhood was no longer suitable to visit.

"Shame on you. God have mercy on Shaarawi, the only one to visit me regularly!"

A few years after the war, official prostitution was abolished. Sayyid was forced to reappear above ground—forty years old, with a few thousand pounds, and a wealth of corrupt experience. We met at al-Fishawi café.

"You have an opportunity, start a new decent life," Reda Hamada told him.

"Isn't preaching ugly?" responded Sayyid with a laugh.

He decided to relax for a while. He stayed in a suspect hotel in the Muski, overindulging in drugs and alcohol, hunting women who could only be considered whores, his day spent playing cards and smoking the narghile. He stood outside time, and major events—the Palestine War, the Cairo fire, the July Revolution—simply passed him by.

When he was fifty, he married a drug dealer whose husband had died in prison; she was forty. Despite the strict penalties the revolution imposed on drug trafficking, he recklessly traded with no regard for consequences. He built himself a large house at the edge of al-Darrasa near the desert leading to the Muqattam hills. It stood on an acre of gardens he planted with palm trees, vines, guava, lemon, henna, and jasmine trees, and furnished in oriental style with pens for chickens, and with geese and rabbits on the roof.

We all met again at the funeral of Reda Hamada's wife. Around midnight, Sayyid and I left together, chatting as we walked.

"Haven't you made enough to stop drug dealing?" I asked.

"I make a lot and spend even more," he said disdainfully.

"But you don't consider the consequences."

"Damn the consequences!" he replied patting my shoulder. "Do you remember my old girlfriend who left me during the war?" he asked soulfully. "I heard she bore me a child, but I've not found a trace of them."

"Would you like to have a child?" I asked.

He laughed, ignoring my question. "I'm happy with my wife, and I don't think of marrying another. It would mean a life sentence!"

He sighed. "It all pales compared to what happened to our gallant friend Reda Hamada!"

"He has the greatest character and the worst luck," I replied with sorrow.

"Compare his luck with the bastard Khalil Zaki!" he said angrily.

"Yes indeed. An ironic comparison."

"He's low and despicable. But me, what's wrong with selling drugs?"

"I fear for you."

"Just remember what happened to Reda Hamada, who never sold drugs!"

He insisted on taking me to his bountiful house in al-Darrasa.

Still our meetings were rare; years would pass, then we'd meet by chance at al-Fishawi. I'll never forget the day he approached me a week after the 1967 disaster. I sat alone, mulling over the heavy burden I'd never known before. He sat down and asked, "Will the occupation of Sinai

Sharara al-Nahhal

really end smuggling?"

His question infuriated me. I considered it the limit of lounging outside time. He sensed my anger and silently smoked his narghile, then muttered, "As usual, you're only concerned with politics and headaches."

"It seems you haven't heard what happened," I replied angrily.

"We've heard and seen the wonder of wonders!" he said, suppressing sarcasm.

I saw him two years later at Eid Mansour's office—bloated in the face and belly, obviously ill.

"How are you?" I asked.

"Fine, as you can see!" he replied simply.

"But you're not your usual self!"

"Praised be Who never changes."

"At last he knows God!" laughed Eid Mansour.

"Have you consulted a doctor?" I asked.

"Do you really believe in doctors?" he retorted. "I've never seen a doctor or tasted medicine!"

After he left the office, Eid Mansour laughed. "It seems a funeral will reunite us soon."

Sharara al-Nahhal

I met him when I joined the civil service—a telephone operator in his twenties, fresh from primary school, attracting attention with his beautiful face, slender figure, and gentle nature.

"Take off that suit, put on a dress, and I guarantee you a husband in twenty-four hours," teased Amm Saqr, the messenger.

A seventh-grade post, vacated by its occupant's death, set the heart of every eighth-grade clerk on fire. No regulations governed promotions; university degrees were a curse that aroused resentment from department heads with only the old primary certificate. Eighth-grade clerks rushed to people of influence as recommendations flooded the undersecretary's office. My old classmate, Abduh al-Basyuni, then a member of congress, was my connection in the race.

Ustaz Tantawi Ismail stopped me in the corridor outside the secretariat. "Have you heard who's been promoted to the seventh grade?" he asked with a frown.

"No," I replied, my heart pounding.

"Congratulate Sharara al-Nahhal."

"Sharara al-Nahhal?!" I shouted.

"Yes."

"The telephone operator?"

"Yes."

"But he only has the primary certificate, and his job is outside the authority!"

He raised his head. "God bear witness, there are still people in Egypt who appeal to logic!"

He continued to his office; I went to the secretariat where it was the news of the day.

"Have you ever heard of a telephone operator in the seventh grade?"

"Who said he's a telephone operator? He's been assigned to the undersecretary's office."

"How?" I asked. "Why?"

"Don't be surprised," said Amm Saqr as he poured my coffee. "You're relatively new, that's all. Someone had already been selected for the promotion. Sharara had asked to meet the undersecretary, but was thrown out of the office, so he waited in the corridor until the his excellency passed. He threw himself at his feet, and theatrically declared he was responsible for a large family and his only connection after God was his excellency. The undersecretary glanced with revulsion, but something in Sharara's face held him and he stared, reluctant to take his eyes off."

The messenger paused with a malicious smile. I was perplexed. "What do you mean?"

"How I cried in love!" he whispered with a smile as he withdrew.

Sharara al-Nahhal was transferred to archives in the undersecretary's office. His appearance matched his new job. He replaced the old, threadbare suit with an elegant new one, black shoes instead of rubber sandals, a silk tie—apparently a donation, an embroidered handkerchief in his top pocket. When we met, we now greeted each other as equals. He was probably aware of what went around but didn't bother—either he was brazen or believed power would wash disgrace and silence tongues. Within two years, he became private secretary to the undersecretary, promoted to the sixth grade. As usual, the staff whispered. "You'll see him soon in the governing circle," Ustaz Abbas Fawzi advised.

Soon recognized in the ministry as the most important figure in the undersecretary's office, more important than the chief of staff, he became the mecca of petitioners, showered with gifts—a smile or greeting from him was the pride of their recipient, who thanked God's bounty.

A minister 'of that kind' was appointed to our ministry and an unforeseen crisis erupted, although both minister and undersecretary belonged to the same party. The conspiracy was plotted by a member of the minister's clique to settle an old score with the undersecretary. He seductively described the undersecretary's 'beautiful' secretary to the minister, and arranged a meeting for him to present the minister with some documents. It was said the minister was convinced of the secretary's competence at first sight, and that the secretary welcomed the minister's appreciation as befitting a young man with unlimited ambition. The undersecretary, informed of the minister's wish that his secretary be transferred to his office, furiously informed the messenger that he could not part with him. The angry minister transferred Sharara to his office by decree. The undersecretary sulked in his palace. It was said the president of the party reprimanded both men, warning them their dispute might leak to the wafdist press. The undersecretary returned to work, stifling his anger.

Sharara al-Nahhal's advance continued. He was promoted to the fifth grade and attached to the fourth—a wide and glamorous future stretched before him. But he did not make his way on beauty alone, or rather, it was not his only asset. He was intelligent, highly motivated, with more than one key to success. During his hectic work, he catapulted into an industrious student again, earning a high-school certificate, a baccalaureate, and finally a degree in law.

"He's not like others of his kind who rely on beauty, rapidly withering with age, forgotten old men in the fourth grade, or at most the third. Our friend is preparing for high office!" Abbas Fawzi commented, mocking and serious.

As a civil servant, he was among the most competent I've known—hardworking, persistent, and resourceful, an important reference in the administration, notorious for ambition, selfishness, and cruelty to subordinates—his former colleagues—never forgiving them a mistake or slip of the tongue, his greatest happiness realized in humiliating them.

The cabinet resigned while he was the minister's chief of staff, third grade. The Wafd formed the government, and the undersecretary was retired before he could take revenge on his old amour. Envious rivals rushed to the new minister, accusing the chief of staff of partisanship and moral deviance. Sharara defended himself—he was a 'civil servant,' his only loyalty to his work and employer—but he was transferred to records, a backstage position devoid of ambition. There, he reorganized the archiving system, breathing in new life, and invited the minister for an inspection. The man was pleased by his industry and complimented him. Then he published an article in al-Muqattam, entitled "A Wafdist Minister Compliments an Enemy of the Wafd," praising the minister's fairness, sincerity, and predilection for public good, how he encouraged him instead of crushing him, concluding that a man needed superhuman effort not to throw himself into the arms of the Wafd.

Ustaz Abbas Fawzi told me he was with the minister when he summoned Sharara al-Nahhal to thank him.

"Where did you find such eloquence?" the minister asked.

"Your Excellency," Sharara replied immediately, "it's a quality I acquired by memorizing the speeches of the immortal Saad Zaghloul Pasha!"

Sharara al-Nahhal was transferred to director of personnel, then promoted to the second grade before the Wafd cabinet resigned. The envious were delighted and said, "The bear has fallen." The former minister returned with the undersecretary. What could Sharara al-Nahhal do? We expected his finale, but were stunned when he was promoted to the first grade as director-general of the department.

"What does this mean?"

News filtered like drops—we learned Sharara had been secretly visiting his former minister and carrying out his wishes. He even reconciled him with the retired undersecretary. When they returned, he said confidently, "Our reign is back!"

It was also said he was tutoring the wafdist minister's son, a student in law school. But he intelligently realized that real power resided in the palace, a more satisfactory and permanent anchor for one with foresight. He wrote his only book, *Makers of Modern Egypt*, a biography of Muhammad Ali, Ismail, and Fuad, and dedicated it to the Royal Person. He received a thank-you letter from the Royal Diwan that was published in all the newspapers. He said to Adli al-Muadhin, his colleague and rival, "Now I've become a palace man, no party will dare touch me."

In the last days of the Second World War, he married into a respectable family, siring a son and daughter—like him, they were portraits of beauty. The daughter married his secretary, and the son became an army officer.

After the war, before the senate elections, he summoned me to his office and allowed me to sit down in front of his desk.

"The elections are very important. If the Wafdists win, they can change the whole regime."

I gave him a quizzical look.

"I'm thinking of recommending you to chair one of the election committees."

I smiled without uttering a word.

"You'll find a man from our party in the polling station."

"Which party?" I asked deviously.

He laughed loudly until his pink face reddened. "The party doesn't matter. Loyalty to the sovereign is what's important!"

"But I've no experience with this kind of work," I replied anxiously.

"Close your eyes and let our man work. You won't be required to do anything else."

I was dumbfounded as he stared at me.

"I recommended you because of your good character, but I won't burden you," he said.

He got up, we shook hands and I left the room. In forty-four districts, ten wafdists won; the elections, as usual, had involved every form of pressure, terror, and rigging. I thanked God I had not participated in that historic crime.

Opinions differ about his honesty. Some say he was honest despite his many faults, others claim he was a very careful, shrewd thief. He owned a lovely villa in Helwan and a building in Dokki, but always maintained they were bought with his wife's money. After the 1952 revolution, petitions brought him before the Purge Committee but nothing could be proven, so he continued in his job—it was said because of his officer son's intervention, but God knows. He was later promoted to undersecretary, then president of a corporation after the socialist laws.

Grief attacked him twice, once when his son was shot and injured during the Yemen War; then when his son-in-law was accidentally injured as he sat in a café during the student demonstrations after the June 1967 defeat. I haven't set eyes on him since he left the ministry, losing touch except for a few snippets that come my way. The last I heard came from a friend who saw him on the pilgrimage to Mecca in 1970.

Shaarawi al-Fahham

He was probably the kindest of the Abbasiya friends, kindness mingled with insouciance and an intelligent, thoughtful simplicity. I remember him laughing, with or without reason: hearing a curse or a passing comment was enough to drown him in laughter. Our heated political discussions made him laugh, when we argued about soccer or cinema, he laughed, if we attended a funeral, we'd not look his way for fear of a scandal among the mourners. At the funeral of a young relative of Gaafar Khalil, the dead boy's mother came out as the coffin left the house, barefoot, hair awry, beating her cheeks with a slipper, dancing like a madwoman. It brought tears to our eyes, but Shaarawi al-Fahham was gritting his teeth as his thin frame trembled under the pressure of suppressed laughter.

He was not cruel, dim-witted, or a fool, just a strange, different type. He lived with his mother in the house next to Sayyid Shouayr, with no father or siblings. His father had died when he was an infant, leaving Shaarawi and his mother the house and a pension of ten pounds. The mother devoted herself to his upbringing on the fixed pension, which held out until Shaarawi grew up and his demands increased. He didn't do well at primary school and was expelled for continuously failing, and there was nothing but the house, the café, and the street. His refined nature disdained Khalil Zaki's company, but he found a haven with Sayyid Shouayr, accompanying him on evening jaunts in al-Husayn and later the prostitutes' quarter. Sayyid introduced him to alcohol, and he was an alcoholic until he died.

Once, while he was still in primary school, he said to me, "I know."

I asked him what he meant.

"You're in love with Hanan Mustafa."

I kept an angry, embarrassed silence.

Shaarawi al-Fahham

"And I'm in love with Hanan Mustafa!" he continued.

I expected a struggle, but he laughed and said, "God's hand is with the congregation!"

"What do you mean?"

"Let's seduce her together in the prickly pear forest."

"Damn you!" I yelled.

That was a few days before the Mustafas moved, and the misunderstanding soon dissolved. Since then, I've never known him to have a love story or a marriage, his activity in that field confined to prostitutes. When his mother despaired of his education, she decided to find him a job—any work was better than none, she always said. Her important relative, Ahmad Pasha Nada found him a job in the Ministry of Endowments; but he couldn't persist: he spent the day at al-Fishawi café waiting for Sayyid Shouayr to get off work in his father's store, and was soon fired from the ministry. Never once did he miss our weekly evening, whether we were students or employed. Alcohol got him, he drank every night the cheapest and foulest kinds he could afford. You can imagine what anguish it did to his mother. He said one night as we partied at Sayyid Shouayr's café in Wagh al-Birka, "My mother won't comfort or be comforted. She wants to create me a job, but what job? She wants to get me married, but which wife?"

"You have a steady income of ten pounds. That's a decent income if you're content with one drunken bout a week. You just have to find a wife with an income," Eid Mansour told him.

He laughed as usual. "I'm waiting for relief, and it's coming soon!"

He meant his relative, Ahmad Pasha Nada, then chief of the Royal Diwan.

"Have you any idea of his fortune?" asked Eid Mansour, the keenest in monetary matters.

"Twenty thousand feddans," Shaarawi replied, filling his glass with hellish cognac. "As for cash, only God knows."

"And no heirs except you?"

"My mother's his sole surviving relative."

Reda Hamada confirmed the facts. It was funny, we only learned he was related to Ahmad Pasha Nada relatively late. He hid it in primary school because of the pasha's bad reputation as a sultan's man and an enemy of Saad Zaghloul.

"My mother is his only heir, and I'm her only heir, and the pasha is seventy-five, and what's coming is near," Shaarawi continued.

"Tell us what you'll do with the inheritance if it comes to you," Gaafar Khalil asked.

He laughed. "Ah, if dreams come true, I'll build a palace in Cairo, another in Alexandria, like the pasha himself. I'll fill the cabinets with every kind of aged liquor. As for women . . ."

"And what will you do for us, your friends?" Sayyid Shouayr interrupted.

"Your party will be in the palace garden. You'll be served the finest food, liquor, and women. God's covenant between me and you," he replied.

"It'll be a historic day when our friend inherits his imaginary legacy," Reda Hamada whispered in my ear.

He drank and dreamed of the inheritance. Wilting with time, his skin dried up, and despite his youth his hair turned gray. Then the pasha surprised the country, returning from a trip to Austria with a gorgeous blonde in her twenties. It was said he was going to marry her according to Muslim tradition. Public opinion rose in protest, our group quivered, and our friend almost went mad. The next thing we knew, Shaarawi went to court to have the pasha declared senile and incompetent. We discovered that Khalil Zaki had counselled him! Factors unknown interceded to restore balance. The Austrian girl left the country suddenly—it was said she had refused to travel until she received twenty thousand pounds. When the palace intervened, the press refrained from pursuing the matter and the incompetency suit was rejected. The pasha retired to his palace, then he announced his famous bequest, endowing his land to charities and mosques. We remembered our friend, saddened by his disappointment. He came to Fishawi's, drunk as usual, red-eyed and stunned. He stared at our faces, then he burst into laughter! Taking his shoes off, he jumped on to a divan in the center, crossed his legs, and sang, "If luck fails, what can you do with your cleverness?" He drowned in laughter again, infecting us, and we all laughed like lunatics.

Nothing new came over him, except more drinking. He drank day and night, affording only the cheap, demonic wines from al-Silsila, Darb al-Mubillat, and the bars on Muhammad Ali Street. His other appetites, food and women, diminished, and he lived in an exile of his own, communicating in a language of gestures, laughing at his dancing fantasies, or bending gloomily toward his ghosts, heading forcefully towards dissolution.

Gaafar Khalil tried to drag him into the world of cinema as he had done with Khalil Zaki, but he rejected the idea and laughed. Sayyid Shouayr offered him work in his café provided he didn't get drunk, and again he laughed. He had no ambition, no desire.

His mother died the year the Second World War started, and he rented out the house and lived in a room on the roof. In 1941, Italian warplanes raided Cairo after midnight. He was sitting on the roof in a drunken stupor. It seems he never left his chair. He was found slumped on it with a splinter through his head. His death was the first experience of that nature in our communal life, the first life friend we lost. Gaafar Khalil was the saddest among us, known always for his empathy toward our delinquent friends like Sayyid Shouayr and Khalil Zaki. The funeral reunited us, even those separated by circumstance. And Sayyid Shouayr said with genuine sorrow, "God have mercy on Shaarawi, the only one to visit me regularly!"

Sadiq Abd al-Hamid

"Doctor Sadiq Abd al-Hamid," said Gad Abu al-Ela, introducing him at his Dokki salon.

A shudder run through me as I shook his hand, recalling the name his wife Durriya had mentioned. Might it be someone else? Hope was dashed as Gad continued.

"He was on a short mission to England—he'd previously earned his doctorate there. A superb internist, but also a man of letters, an artist, philosopher, and politician."

Then he was my mistress's husband—this man, just forty, brimming with vitality and twinkling intelligence. I liked his luminous rambles through art, thought, and politics, finding myself drawn by his brilliant conversation, profound and diverse, and by his spirit; a firm friendship was mysteriously kindled, growing deeper with time, and clearing when I broke the affair with his wife, although I was never free of anguish whenever I remembered her.

Upon his insistent urging, I introduced him to Doctor Mahir Abd al-Karim's salon and Ustaz Salim Gabr's meetings, and to Zuhayr Kamil. I think he itched to try his hand at writing, but was content—for a while—to listen and debate, both giving him immense pleasure.

He was enthusiastic about the July 1952 revolution, a true believer who had dreamed of socialism since he was a student, with no party or feudal roots to hold him from embracing it.

"Have you got no complaint, even about some of its actions?" Reda Hamada asked him.

He replied with enthusiasm—he always talked with enthusiasm. "No. I supported its position on political parties, the Muslim Brothers, and even the communists . . ."

"And what's the need for that 'even'?"

"I'm not a communist, but I welcome their cooperation with the revolution. They're two currents from the same source, ultimately pursuing similar goals. I also supported its position on the union with Syria and the Yemen campaign."

"So it's not possible to have been more perfect," said Reda Hamada.

"I'm not unaware of the drawbacks," he said with a laugh, "but they're a necessary evil in times of transition and change. With one fortunate stroke, you can change the regime, but human nature takes a lot longer. Say what you will about cooperatives, but it's an ideal system. Corruption will disappear one day, and cooperatives will persevere. The same applies to the public sector. Do you remember the Agricultural Credit Bank? Ismail Sidqi used it to break his enemies and fragment the nation. He's gone but the bank remains."

When the disaster happened on the 5th of June 1967, he was stunned and lost his balance, stumbling between salons and cafés as though doomsday had arrived. We had a long talk on the telephone, which he concluded with "Was our life a fantasy?"

I met him a few days later at Reda Hamada's home in Heliopolis and found him agitated. "How many gloaters, how many scoffers. No one lost his mind, no one committed suicide, or had a heart attack. I must lose my mind or commit suicide," he agonized.

Slowly he regained confidence, seeing the defeat as a bitter test for self-diagnosis. If the enemy wished the revolution liquidated, his conviction and enthusiasm intensified, eventually its survival became more important than recovering the occupied land. What good was recovering land and losing ourselves? Its continuity was our guarantee for recovering the land, and for Arab resurrection.

"We're fugitives, pursued by backwardness—our real enemy, not Israel. Israel is our enemy only because it threatens to freeze backwardness."

One evening we left Doctor Mahir Abd al-Karim's salon together. I sat beside him in his car as it slowly carried us through a darkness pierced by its blue-painted headlights.

"Abduh al-Basyuni told me something strange," I found myself telling him. "He said Zuhayr Kamil has recently fallen in love with an young journalist named Nimat Arif."

"What's strange about that?"

"He's sixty, she's only twenty."

"Love is love, regardless," he replied with a laugh.

"He also said he's going to marry her," I continued.

"My dear friend, a war might kill thousands, an earthquake might destroy multitudes. Zuhayr's marriage might pass peacefully, maybe leaving a couple of victims behind!"

We were silent.

"I confess that I'm in love," he told me.

I recalled Durriya's words at our final meeting, but asked with feigned interest, "Really?"

"An Italian dancer at the Auberge."

"A whim, perhaps."

Sadiq Abd al-Hamid

"A love that's lasted more than ten years."

"What a great love!"

"Sometimes I feel it's lived longer than it should!"

I hesitated, almost asking about his wife, but he continued as if he'd read my thoughts.

"I also loved my wife once."

Tepidly, he talked of their love, the love of the intern and the nurse, as I had heard before.

"She's poor. Although we aren't rich, my family never accepted the idea of marrying her."

"But you married her."

"And we drowned in love like maniacs."

My tongue rebelled against my reticence. "Then the wells of love dried up?"

His voice rose, as though its pitch afforded him some defense. "The truth is that her attitude to love changed completely once she became a mother."

"How?"

"I don't know!"

"Of course you know."

"Maybe her love became greater, but I missed the first love, and then . . ."

"Then?"

"I withdrew, permanently."

"She's to be pitied!"

"I provide her with all the means of comfort. Sometimes I wish she'd love another man and leave with him peacefully."

I thought Durriya's story complete, but I had—and still have—many doubts. Fate had it that Sadiq and I should be introduced to Zuhayr Kamil's wife. He invited them to the Fayyum Auberge and made an excuse for his wife—that she was busy with the children.

A year later, Ustaz Gad Abu al-Ela, in his salon, told me, "I saw them together. Nimat Arif and Sadiq Abd al-Hamid at King Maryout."

I stammered to hide my discomfort. "Maybe . . ."

He interrupted me sardonically with a verse. "They said, you see her changed, fair one/Changed by the slanderer, and you said maybe."

I told myself the great doctor's emotional side required further study. He still talked about politics and art but never mentioned his new love, and continued his visits to Zuhayr Kamil as friend and admirer, filling me with anger and disgust. My anguish doubled when I saw Durriya in Gad Abu al-Ela's car speeding toward the Pyramids—I remembered the villa Aglan Thabit had told me about when he described Gad's affair with Amani, Abduh al-Basyuni's wife. Durriya was trying her luck once more with a frivolous man who offered no security.

My moral scruples exasperated me, as I remembered those who called them 'bourgeois.' Fortunately, I told myself, we don't have that much time left in this tiring, fascinating life.

Sabri Gad

He was appointed in the secretariat toward the end of the year of the defeat. He was twenty-two, with a degree in philosophy. From the first day, I eyed him with curiosity, eagerly anticipating when he would reveal himself and connect me to that strange new world. He was of provincial stock; born, raised, and educated in Cairo in a middle-class family, the only son among three daughters, all employed and married.

"Do you know Ustaz Abbas Fawzi?" he asked me one day.

"Of course," I replied. "He was our chief until he retired some years ago."

"Where does he live now?"

"In Abdin. Would you like to meet him?"

"Yes, I want to interview him for *Science* magazine."

"Are you a journalist there?"

"An intern."

"What do you say we visit him together? I haven't seen him for quite a while."

We went together to Abbas Fawzi's villa, constructed on top of the building he owned in Abdin. He welcomed us with his usual kindness. Sabri Gad interviewed him about his writings on classical texts. When he had finished, he excused himself to leave, but Abbas Fawzi said, "I won't let you go until you've answered my questions. Questions about your generation prey on my mind. Are you prepared to reply frankly?"

"Of course," the young man said with a smile.

"Frankly, please. This is private. Don't withhold the truth from me."

"At your disposal."

"The Ustaz wants to learn about the generation as a whole, not you personally," I said.

"That's exactly what I mean," Abbas said.

"At your disposal," Sabri Gad repeated.

Ustaz Abbas Fawzi sat up on the turkish sofa. "What's your position on religion?"

"Nobody cares about it," Sabri Gad replied simply.

"Nobody?"

"The majority are not interested."

"Why?"

"It's not of interest, maybe its illogical aspects oppose what we study."

"But I know the state teaches it and requires passing it in exams."

"We memorize it and pass."

"You mean that teaching it is fruitless as far as faith is concerned?"

"Yes."

"What about at home? Don't you learn about it there? Are your parents believers?"

"Yes, but they don't pray or fast, or talk about religion."

"Aren't there any Muslim Brothers among the students?"

"No, at least not in any numbers."

"Aren't there any students who are believers?"

"In my opinion, very few." He paused. "After the defeat, there was a tendency toward religion—some said the defeat was caused by neglect of our religion."

"Then there is a leaning toward belief?"

"Yes, some."

"I'd appreciate more precision," Ustaz Abbas said with a smile.

"I've told you what I know from my recollections of secondary school and university."

"Let me help you. Perhaps you mean that faith in general doesn't play an important role

Sabri Gad

among you, but the situation might have changed after the defeat?"

"Yes..."

"What do you think is the extent of this change?"

"I don't know."

Ustaz Abbas was pensive. I followed with alert senses and pointed interest.

"What values do you respect?" the Ustaz asked.

"Values?" Sabri Gad muttered, looking at him in bewilderment.

I quickly interrupted. "Please avoid abstractions as much as possible," I told the Ustaz.

"Why do you learn at school?" he asked again.

"It's better than loitering in the streets!"

"Just that?"

"And to get a job that would afford us a happy life."

"What's a happy life?"

"A clean home, good food, elegant clothes, and the other pleasures of life."

Unintentionally, I interrupted again. "Don't you like knowledge? To excel in it?" I asked.

"We all want to study, except those defeated by their grades."

"Why?"

"Degrees ensure the best jobs."

"And excellence, new contributions to knowledge?"

He wavered for a moment. "I believe the best students dream of that."

"Don't you read books in your spare time?" the Ustaz asked.

"We prefer the cinema, radio, and television. A few read."

"Do they read the classics?"

"I don't think so!"

"Didn't you have to read the classics as a liberal arts student?"

"Their language is complicated, the rewards shallow, and they're irrelevant to our time."

A sharp tone crept into the Ustaz's voice. "And the homeland? Do you still love it?" he asked.

"Of course."

"And Israel? Do you want to fight it?"

"We will liberate the homeland with our blood, the homeland you caused defeat."

"Us? Our generation isn't in power ..."

I signaled Ustaz Abbas to avoid sharpness. He calmed down and smiled.

"Which do you prefer, socialism or capitalism?" he asked.

"Terms don't concern us," shrugged Sabri.

"Terms?"

"Yes, we're bored with that. We want every individual to be free, successful, and happy."

"That means you prefer socialism," I said, intruding again.

"I don't know."

"Do you prefer the capitalist system?"

"I don't think so."

"Do you have a new system?"

"No. But we're bored with all that."

"And where do you stand on love?" Ustaz Abbas Fawzi asked. "Does love still have any value, or has sex become everything?"

"Sex is in control. A few still love and want love to go as far as marriage."

"And the majority?"

"They indulge in sexual adventures."

"With whom?"

"School girls, university girls, girls!"

"Do they accept marrying their adventures?"

"Many would, but some follow the tradition of the past generation."

"I don't think girls would give up the dream of marriage."

"That's their major fault."

"It's not impossible that you marry one day."

"Yes, even though my salary's a joke and my future's a void."

"But something surely attracts you to life?"

"The instinct of preservation."

"Isn't there some joy in your life?"

"A tasty meal, a good film, an innocent sexual relationship."

"Innocent?"

"One that isn't a trap to marriage."

"Do you think you're better than your father?"

"My father was a wafdist, he adored Saad Zaghloul and Mustafa al-Nahhas. It's laughable."

"Why?"

"It's been proven they were stone idols, no more, no less."

"I don't see you have an alternative ideology."

"I had, but everything collapsed after the 5th of June."

"What do you suggest to improve things?"

"The whole world's a vacuous nothing."

"What do you suggest to improve it?"

"Doing away with all its officials!"

"Then what?"

"It doesn't matter. Things will improve on their own."

"My dear boy, you've come to interview me about heritage when you don't believe in it."

"I'm a trainee journalist."

"Isn't your conduct a little opportunistic?"

"Anything, in this overpopulated world, that can get what you want is legitimate!"

"Thank you very much."

"Not at all."

We left the Ustaz's building, my heart was pounding like a storm.

Safaa al-Katib

The al-Katib residence was one of the noblest houses in old Abbasiya. It stood in the eastern quarter, an imposing structure with a sprawling garden that extended between two tram stops. We often walked along its wall on our way to the desert to play ball. I never saw more than tree tops, jasmine bushes, and drawn curtains. One day, on my way to the desert, a carriage pulled out of the east drive toward the main street with an old woman, her face showing a pair of sleepy eyes above the rim of her veil, and a girl glowing with youthful light. As my eyes fell on the girl's face, they embraced one of life's explosive secrets. The gates of heaven opened and showered me with a deluge of love's blessings.

"It's Safaa, daughter of the master of the palace," said Shaarawi al-Fahham, our most knowledgeable about the eastern quarter.

"She's twenty," added Khalil Zaki. Whenever he got a chance, he burglarized the gardens of the eastern quarter for a bunch of grapes or a mango.

"And you're only fifteen!" whispered Gaafar Khalil in my ear, noticing my change.

Her image, despite the passion she had created, vanished completely into a mist of the past; never in focus even while I was prey to her magic. I don't know the color of her hair or its style, or the color of her eyes, her height, or her shapeliness—that dissolved in a magical potion. When I remembered—or imagined I did—it came indirectly, an inspiration, like the scent of rose that surprises you from behind a wall as you pass by—nothing moved my heart unless it mysteriously led to her. I became infatuated at relatively late stages with features, looks, characteristics, and glances I imagined reminded me of what I had missed of her. I never loved a feature in a human face that she did not loom behind, in truth or imagination. Because of this fleeting love, my emotional life suffered continuous, complicated crises, as though she were black magic. It was a love without places, incidents, or a history. I saw her in the carriage for an instant, lost my will, and was thrown into a new world. My love for Hanan Mustafa had been recent—I realized my error and was convinced I was in love for the first time. I understood how one can be absent while present, to be awake while asleep, to vanish in a crowd from loneliness, to befriend pain and penetrate to the roots of plants and waves of light.

I hovered around the palace—locked windows, drawn curtains, and no souls except the doorman, the gardener, and some servants. Once I heard a soft voice calling the doorman, my heart trembled, immediately assumed it was her voice, then believed it. I saw her the second time on a sad occasion, in the window of an ancient house on Muhammad Ali Street where a group of women crowded to watch Saad Zaghloul's funeral procession. I noticed her only after the coffin had passed. Through my tears I glimpsed her shining face as she wiped her eyes, stretching her neck toward the blessed coffin. My heart gave a sudden leap, but I wasn't rewarded with a vision, and lost the thrill in a sad, broken heart. I was overwhelmed by conflicting emotions and the wave of weeping people. I only saw her again as she descended the steps of the salamlek in her bridal gown to mount the car that carried her to the bridegroom's house. I was in the crowd of onlookers on the opposite sidewalk.

This period lasted almost a year, the most incredible year of my life.

My affair was discovered by my friends. The jokers ridiculed me and called me Magnun Safaa, others warned me of persisting in a useless passion. We were young, our naive ideas borrowed from novels and what we had learned of Arabic literary history.

"Don't give up, or you'll go mad like Magnun Layla," Surour Abd al-Baqi told me.

"Your love shows that you loved her in an ancient time, maybe during the time of the pharaohs, like Rider Haggard says," said Reda Hamada.

This love, a powerful, consuming force, sought nothing less than devouring body and soul,

Safaa al-Katib

tossing me into painful purgatory. It smelted me into a new metal that craved existence, attracted to all that was beautiful and true. The love remained—after its creator had vanished—no less than ten years, burning like incurable madness. Thereafter, it resided dormant in my depth; roused by a tune, a view, or a memory, it would pulsate with momentary life, proving it had not yet been annihilated.

I'm bewildered when I recall those days, at the secret of the life I led. Was I touched by madness? I regret my love did not experience reality, that in its violent vortex heaven and earth did not meet, that I could not test my true abilities in endurance, in confronting its secrets under the cruel, coarse light of reality.

How wise Reda Hamada was when he told me one day after we'd reached some maturity, "Safaa was thrown into your life as a stimulant, she was a code that pointed to something. You had to discover her symbols to reach it."

"Our life has dissolved into ironies, but I hate to recall those days with scorn," I replied.

"Scorn?! How can one scorn the best days of his life?"

I walked by the Katib palace in the sixties and found it had been torn down and its rubble removed, the open space was being dredged for four apartment blocks. I smiled as I surveyed the lot, and sadness fleeted by. I remembered Safaa, whom I had not seen since she descended in her bridal gown. I knew nothing about her: alive or dead, happy or miserable? How had she aged now that she was sixty? What had happened to her, what did others think of her? Did she not deserve to know that she had been worshiped as a deity, that she had exploded into a heart life that still pulsated, now and then, with her memory?

Saqr al-Menoufi

Amm Saqr al-Menoufi was the secretarial department's messenger, but there came a time when our august department was almost called Amm Saqr's department. He was short and portly, but his energy surpassed the demands of his job. A self-serving spy by nature, as he served the morning coffee his whispers divulged the secrets of the ministry and its employees. He was the first to enlighten me about the real reasons for Sharara al-Nahhal's promotion from telephone operator to the undersecretary's personal secretary; his intelligence poured successively about Abbas Fawzi, Adli al-Muadhin, Abd al-Rahman Shaaban, Abda Sulayman, kind, unfortunate Tantawi Ismail, and others.

One day, as Ustaz Abbas Fawzi and I discussed rising prices and the hardship of employees on fixed salaries during the war, he said, "No one eats what they crave except Amm Saqr."

I expressed amazement.

"He loves good food," he explained.

"Love is one thing, affording it is another," I replied.

"He's a bureau of investigation, no wedding or funeral takes place without him knowing. You find him among the staff volunteering his services so that he can get to the banquet at the end. He's always at major mosques on *mulid* nights. A night never goes by without him attending a banquet. Which pasha matches him in this unrivaled gustatory fortune?"

Hence his constant brilliance with health and vivacity, and his gentle flirtation with meats, pies, and sweets. Other aspects of his life flowed at the normal, miserable level of a poor messenger, living with his wife and children in a ground floor room on Dibes Alley in al-Husayniya. When did he conceive the plan to get rich, no doubt devised and executed patiently and diligently? Perhaps around the time I joined the service in 1924.

He launched himself by selling off some jewelry and copper he had inherited from his mother and investing the money in lending to employees at an exorbitant interest—strange behavior for a Muslim man from poor country stock, but he undertook it, with no qualms until the end. His reputation spread among the poverty-stricken employees, who flocked to him greedily, as he became the center of a secret banking operation. His money piled up, and within a quarter of a century, he'd bought the building where he lived for a thousand pounds, demolished it, and constructed a small, two-story building with two shops.

He had two sons and a daughter, neglected as poor people neglect their children. The eldest became an orderly in a provincial health unit and cut himself off from the family, the middle boy worked as a butcher; and the teenage daughter disappeared—people said she had been abducted, gotten lost, or had run away. The middle son was killed in a fight at the slaughterhouse. Amm Saqr was grief-stricken and believed what had befallen him was God's punishment for usury. He halted his loans and penitently went on the pilgrimage.

Strangely, his improved means did not affect his appearance or conduct. He kept his menial job serving employees of whom he was financially master, sought weddings and funerals to enjoy free meals, and sniffed out news to spill as he served coffee. In his solitude, grief overwhelmed him for his lost daughter and dead son.

I was at Gaafar Khalil's funeral when Adli al-Muadhin came to present his condolences. We sat together for a while.

"Saqr al-Menoufi has been arrested," he told me.

Why, I asked, stunned.

"He lost his mind, no doubt. He was alone at home when the presser's daughter brought his suit back. He assaulted her, she's a minor."

He disappeared from my mind for a long time until he approached me at Fishawi's café, around 1960, a few months after his release from prison. Every time I inquired about his state of affairs, he'd reply tersely, "*Al-hamdulillah*, God be praised."

I learned that his wife had died while he was in prison and that he was living alone.

"I went to visit my son, but I wasn't comfortable, so I returned after one week."

I tried to console and encourage him.

"I accept what happened, it's just retribution. But why doesn't God treat people like Sharara al-Nahhal and Adli al-Muadhin the same way?!"

Sabriya al-Hishma

Around 1930, when she ran a brothel and four beautiful girls in Darb Tayyab, a strong friendship grew between her and Sayyid Shouayr. He introduced us and we became part of the *muallima*'s intimate circle with valuable privileges—private evenings in the house, after the *darb* closed down for the night, singing, dancing, and nocturnal reveries until dawn.

She was forty, fleshy, imposing, attractive in her features, with a dominating personality as befits a muallima. Her mere presence constituted natural law: all yielded, each in their sphere, no concubine, pimp, customer, or servant daring to belittle it.

Gaafar Khalil admired her, and Shaarawi al-Fahham fell in love. Sayyid Shouayr was forced to tell him, "The *muallima* manages, but doesn't work."

"Do you mean there are no men in her life?" Shaarawi asked.

"No, she has affairs, but not for money. She has a Greek man, a wine-dealer."

When the Second World War started, she was among the first *muallima*s to respond to change. She rented a large apartment on Champollion Street for secret prostitution, and expanded by opening a bar on Queen Nazli Street, maximizing the benefits of entertaining soldiers of the British Empire. That tense period revealed her talent for administration.

"I was worried about her expanding, that she might lose control, but she's cleverer than the red jinn," Sayyid Shouayr said.

He visited her regularly and kept us updated about her adventures. We learned how she traded on the black market, making huge profits from liquor and junk.

"She's more capable than any minister, although she's illiterate. She doesn't miss a millieme in the accounts of the house, the bar, or her commerce. She knows clients by name, and woe to anyone who tries to trick her. She's generous to those who work for her, the distributors, pimps, and girls. Everyone loves and respects her and holds her in high regard," Sayyid Shouayr told us.

"I wish our government followed her example in treating employees," I said to Reda Hamada.

He laughed. "To me, she's better than our religious friend, Zahran Hassouna!"

"Better than ministers and leaders who play the same game with the English, at the country's expense," I replied.

"God have mercy on our poor friend Shaarawi al-Fahham, she's probably the only woman he ever loved in his short life," said Gaafar Khalil sadly.

By the end of the war, she had amassed an enormous fortune and proved she was wiser than most. At fifty-five, she liquidated her affairs, deposited her many thousands in the bank, and built herself a villa in Maadi. Her Greek friend had died, she had no family or heirs, so she lived a quiet, comfortable life. Then she decided on radical change. She went on a pilgrimage, gave generously to her old friends, and donated to charity. In 1950, when she was sixty, I heard she had married a man in his thirties, a civil servant in the Survey Department. I realized her period of serenity had come to an end, and a time of troubles had started. I've heard no more; marriage had closed her door in Sayyid Shouayr's face and I lost track of her.

Tantawi Ismail

Probably the one civil servant in whom I found nothing of the customary civil servant's 'essence.' When I joined the service, he was chief of the general secretariat, fifth grade, fifty years old, and held that position until he retired in 1944.

Looking over over my employment file, he asked, "Were you a student of Ibrahim Aql?"

"Yes, and Doctor Mahir Abd al-Karim as well," I replied proudly.

"Mahir Abd al-Karim is a great man, but Ibrahim Aql is a heretical bastard, a tail of the missionaries," he said in a voice with a coppery ring.

"He has retired from intellectual life, a ghost remains of his professorship," I replied, with no motive to defend the man.

"All that remains is a mercenary," he retorted angrily.

I witnessed Tantawi Ismail several times in the director-general's office: dignified, he never bowed or flattered. He corrected letters submitted to him for style and language, not only technical mistakes. He inspected every office in the department to check work order, showing no sympathy to the sluggish and negligent. Yet I never found an employee who acknowledged his qualities. His conduct was usually described as idiotic or megalomaniac.

I remember just before the Islamic New Year, he told me, "I was the first to demand that Islamic New Year's Day be an official holiday," and showed me the article he had written. When he was promoted after many years, as a result of a cabinet decree for forgotten employees, I congratulated him.

"If they were just, they would give power to the forgotten, the noblest civil servants."

Amm Saqr, whom he treated kindly, was there.

"Maybe this will change your mind about the Wafd, sir!" he said to Tantawi.

"This isn't fairness," he replied. "It's camouflaging evil in a panic, a half-solution. That's the Wafd's real secret motto. Truth is truth, false is false, the real good is to empower the deserving and throw the corrupt in jail. God have mercy on the Nationalist Party leaders, their lives were sacrifice and struggle, not politicking and parlaying!"

One day, reading the names of officials awarded ranks and decorations, he said, "But for faith in God, that His wisdom is beyond man's understanding, I'd have gone mad!"

"He still thinks he's sane," whispered Abd al-Rahman Shaaban, the ministry translator.

He was considered insane and much of his behavior ignored. I learned about his past from Abbas Fawzi, Amm Saqr, and others. He was twenty when he was employed at the ministry with a diploma in commerce; within five years, he became inspector of accounts, discharging his duties with an honesty that brought panic to clerks and auditors. They operated a tight, cooperative system of bribes and gifts; the man exploded in their midst demolishing their real source of income. Had they been brave, they would have murdered him, instead they forged his signature. He found himself accused and unable to prove his innocence; a disciplinary council dismissed him. Imagine someone honest to the point of insanity finding himself fired for dishonesty! He left screaming, "I'm honest, I'm honorable, I'm innocent!"

For five years, he endured pain, hunger, and insanity until his nerves cracked. His uncle committed him to the mental asylum in Helwan, where he spent a year until he recovered, but he had lost something essential and irreplaceable.

The man in charge of accounts fell ill; sensing the end was near, he summoned the head of investigations and confessed the conspiracy to trap Tantawi Ismail. An investigation, secretly reopened, reinstated him in a 'non-financial' department to avoid damage to himself or others.

I worked ten years with him and knew him closely—boundless belief in God, purity of character, and a fanatical patriotism. He was well read in religion, conservative to the degree that new ideas or conduct were a deviation and a fall.

We shared a corner at al-Husayn mosque on the annual evening of Shaykh Ali Mahmoud's recital. "Are virtues still virtues or have they become old-fashioned?" he asked people around him, launching a tirade on cowardice, flattery, corruption, and decay. "We need a new flood, the ark will carry the few decent people who will recreate the world!"

I always wished to know more—his private life, upbringing, relationship with his wife and children, behavior with life's temptations—but satisfied myself with what came my way. He cultivated purity but lived in a swamp of bacteria; his violence for truth sometimes pushed him unaware to the verge of inhumanity; his bluntness marred by unnecessary hurtfulness brought on him a general feeling of distaste, even hatred. Abd al-Rahman Shaaban, the ministry translator, referred to him as 'son of a crazy woman.' Ustaz Abbas Fawzi sarcastically called him 'our master Tantawi ibn al-Khattab, God be pleased with him.'

Yet he could not stop the wave of modernity from invading his lair. One day—I was still a new employee—I saw a beautiful, attractive girl sitting beside his desk. He introduced us.

"Soraya Raafat, my brother's daughter." With a protesting smile, he added, "She's a student at the Higher Institute for Education. Knowledge is light, but I don't approve of the working woman. But I have no say in my elder brother's household except to offer advice."

The last incident to leave me with an imprint was the day following the 4th of February, 1942. Before he sat down at his desk, he said, "What do you think? British tanks returned your leader returned to power."

I always avoided arguing with him when he was steaming.

"Have you ever heard of such leadership?" he asked with blazing eyes. Anger overcame him and he shouted like one possessed, "The flood, the flood, the flood . . ."

Taha Enan

He appeared in our world during our fourth year of secondary school. His father had been the police *maamour* in Asyut, then was transferred to Cairo as *maamour* of al-Wayli, and set up home in Abbasiya.

At school, Taha met my friends Gaafar Khalil, Reda Hamada, and Surour Abd al-Baqi, but he grew closer to Reda Hamada and me as we shared wafdist ideology and cultural interests. He participated in the strike when our friend Badr al-Ziyadi was killed. His father was part of the force that surrounded the school then attacked with brutal strength. We debated his father's position; he was ashamed and hurt.

"My father's a nationalist, just like us," he said in his defense. "He believes in Mustafa al-Nahhas as he did in Saad Zaghloul. But he's performing his duty."

"We've heard of officers like him joining the revolt in 1919," Reda Hamada replied.

"Those were days of revolt, there's no revolution now," defended Taha as best he could.

Seriousness dominated his attitude, so he rejected Gaafar Khalil's humor. We read together the classics and the works of contemporary intellectuals, debating with enthusiasm, aspiring to a common intellectual future. Taha believed in books, referring to them in all that concerned him about life. When he heard about my love for Safaa al-Katib, he was surprised.

"Your feelings aren't normal," he said.

"But real!" I replied angrily.

"I'm in love with my cousin. We're thinking of announcing our engagement."

Following his predilection for consulting books, he took me to Dar al-Kutub, where we looked under the word love in the *Encyclopaedia Britannica*.

"Here is love from all angles, physiological, psychological, and social. You can see now that

Taha Enan

what you have isn't love, it's madness."

"Madness..." I muttered furiously.

"Don't be angry, maybe we need more reading," he said with a smile.

We didn't read more about love, but we read a lot, especially during the summer vacation, about new and diverse phenomena. Everything was new. Severe mental and psychological crises ravaged us.

Sitting at Fishawi's, he made a strange suggestion.

"We must start from nothing!"

"From nothing?"

"We can only face this torture by starting at zero," he said with a confidence that belied our breakdown.

I gave him a quizzical look, although I understood what he meant.

"From zero," he went on. "Recalling the story of civilization again, relying on reason alone."

"And if we encounter what reason cannot answer?"

"Let's start with reason, considering it man, and see where it leads us."

We continued our journey over the first two years at university, but unexpected events obstructed our way. Ismail Sidqi abolished the 1923 Constitution, and the Wafd rose to confront him with all its popular might.

A fearsome day, tension was at its peak, police and army occupied the crossroads, the people couldn't congregate to form a great demonstration. Assembling in alleys and side streets, they burst out, shouting, throwing rocks in all directions, then dispersed quickly for another round as bullets chased them.

We participated, Taha Enan, Reda Hamada, and I. From the beginning of the day, we joined the scattered gatherings, sudden forays, and rapid dispersals to the tune of whistling bullets. Hundreds fell, we saw soldiers pounce on them like vultures, carrying them off into trucks with inhuman brutality, hiding bloodstains with sand. Before sunset, the fighting died down, and gatherings became rare, although the air remained charged with dispersed shouting, and few but constant gunshots.

We decided to go home, walking along Hasan al-Akbar Street, arm in arm from fatigue.

"For months, the people have been resisting, uncounted victims have fallen, no one cares," said Taha Enan, who was in the center.

"He's a bloodthirsty murderer," said Reda Hamada.

"Anyway," Taha went on, "the people's positivism is better than the cold debates at Doctor Mahir Abd al-Karim's salon."

He felt heavier. "Are you tired?" I asked. He didn't answer, getting still heavier. We looked at him and saw blood gushing from his mouth.

"He's been hit," Reda Hamada yelled.

The shooting hadn't stopped. We saw a dentist's sign and, shivering with anxiety, carried him inside. The clinic was empty, but the nurse laid him on a couch and rushed to phone the ambulance. Taha took his last breath in our arms before the ambulance arrived.

Abbas Fawzi

We became friends the day I joined the civil service. Our desks shared the same corner of the secretariat: me, Abbas Fawzi, deputy-director of the secretariat, and Abd al-Rahman Shaaban, the ministry translator.

Our chief, Tantawi Ismail, introduced him. "Ustaz Abbas Fawzi, the deputy-director."

I looked at him with interest and asked, "Are you the famous writer?"

When he replied affirmatively, I shook his hand with enthusiasm, as the other employees looked on in disgust.

"We always found your books on the classics very useful," I told him.

"But the university only recognizes degrees," he replied.

"There's a level of knowledge that transcends degrees."

"Your professor Ibrahim Aql doesn't believe that," he retorted angrily.

I considered him a jewel in my new world. We worked together, and met at the salons of Doctor Mahir Abd al-Karim and Salim Gabr, and later, Gad Abu al-Ela. I was surprised that he was still on the sixth grade, despite his fame and fifty-three years of age. His colleagues believed he had usurped the grade in the name of the gibberish he wrote. The strict civil servant respects only a real bureaucrat, expert in administration and regulations; writing books was seditious, not worthy of respectable men. They tell the story of his leap. He was a clerk in the archives where he belonged; he didn't even have the primary certificate. Whenever a new minister was appointed, he would present him with a collection of his works, accompanied by a dedication in verse. The ministers would accept the gift, he would return to the archives, and the curtain went down on the recurring drama, until a lover of literature became minister. He admired Abbas Fawzi and promoted him to the seventh grade, and two years later, to the sixth, appointing him deputy-director of the secretariat, where he was imposed on them.

Ustaz Abbas Fawzi knew what was said and returned their contempt. Frequent verbal battles occurred until conciliatory forces intervened. He considered the civil servant a poisonous insect and defined man as a talking civil servant.

A man of Tantawi Ismail's distinction told me, "Beware, he's learned, but has no morals."

He was burdened with children and poverty, struggling to satisfy himself and his family. I've never known a man to exude such bitterness, expressed in vicious sarcasms that spared none. He disdained the bureaucrats' morality that soaked him up to his head, and derided successful intellectuals, although he failed to match their achievements, even in his own field. He kept an inexhaustible supply of information that questioned their talents or impugned their personal conduct. His real value was in Arabic-language classics—with no exaggeration, he knew it all, prose and verse, by heart.

"You're dazzled by Western literature, you think it's everything, yet you know nothing about Arabic literature," he told me one day. "I challenge you, cite me any piece of Western poetry, and I'll match it from Arabic literature."

I quoted what came to mind from poetry and prose, and he countered in Arabic, with almost defying perfection. He stalked us, whenever we spoke, correcting our pronunciation.

"Our words should not be printed without vowelling," he would say.

One day Abd al-Rahman Shaaban and I paid him a visit because he had been ill with

Abbas Fawzi

kidney trouble. We found him in bed, wrapped in a blanket that showed only his head.

"How's the kidney, Ustaz?" I asked.

I pronounced the 'k' in kidney with an 'i' vowel as we normally do in colloquial Arabic. In a feeble, almost inaudible voice, he corrected me: the 'k' should be pronounced with the 'u' vowel.

"When he dies," the translator said on our way home, "he'll correct the pronunciation of the angel questioning him!"

His attention focused on Arabic classics. He had no other interest; no other art appealed to him, not even singing. He knew nothing about modern culture, he was not interested in politics, making no distinction between one party and another, the only minister he respected was the one in office, and he didn't believe in any values or religions—his only loyalty was to himself, his family, and the Arabic language. His office at the ministry was a meeting-place for poets, writers, journalists, and song-writers of different generations. Many asked him to revise the grammar and syntax of their texts for a small fee. He always welcomed them warmly, showering them with praise, then stoned them as soon as they left.

"That poor song-writer, he divorced his wife when he fell in love with her son by a former husband!...This one may be the only contemporary poet who's homosexuality surpasses that of the late famous poet so-and-so!...This author really has a big heart. He loves all political parties and only when they're in power!"

He was once visited by an old Englishman who had remained in Egypt after his retirement, and who spoke Arabic as well as he did English.

"I admire English ethics," he said after his visitor had left. "There's a tremendous difference between an English homosexual and an Egyptian homosexual. The Englishman carries his homosexuality with him to the ends of the earth, but it never stops him serving the empire until death. The Egyptian homosexual has neither principle nor belief!"

And as he showed no compassion, he was shown none. He claimed his father had been an engineer; they said he was a grave-digger and his mother a washerwoman. They also accused him of sexual perversion. The only person he spared was the minister who had been kind to him or, as he put it, had discovered him. "He was cultured, dignified, and fair even though he was a minister," he would say.

But he held the reins on his aggression with influential people, in power or outside it, not participating in partisan discussions or offending a palace man even if he were a cook. During the war, he pretended to support the allies, but after Dunkirk, when many thought the war was about to end with a German victory, I heard him recite the verses of Bashshar: "We sent them sudden death/We are death's children, over us flutter its strands/A group were taken prisoner/Others killed, and others took to sea in flight."

When the the tables were turned on Germany at al-Alamein, I quoted the same verses of Bashar. He realized my trick and said, "God have no mercy on Bashshar, he was a Nazi faggot!"

The day after the 4th of February 1942, party lackeys among the employees accused the Wafd of betrayal, while wafdists rejoiced and Amm Saqr danced around the department. Abbas Fawzi feared his reticence might be construed as unfriendly to the Wafd. He seized the opportunity of Tantawi Ismail shouting, "The flood, the flood, the flood . . ." and said wisely, "Say what you will about last night's events, but we must admit that Mustafa al-Nahhas has rescued the nation at this critical point in its history!"

It was his good fortune that the wafdist minister was fond of literature. He promoted him to the fifth grade and appointed him chief of the secretariat after Tantawi Ismail's retirement. But his books did not flourish as university professors debated with him, their modern intellectual approach giving them an edge. His anguish increased when one of his students used his knowledge of the classics to write religious works about the Prophet and the Quran, making an incredible amount of money. Abbas Fawzi almost went out of his mind.

"In my day, atheism was the fashion, so we faced that direction." He shook his head sadly. "How could I have missed that golden gate?" Then he asked me angrily, "Do you know what is the real wealth of the Arab world? It's not oil! It's the story of the Prophet and the Quran!"

"What do you say we translate together some Western books that deal fairly with the Prophet?" Abd al-Rahman Shaaban asked him.

Abbas welcomed the idea, and though they were both atheists, they carried it through, bringing them a profit that was the first real money Abbas ever made in his life. He followed with biographies of all the prophets, his affairs improved, and he faced the post-war rise in prices with confidence.

"If only God had sent many more messengers and prophets," he told me one day.

His sons graduated from university and were employed, so he decided in 1950 to take his first summer vacation. He had never asked for a vacation, and kept on working year after year.

"Why don't you take a vacation to relax for a while?" I had asked him.

"You're kind-hearted," he laughed. "You know nothing about those who are after my job. They meet me with embraces, hiding their daggers behind their backs. If I left for a month, they would immediately start intriguing to get my job. We live in a jungle of wild beasts, but they are lower and filthier than beasts."

I failed to understand his logic. In any case, in 1950 he was confident enough about himself and the revenues from his books to give himself a holiday. He took his wife and daughter to Alexandria. He was seeing it for the first time in his life. But he found himself a lost waif, having never before dealt with leisure. His days were filled with work—at the ministry, at home, at literary salons—but he never knew cafés, cinemas, or theaters, not to speak of Alexandria. He was fed up with the beach, and his wife was terrified of the crowds. So they decided to return after one week, despite their daughter's desperate pleas.

The July revolution hardly had any effect on him; he neither grieved for the passing world nor was joyed at the coming one. He doubled his efforts at religious writing until he had made a real fortune. In 1959, he retired and devoted more time to his work. He constructed a building in Abdin, with a villa for himself on the roof.

Until today, he remains recalcitrant and sarcastic. Whenever I visit him, he regales me with his latest sarcasms and complaints.

"Imagine, I haven't yet been elected to the Language Academy! As if its foreign members are more knowledgeable about the language than I am. And the Supreme Council for Literature doesn't count Abbas Fawzi among its members! Is it destined to have only plebs as members?!"

When he noticed my depression after the June defeat, he said with a smile, "Your hair's gone gray, but you still haven't learned any wisdom." Sarcastically, he asked, "Is there any real difference whether you're ruled by the English, the Jews, or the Egyptians?!"

Adli al-Muadhin

He was employed at the university when I first enrolled. We frequently met in the library, and he also attended Monsieur Coriet's lectures on philosophy which he found useful in preparing his master's thesis. We called him 'The Egyptian Scribe' because of his amazing resemblance to the statue, except he was tall, broad-shouldered, and in his dark face two falcon eyes flashed provocatively, radiating intelligence and cunning.

We met once in the Urman Garden on our way to college.

"I'm presenting my thesis next October, but I'm already thinking of the next step," he said.

"A doctorate?" I asked.

"No," he replied. "Do you have you any idea which philosophical books would be popular?"

"I didn't think philosophical works were written to sell."

"But if we published a series of books on the victims of free thought in philosophy and sufism, wouldn't we contribute to the defense of freedom, assassinated in our era?"

"A magnificent idea," I replied enthusiastically.

"And successful, don't you think?"

"Most certainly."

He received his master's, but did not implement his idea. The only books he published were revised editions of *The Absurdity of Philosophers* and *The Absurdity of the Absurdity*. My classmate in college, Aglan Thabit, told me about an unknown side of his past.

"He's our neighbor in Sayyida Zaynab. His father was a tram driver, and now he lives with his mother and sister."

"His staid, imposing appearance affirms that he's from a lineage of rulers," I commented.

Aglan laughed. "He was employed with the primary certificate and continued to study until he reached this level of learning." Then he whispered, "It seems his sister is a devilish flirt who missed her marrying age!"

He had a humorous side; at an end-of-year party in college, he volunteered to do imitations of the professors, succeeding wildly with Doctor Ibrahim Aql, hardly mentioning the highest ideals before the hall burst into loud applause. Nevertheless his relationship with Doctor Ibrahim Aql was close. When the Doctor got his important position after currying the palace's favors, he depended on Adli al-Muadhin in his administration; before the Second World War, he introduced him to a minister who had him transferred to his ministry, a wider field for his ambition than the university.

Thus he arrived at our ministry, an important man close to the minister. I went to visit him with congratulations and anticipation, only to find a new person—a dangerous administrator hardly connected to the man who groped with difficulty along the path of philosophy. His latent talents epiphanized in the service of minister and ministry. He had a sharp intelligence, exceptional administrative ability, and an unbelievably cool temper, uncommon among Egyptians. Immediately, Sharara al-Nahhal realized his threat, taking it carefully into account. Ustaz Abbas Fawzi imagined that an important, educated employee had arrived at the ministry at last, and that he had better present him with his works. I made the introduction.

"It's not my habit to offer my books, but books are written to be presented to people like yourself!"

"I admit that I've already read them," replied Adli with his rare coolness.

Adli al-Muadhin

Delight shone on Abbas Fawzi's face.

"And I must admit that I found them superficial, adding little to the original ..."

Abbas Fawzi paled, but pretending humour, said, "Don't judge by your mind, Ustaz. We write for the simple folk, to educate them, but philosophers are beyond us."

Returning to the department, he said, "Don't repeat this to the any of the rabble."

"Of course not," I replied, secretly lamenting.

Regaining his sardonic nature, he said, "Philosophy began with the son of Rushd and ended with the son of a dog."

In a short time, Adli al-Muadhin had the ministry and its employees under control. He was head of the advisory office, connected to every branch. His superhuman energy earned him trust without falling into the quagmire of party politics. He maintained his probity, not leaning toward what might impinge on honor except in extreme necessity, raising the parvenu to sublime heights. Deep down, he leaned toward the Wafd and its popular, democratic values, but he stifled it with his cool nerve.

He was never known for a charitable act in his life, and he never hesitated to harm if he could, undoubtedly finding pleasure in evil provocation—debunking enemies and even friends. He didn't care to be loved, I often thought he was striving to be the object of anger, hatred, and envy. In that, he was different from Sharara al-Nahhal, who covered misdeeds with compassion, sweet words laced with poison, eager to gain confidence even through lies and hypocrisy. The staff hated Adli like Satan. They whispered his weak points, like his roots and his sister's story. Some interpreted his bachelorhood as a sexual perversion hidden under stern haughtiness— which was why the only employee to help him was a handsome, dissolute young man.

I often wondered how he kept his dignity and job despite the continuous flow of ministers and parties. With investigation, I learned he gave protection to employees from various political parties. When the party of one came to power, the favor was returned, recommending him to his minister. He kept his position through all the reigns, justifying his success with competence. He sailed from one promotion to the next until he was appointed director-general before the July revolution.

And in spite of our old relationship, he had no qualms about sacrificing me at the first opportunity. The personnel committee nominated me for a vacant position after lengthy comparisons between me and my rival, a clerk in the records office. The committee submitted its decision and it was signed by the minister. I left the ministry that day promoted and congratulated. When I returned next morning, the decree had been rescinded and my rival promoted in my place. I almost lost my mind. I learned that a senior official in His Majesty's court had called Ustaz Adli al-Muadhin the previous evening to recommend my rival. Adli hurried to the minister's office (the reign being royalist) and informed him of the recommendation. Immediately, my promotion decree was torn up and another one issued. I went to Adli al-Muadhin's office in a rage, but he remained silent and cold until I tired.

"Prepare the report on the new budget for the press," he told me calmly.

I learned more from the deputy-director of personnel, as much my friend as he was his enemy. "What happened is a clear contravention of the law. A ministerial decree can only be changed by another ministerial decree. I myself saw your promotion decree. When was a second one published rescinding the first?"

"Can you raise the matter officially?" I asked.

"Only the British ambassador could manage that!" he replied with a laugh.

"But what's the relation between the other employee, who is a small person like myself, and the palace official?"

"Praise our master Lot!" He laughed again.

After that incident, our relationship waned, almost confined to official business. Before, we met in Sulayman Pasha Square every morning, walking together as colleagues despite the difference in rank, had breakfast at À l'Américaine, then continued to the ministry, remarking on events, passers-by, and things. He was charming, friendly, laughing, and humorous. He would even tell me the latest political jokes he had heard about the king, his entourage, and family, or he would invite me to his new home in Maadi where he moved after his rapid rise. Fifteen minutes later, he would summon me to his office and appear with a new face, stern, cold, commanding, threatening, with no mercy or taste! I'd leave clapping one hand against the other. Once, to relieve myself I confided to Ustaz Abbas Fawzi.

"He has a split personality, the son of an old hag," he replied. "We're doomed in this ministry with all sorts of perversion."

The 1952 revolution offered him an opportunity to eliminate Sharara al-Nahhal, his greatest rival for undersecretary. I believe he was behind some of the petitions that sent Sharara to the Purge Committee. But the man escaped miraculously and was promoted to undersecretary—the biggest blow Adli al-Muadhin received in his life. He soon found himself a stranger among new employees he did not know. Most of his associates disappeared in the purge, and he faced a new life. He sought my friendship again as he had done at the Urman Garden, and we returned to our meetings in Sulayman Pasha Square.

"The ministry has fallen into the hands of a group of boys," he said sarcastically. "What's the value of knowing the laws and principles of administration? Now you can do what you please, as you please, in the name of the revolution."

For the first time in my life, I felt a wave of justice sweeping through decay with no complaisance. I hoped it would continue without hesitation or deviation, pure forever.

He tried to ingratiate himself with the new leaders but failed. He was attacked by leukemia, retiring at home for a while until he died around 1955. I'll never forget the moment his death was announced in the ministry. Employees broke our time-honored tradition. I heard scores of them saying in loud, malicious voices, "God send him to hell! . . . a thousand hells!"

His funeral was the poorest I'd ever seen; only ten people attended, one relative and nine of his old university colleagues. One important person attended, Doctor Ibrahim Aql, in his mystic phase after the death of his two sons.

One day after Adli al-Mudhin's death, his spinster sister committed suicide.

Abd al-Rahman Shaaban

Unforgettable. When I sat at my desk in the secretariat for the first time, he shook me like an electric shock. A giant of al-Aqqad's height, huge like Zeywar Pasha, elegantly dressed, resplendent, you'd take him for a reactionary minister or a bank director.

"Our great Ustaz, Abd al-Rahman Shaaban, the ministry translator."

Later I learned that his salary was only twenty pounds. That first day, he seemed morose and foreboding like a fortress, and I assumed there would be difficulties in this association fate had decreed, but he could open his heart easily and quickly, his laughter exploding like bombs, blood pumping his round, fleshy face, which was childishly innocent.

When he spoke, information poured like rain. He loved subjects that broached what he had accumulated of knowledge and abhorred topics where he was ignorant and was forced to listen—the most repugnant of all. He worshiped talking, producing countless tidbits about innumerable things: cars, furniture, oils, diseases, politicians, films, countries, jokes, history, geography, astronomy, law, banks, prostitution. A big baby of thirty-five, light in spirit, his jokes blossoming flowers, his anecdotes intricate miniatures, and his anger, woe if it should explode—easily, for something or nothing—earth shook, volcanoes erupted, and tornadoes raced; if unchallenged, he subsided, apologized, offered a cigarette, or ordered a round of coffee.

He argued once with an employee. The man stubbornly aroused him, then wanting to nonplus him, cited a story from Islamic history—Abd al-Rahman knew nothing about Islamic history—"A Bedouin went to see Abd al-Malik ibn Marwan, and said ..."

Abd al-Rahman Shaaban shot to his feet, shouting in rage, "Abd al-Malik ibn Marwan! Who is Abd al-Malik ibn Marwan? You cite me an animal, you animal! Damn your father and Abd al-Malik ibn Marwan's ..." And attacked him like a beast. The other man escaped, but did not make a complaint. Even Tantawi Ismail, chief of the secretariat, overlooked this flagrant breach of regulations, saying, "He's a fool but he's the cleanest in this ministry."

I realized that opposing him was unsafe and discussing a topic you knew and he didn't was insane. Abbas Fawzi was the first to hoodwink him; Abd al-Rahman secretly despised him but treated him with friendly respect.

His father had been a minister of war. He sent him after high school to study medicine in France. He spent ten years between France and England without success, a year or two at medicine, two more at science, the same with law and literature. He couldn't focus and failed to get a degree. When his father died, he returned to Egypt at thirty, carrying a jangling, incomplete encyclopedia in his head, and considerable experience in English, French, women, gambling, bars, theaters, cinemas, and brothels. He also brought back a Lebanese wife. His father left him no money, his elder sister was married to an ambassador living abroad, so he worked as a translator in the French embassy.

"I didn't last a year, then I had to leave because of a blow I gave the press attaché."

He worked for the radio, before it was Egyptianized, but had to resign after a violent quarrel. Then he moved to al-Muqattam newspaper until he directed an obscenity at the owner that almost got him sued. Finally he joined the ministry, after passing an exam that was announced in the newspapers.

He had become accustomed to a life of plenty, European style. His salary not satisfying his requirements, he translated for the press, publishing houses, and pocket-book stories, his energy devoted to life's luxuries and an only daughter he worshiped. He lived in an apartment on Fuad I Street, surrounding his family atmosphere with the friendship of European families—French, Italian, occasionally English—to afford himself the environment he loved, with its trimmings of fine furniture, good food, enjoyable drink, refined company, and elevated conversation.

Abd al-Rahman Shaaban

"Europe's the spirit of the world, and its people the angels of creation. All others are animals or insects," he said with ardor.

"Sometimes I get physically shocked when I look around me. I see myself a stranger amid a cluster of employees, wretched, ignorant, cringing, fawning hypocrites. God have mercy on you, father, why did you lose your money in gambling?!"

Nothing apart from his birth certificate showed he was a Muslim. All he knew of his religion was the name 'Muhammad.' I discerned no interest in any values, although he was courageous, generous, and honorable. He was a mad smoker, a riotous drunkard, a reckless gambler, and a ravenous eater.

We'd leave the ministry at the end of the day, walking together to the tram stop below his house. He didn't stop talking for a second, my eyes and ears following him. He criticized whatever his eyes fell on, comparing it with its equivalent in England or France.

"Do you like these shops and stalls? They're commercial prison-cells . . . Look at the filthy streets in the middle of the city, the day will come when flies demand citizen rights! . . . What do you think of those barefoot boys on Sulayman Pasha Street? . . . Look at that unique scene, the cart, the camel, and the automobile in a single caravan, and you say independence or death? . . . Do you really like that reciter Ali Mahmoud? A blind, repulsive man who croaks like an idiot—compare him to a Catholic Mass, its air floating with eternal music! . . . Believe me, the politicians you admire are not fit to be junior employees in a foreign embassy . . . By what logic do millions of dirty peasants deserve life? Why don't you replace them with modern machinery? . . . The best Egyptian civilization has produced is hashish, and how foul it is compared to whisky! . . . Do you really appreciate these authors and writers? Believe me, they're illiterate on a world scale . . . Allow me to urinate on all the leaders, authors, and singers you admire . . . Do you know the greatest blessing bestowed on us? European colonialism. Future generations will celebrate its memory, just as you do the birth of the Prophet . . . Nothing infuriates me more than your citing examples of Umar's justice, Muawiya's cunning, and Khalid's militarism. Umar was a beggar, Muawiya a charlatan, and Khalid a cheap thug who had no one to put him in his place. The Egyptian woman is the only creature worthy of respect. She's a bitch. She could, if she had more freedom, make this people that deserves to be annihilated happy . . . Wouldn't it be better for humanity if Europeans spread over the face of the earth and eliminated everyone else?"

This was not a product of envy or opinion in any sense, but an emotionality amid ripples of innocent laughter. If he had met someone fanatically pro-Europe, he would have defended the East with the same enthusiasm. He was by nature a controversialist: if you said sweet, he'd say sour, if you said sour, he'd say sweet, seizing the opportunity in either case to talk.

I found no profundity in his emotions, except what concerned his daughter. He worshiped her, relating her trivial events as though they were sagas, citing her foolish words as universal wisdom, relaying to us her opinions—that he falsely claimed for her—about the events and wars of our homeland, extolling her precocious intelligence far beyond her years.

I was afraid that he might clash with a strong and vicious person like Adli al-Muadhin or Sharara al-Nahhal, but his size gave him an aura that forced senior employees to respect him. He, on the other hand, after his unfortunate experiences in the French embassy, the radio, and *al-Muqattam*, avoided influential people.

"Damn these times that have taught us to respect bastards. God forgive you, my daughter."

I invited him to Fishawi's and introduced him to some friends, Gaafar Khalil, Reda Hamada, and Shaarawi al-Fahham. He liked the place and the people. At the funerals of Shaarawi and Gaafar, he cried like a baby. But despite our close friendship, I did not escape his anger. One day I was reading the paper and came across a page devoted to the memory of Salama Hegazi. I turned to Abbas Fawzi and said with delight, "Can you believe Verdi said that if Salama Hegazi had been born in Italy, Verdi would not have had a chance?"

Ustaz Abd al-Rahman hurled the book he was reading and yelled at me like a volcano, "What's this rubbish? Do you believe anything those savages put in the newspapers? Who's this Salama Hegazi? Any car hailer in France has a better voice. But that's how you Egyptians are, you'll stay drowning in fantasies of words until you die. Star of the Orient, Serenader of Kings and Princes, the Sultana of Song, if I weren't Egyptian I'd wish to be Egyptian. And why not wish to be an ass? At least you'll have some use. A dark night take you and your country!"

In 1950, he married his beloved daughter to an employee in the National Bank, celebrating the wedding at the Auberge. He was happy as never before, and we were happy for him. Two years later, the morning of the 27th of January 1952 to be precise, the ministry adjutant entered the office and announced, "May the rest of your lives be long: Ustaz Abd al-Rahman Shaaban."

We were shocked, as if we had never heard of death before. Just yesterday, he was with us in the office, I had walked with him to his house along streets packed with demonstrators and saboteurs, as fires burned public places, dance halls, and cinemas. We learned, as we followed his funeral procession, that he had spent the evening at the Turf Club with some English friends. Demonstrators attacked the club, killing everyone in it, and his remarkable life ended.

Abd al-Wahab Ismail

Today he is a legend, and as a legend, interpretations vary. Although he always showed me generous fraternity, I was never comfortable with his face or the look in his bulging, serious eyes. We met at Doctor Mahir Abd al-Karim's salon during the Second World War; he was in his thirties, an Arabic teacher in a secondary school, occasionally publishing pieces of criticism or traditional poetry in literary magazines. An Azhar graduate with no knowledge of foreign languages, still he earned my respect and interest with his powerful logic debating with people known for broad culture and extensive readings in foreign languages—like Doctor Ibrahim Aql, Salim Gabr, and Zuhayr Kamil. He was a calm, polite conversationalist who never lost his temper, digressed from objectivity or appeared below their refined levels, their peer in every sense. I was convinced of his sharp intelligence, debating ability, and broad reading despite his complete dependence on heritage and translations, not doubting that he was brighter than them. Even his criticism of contemporary works was not marred by wit or superficiality as in the case of the specialists with degrees from Paris and London, except for a subtle difference revealed only to the eyes of meticulous cognoscenti.

"He's a talented young man, it's a pity he wasn't sent on a scholarship abroad," Doctor Mahir Abd al-Karim, who always weighed his words carefully, told me.

Although Abd al-Wahab Ismail never spoke about religion, pretended modernity in his ideas and dress, and adopted European habits in food and going to the cinema, yet the effect religion had on him, his belief, even fanaticism, were not a secret to me.

A young Coptic writer had offered him his book of articles on criticism and sociology. He talked about him one day at Fishawi's.

"He's intelligent, well-informed, sensitive, original in style and ideas."

"When will you write about him?" I asked innocently, as I was fond of the writer.

He smiled mysteriously. "Wait, and it'll be a long wait!" he said.

"What do you mean?"

"I will not help build a pen that tomorrow will slander our Islamic heritage in every twisted way," he replied decisively.

"Do I understand then that you're a fanatic?" I asked angrily.

"Don't threaten me with clichés, they don't move me," he jeered.

"Your position saddens me."

"There's no point arguing about this with a wafdist, I was a wafdist once. Frankly I don't trust people of other religions."

He had been a wafdist, but broke away with Ahmad Mahir whom he greatly admired. When the saadists were in power, he was promoted to inspector. But his dream was lost with Ahmad Mahir's assassination, as though he had been hit by the bullet that killed the man.

"The nation's greatest man is lost," he told me in despair.

He complained about his health at every opportunity, using it as an excuse not to fast in Ramadan, but he never told anyone the nature of his malady. He was not interested in women and never married—in that regard, he was upright. Yet despite his serious morality and sincere crusades against corruption, an aspect was disclosed that I would not have believed had I not seen it. Abd al-Wahab despised a writer who owned a magazine and printing press that published a monthly series of books.

"If it weren't for his magazine, he'd never find a place to publish a word of his," he said.

I was stunned to read an article by him in *al-Risala*, praising the magazine owner to seventh heaven. I had difficulty explaining it until I learned they had agreed to publish one of Abd al-Wahab's books in the monthly series for an extraordinary fee no other author had yet received! Recalling his blind attitude toward the Coptic writer, I was disturbed by this opportunistic side, doubting his integrity. A permanent revulsion, despite our friendship, settled in my heart.

He continued as an inspector and writer until the Wafd formed the government in 1950. Uncomfortable with the wafdist minister's treatment, he resigned and devoted himself to the press. He was known at that time for his relentless attacks on the wafdist government, simultaneously publishing contemporary books on Islam that were extremely successful. The 1952 revolution found him immersed in fighting the Wafd and defending Islam.

Some two years had passed without our meeting, and I had lost track of his news. On a visit to Salim Gabr, he told me, "It seems Abd al-Wahab Ismail's star will shine soon."

"What do you mean?" I asked with interest.

"He's in the inner circle," he replied.

"As a political writer or a religious writer?" I asked.

"As a member of the Muslim Brothers."

"The Brothers?" I asked in amazement. "But I knew him as a fanatical saadist."

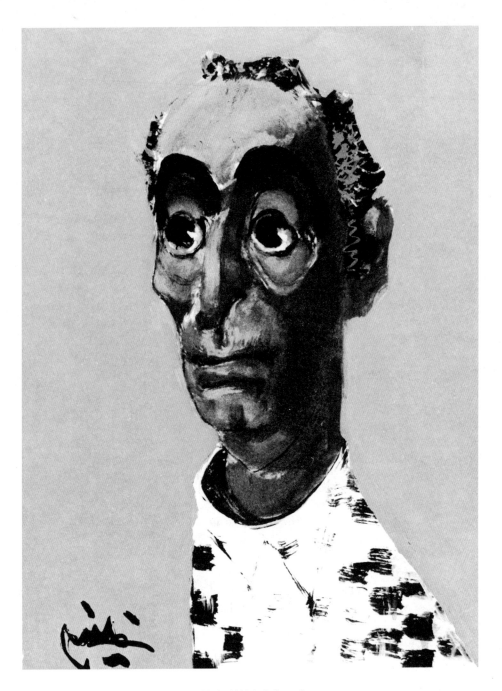

Abd al-Wahab Ismail

"Praise be to Him Who causes change but never changes!" he replied sarcastically.

A year later, we met in front of the Anglo Bar; shaking hands warmly, we strolled and chatted until the revolution came up.

"A blessed revolution, but it's difficult to know what they're after," he said with reserve.

I sensed a bitterness—I could not fathom its secret, nor did he reveal it. He had the ability, rare in Egyptians, to keep his secrets.

"I heard that you've joined the Muslim Brothers," I said.

"Any Muslim is liable to that," he replied with a cryptic smile.

"It's a pity you've abandoned literary criticism."

He laughed. "What a pagan wish!"

As we parted, I felt that henceforth we'd meet only by chance in the street.

At the first clash between the revolution and the Brothers, he was arrested, tried, and sentenced to ten years in prison. He was released in 1956. Carrying my good wishes, I went to his house on Khayrat Street. He had not changed much—his hair had grayed, as expected for a man of fifty-seven or fifty-eight, and he had put on weight. I thought his health had improved. We exchanged questions about our lives. With his usual sedateness and remarkable cool nerve, he plunged straight into public affairs, expounding his views with confidence.

"The Quran must replace all imported laws ... The woman must return to the home. It's alright to be educated—for the home, not for a job. The state may guarantee her a pension in case of divorce or absence of the provider ... Socialism, nationalism, and European civilization are a malice we must uproot from our souls," he said with force.

He launched such a tirade against science that I was shocked.

"Even science?!" I asked.

"Yes. It will not give us an edge. We're behind there, and will stay behind no matter how hard we try. We have no scientific message to offer the world, but we have the message of Islam and the worship of God alone, not capitalism or dialectic materialism."

I listened, politely controlling myself. Rising to leave, I asked, "What about the future?"

"Do you have you a suggestion?"

"Yes, but I'm afraid it might be pagan. Go back to literary criticism."

"I've received an invitation to work abroad," he said calmly.

"What have you decided?"

"I'm thinking."

A year later, newspapers greeted us with news of another Brothers' conspiracy. I knew nothing about Abd al-Wahab Ismail, assuming he had left the country to work abroad. But my friend Qadri Rizq confirmed that he had been part of the conspiracy and had resisted the force that had gone to arrest him until he was shot dead.

Abda Sulayman

She may have been the first woman in our ministry, certainly the first in the secretarial department. She was appointed during the Second World War, the same month Abbas Fawzi became chief of the secretariat. She was twenty-five, soft, full, brown in complexion, of medium beauty, and a light spirit. She had the secondary certificate, but had not wished to be

Abda Sulayman

employed until her father had died.

"Please be worthy colleagues," Abbas Fawzi warned.

"Your friend lives in Sayyida Zaynab," Amm Saqr whispered as he poured my coffee.

"So?" I asked.

"Sayyida Zaynab is full of students, so many of its girls..." He made a suspect gesture.

Attention to personal appearance increased in the secretariat. Eyes glanced at the corner where Abda sat to the right of Abd al-Rahman Shaaban. It was a long time before Abda became a daily habit that did not excite or arouse us. News spread picturing her personal conduct in Sayyida Zaynab as reckless.

"Don't believe an honorable girl would accept to work among men," Amm Saqr told me.

"But she's polite, and rejects all propositions without exploiting the publicity," I replied.

"A nice policy to keep her dignity as an employee and catch a stupid suitor!" he insisted.

We noticed a colleague in archives started paying regular visits to his friend in the secretariat. He was famous, despite his lowly position and rudimentary education—only primary school—and he was handsome, with the air and looks of an aristocrat. He was from the al-Adil family: Muhammad al-Adil, thirty years old, nephew of the pasha who was head of the family, and husband of his wealthy daughter. In spite of his poverty and meager salary, he wore the most elegant suits and spent his wife's money lavishly. It was known he was chasing Abda, visiting the secretariat to stalk his prey. Abbas Fawzi refrained from comment grudgingly, aware of the friendship between his uncle, the pasha, and the undersecretary; but Abd al-Rahman Shaaban, the translator, did not: one day, he grabbed him by the lapels and shoved him to the door. "If you come back, I'll break your head," he told him.

Amm Saqr told me that, madly insistent, he was following Abda to Sayyida Zaynab. It was clear the girl had rejected him and held her ground, refusing to be a mistress. We discussed the matter in whispers.

"The boy is handsome and irresistible," said Abbas Fawzi.

"But he's an ignorant scum," retorted Abd al-Rahman Shaaban.

"Woman is woman and man is man," Abbas Fawzi told him.

"It's natural she should look for a husband, why should she settle for mistress?" I put in.

"That's reasonable, but love is not reasonable."

Time passed, and Abda would not relent. One day she asked for a week's vacation. No one noticed until Amm Saqr told us, "Muhammad al-Adil took a week off too."

Guesses flew wildly, but they remained guesses. The week passed, and Abda returned a changed person: her soul had lost something precious. We waited for her to speak, but she went to work silently in a halo of grief, as though she had returned from a graveyard.

Abd al-Rahman Shaaban leaned over and asked gently, "What's wrong, mademoiselle?"

Sensing sympathy, her tears ran. Eyes gazed on her. Abbas Fawzi walked to her desk and asked, "What's the matter? We're colleagues. People are for each other."

"Nothing."

"We don't wish to force you to talk."

"Nothing will stay hidden," she said in despair.

"Then what makes you so sad?"

She hesitated. "I took a holiday to get married," she said.

"Nothing wrong or sad about that."

"Muhammad al-Adil and I got married."

"Muhammad al-Adil!"

"Yes."

"Secretly!?"

"He told me he was gambling with his future. If his wife or his uncle, the pasha, found out, he'd be finished for life."

"How could you accept, knowing his situation?" Abbas Fawzi asked reprovingly.

"Remember your words about love," Abd al-Rahman Shaaban retorted angrily.

Retreating, he asked. "Then what happened?"

"We went to Alexandria for a week."

"Then what?"

"He divorced me yesterday!" she said, trying to control her tears.

"Divorced you?!!"

"Yes."

"Why?"

"He said if it continued, it would be found out and he would lose everything!"

"A new type of love affair," Amm Saqr whispered in my ear.

Abda received both sympathy and blame. Many volunteered to help her with a legal case. News reached the wife and pasha. The undersecretary, at the pasha's behest, summoned Abda, rebuked her and accused her of seducing the stupid boy, and demanded she drop the case in return for guaranteeing her rights. She confided to us that she was pregnant. She gave birth to a girl. Alimony was deducted monthly from the young man's salary.

Muhammad al-Adil had not had his fill of Abda, and she still loved him, a fact that was clear to experienced men like Abbas Fawzi and Abd al-Rahman Shaaban. The affair recommenced—illegal this time, in complete secrecy—until Muhammad and Abda were summoned by the undersecretary, who threatened them, in the pasha's presence, with transfer to the provinces if they did not immediately end their nefarious relationship.

Their voices reached the messengers. Amm Saqr picked up the news and broadcast it in his sadistic fashion. Abd al-Rahman Shaaban reminded him of his missing daughter, and he left the room with a contorted face.

Muhammad al-Adil was transferred to the Ministry of Agriculture. Abda married a contractor who agreed to have her daughter brought up in his house provided Abda resign. She did. This happened at the time of the first Palestine war in 1948.

Twenty years later, I ran into Abda in Tahrir Square. We shook hands warmly. She was fifty and very fat. As we walked, she asked me about the old colleagues. I told her about Abbas Fawzi, about Abd al-Rahman Shaaban's end—she was genuinely sorry—and Amm Saqr's sad turn. She told me her husband had died two years earlier; she had given him three sons who were studying medicine, agriculture, and economics. Her daughter had married an officer.

"Do you know what happened to her father?" she asked me.

I'd forgotten all about him.

"A year after the Agricultural Reform law, the pasha died. The daughter only had enough to raise her children, and stopped giving her husband money. He could no longer lead the life he was accustomed to, he embezzled and was fired. He lives now like a vagrant and had to work in Alexandria as a parking attendant," she informed me.

As we parted, she asked me, "What about the situation, is it war or peace?"

I spread my palms, unable to reply.

Aglan Thabit

He was our classmate at university for a year and a half, then was accused of stealing a tarboush. The scandal forced him to abandon his studies.

At the time, Adli al-Muadhin told me, "He lives with his old mother on a small pension."

"None of us can help him, and success would have been easy," I said sadly.

"He had no manners. Don't you remember his sharp discussions with Doctor Ibrahim Aql?"

"In my opinion, he's better than Doctor Ibrahim Aql," I replied angrily.

At university, I had been convinced of his intelligence, industry, and awareness. He had a knack for foreign languages and was an excellent reader. At that early stage in his life, he translated some of Shelley's poems and published them in *al-Maarifa* magazine.

"Don't respect a student who isn't interested in politics," he told me. "And don't respect someone interested in politics unless he's a wafdist, and don't respect a wafdist unless he's poor!"

"But Saad Zaghloul wasn't poor," I replied.

"Mustafa al-Nahhas is poor."

"Do you mean Mustafa al-Nahhas is better than Saad Zaghloul?"

"Saad Zaghloul was a genius, but Mustafa al-Nahhas is an untarnished will."

He couldn't find a job after quitting the university: jobs were rare without connections. A member of the Wafd found him work in an independent newspaper as a poorly-paid translator.

We separated for about ten years, then a chance meeting at Fishawi's was happily welcomed. I asked him about his life.

"I'm still translating for the press, and the pay is still pathetic," he replied with a laugh. His spirits were high. "But I'm married."

"You're reckless!"

"It's love, damn it!"

He invited me to his home in Khan al-Khalili and introduced me to his wife. She was a beautiful girl, with an average education. I noticed she was dedicated in her love, with a resolute will to face her spartan life. We talked about war and politics.

"I'm no longer a wafdist," he said.

I was surprised. He confided that he was a communist, assuring me that communism was the solution to the world's problems.

"And a solution to mine," he added with a laugh.

His wife laughed. "That's the most important thing," she said.

He explained communism as a scientific theory, but I felt it had become a religion for him.

After the war, he was fired from his newspaper at the instigation of the Interior Ministry of the reactionary regime that ruled the country after dismissing the Wafd government. His

Aglan Thabit

situation looked critical, and he was even threatened with being thrown out of his modest lodging because he couldn't pay the rent. I visited him, occasionally giving him some negligible assistance. Then I realized his home had turned into something new and strange, a meeting place for the war nouveau riche, where the hashish pipe was passed around, and his wife sat among them as the hostess! To avoid embarrassment, I restricted our meetings to the café. To me he appeared blatant and reckless, shameless and frivolous; still his faith didn't dissipate, free of corruption, a gem buried in decay, but retaining its value.

In 1950, he returned to his job at the newspaper without changing his lifestyle, because of his poor pay and the loss of self-confidence. I met his wife after a long absence and was mortified to see a whore who reminded me of a professional—my heart was torn with grief.

He must have noticed my depression. "Whatever our circumstances, there's a part in us that can perform miracles, the part that created God," he said.

After the 1952 revolution, friends found him a better job. His affairs improved, he even moved to an apartment on Giza Square, a symbol of his determination to change his life. He was imprisoned for several years because of his ideological activities, and his wife resorted to the protection of a client from her old house. He came out of prison tired and disgusted. He retrieved his job and income, but he could not rescue his wife.

"She's addicted to opium," he said, shaking his head sadly. "I love her and will love her forever, but she can no longer give love." He continued angrily, "I attack corruption wherever I find it, and I'm not afraid to be denounced."

He sanctified their relationship with devotion and tolerance. He gave her a good life, not permitting himself to question her behavior, present or absent, sensible or reckless. He aged early; his only pleasures were work, conversation, and endless tolerance for his wife.

Despite pains, deprivation, and the degeneration of his beloved wife, he reached the peak of his maturity, producing his best work. His articles on politics and society flowed, elegant and profound. I consider his book on progressive Arab thought among the most enjoyable contemporary works, the most inspiring and optimistic; and I find his populist face, the contradictions of his personal life, his physical troubles, and the sharpness and clarity of his mind, an example of a tumultuous era, throbbing with destruction and construction, unity and fragmentation, despair and hope. It pained me when my professor, Mahir Abd al-Karim, showed no enthusiasm to receive him in his salon.

"They say he's . . ." he said with his usual calmness. His smile replaced a description that would have hurt his refined taste. I learned Gad Abu al-Ela had slandered him—that person with no real existence!

Adli Barakat

He conveys an old image, like old Abbasiya of fields and eternal silence. When the carriage waltzed him from East Abbasiya to school, he would descend and walk, despite his tender age, with haughty grandeur fit for a crown prince, passing us without a glance, alone, with no friend, our sarcasm trailing him, hiding admiration and envy.

The Barakat family—like the al-Katib family—were of the East Abbasiya aristocracy who lived in palaces. Adli's mother was Turkish, his father a wealthy Egyptian peasant. They had two sons, Adli and an elder brother. The mother died when Adli was twelve, and a year later his father married an Egyptian woman. I was told his mother's death settled melancholy in his soul, while another woman replacing her destroyed his equilibrium for life. These sorrows can only be imagined, analysis is not possible, especially since Adli never mentioned his mother to anyone, nor allowed a return to that old past. Although I knew him in his fall, when he showed respect for nothing nor exempted it from sarcasm, it was tacitly understood that his mother was a closed, sacred secret, not to be touched, broached, nor even thought to approach.

We saw him often in our youth, at school and in the palace garden, but no acquaintance ever grew between us, or even an inclination. Once, as we returned from the soccer field in the desert, we found him standing in front of his palace. Khalil Zaki decided to pick on him.

"Do you know Amm Falqous, the seller of *mudammas* beans?" he asked insolently.

He retreated inside the palace without a word. We walked away, suppressing our laughter and cursing Khalil, but a certain pleasure overwhelmed us.

"I'd love to wring his neck," Khalil Zaki often said.

We started university the same year; he became Reda Hamada's classmate in Law School. Reda introduced us as we watched a tough match between al-Ahli and al-Mukhtalat.

"We're from the same neighborhood, and we haven't met until today," I said.

"Yes," he replied with a curt smile.

I inspected him closely: in spite of the elegance and grandeur, he looked exactly like his peasant father—he had not inherited any useful features from his Turkish mother! From the outset, I realized he was tiresome and required special treatment to gain his confidence and friendship, that he despised everything, and that the word 'comic' was a cliché stuck to his tongue to describe any person or action. The professor of civil law was a 'comic' professor, Mustafa al-Nahhas was a 'comic' leader, the Wafd's decision to announce a boycott was a 'comic' announcement, and rules of Islam were 'comic' rules.

"Who deserves your respect?" I asked him once.

"The handsome rogue!" he replied with a laugh. "They say Ismail Sidqi was that in his youth."

"But you surely respect your father?" I asked.

He spat on the ground, spontaneously and savagely. "Damn him and all insects!" he said.

I learned of his hatred for his father. One of his neighbors told me about their strange relationship: Adli, for a long time, no longer hid his hatred for his father, and the pasha glossed over it, surrendering himself to God's will. I asked the reason.

"No one knows for sure," he replied. "Adli doesn't divulge that part of his secrets. But it's thought it goes back to his father's marriage after Adli's mother died."

When we got closer, I asked him why he hated and despised his father. He pierced me with a harsh glance. "Isn't it enough he gave me his looks?"

"You're a handsome peasant," I replied.

"If you flatter me again, I'll hate you more than him," he said with a frown.

To stay out of his father's way, he lived in a separate guesthouse in the palace garden. A month or two would pass without either laying eyes on the other. At the end of his time at Law School, he selected a small coterie known for moral depravity and made them his intimate friends. Through them he emerged from his seclusion and discovered the halls of pleasure and

Adli Barakat

al-Fishawi café, and his house in the garden became a tavern and hashish den! The pasha no doubt was aware of the suspicious new activity, but did not interfere, preferring not to stir up trouble.

"Take evil people for companions, through them you know yourself," he told me one day.

I didn't realize what he meant until I learned that as much as he loved the company of beautiful women, he responded only to prostitutes with monstrous faces.

He completed his studies in 1938, after failing four times. The pasha invested his influence to appoint him in public prosecution, but no one was accepted in the prosecutor's office without investigation. Investigations revealed the hashish den in his house, the application was refused, and the father was told the truth. When his father broached it with him, he replied disdainfully, "The public prosecutor is a comic job."

Both were angry, and the other son mediated until tempers cooled down. It was agreed the pasha would open a lawyer's office for him in the guesthouse, provided he held his personal gatherings outside the house. One of the two rooms was converted into an office and legal library, and a sign with the new lawyer's name was posted at the palace gate. The agreement lasted a few days. The friends returned, and the hashish pipe went around. Hashish had completely enslaved him. The friends brought prostitutes as clients of the new lawyer, and it turned into a brothel. One night, a drunken prostitute undressed and danced naked in the garden under the moonlight.

For the first time, the pasha allowed his anger to explode. He cursed and damned his son, who returned the curses twofold. The father slapped him, the son threatened to slap and kick back. He threw him out the of house and said he never wanted to set eyes on him again.

Adli left the palace in the early days of the Second World War with only his clothes, rotating between his friends' homes, considering the future. Some suggested he take a clerical job until deliverance arrived, but he replied proudly, "I prefer drifting."

Reda Hamada suggested he reopen his law office.

"I've forgotten law, and I don't have the stamina to recover it," he replied.

"Do anything in my office," Reda suggested innocently.

But he realized Reda was offering him a clerical job.

"I despise you, and I despise who created you," he shouted in anger.

He chose vagrancy, borrowing money against his father's death—he was over seventy. He chewed on sandwiches and silenced his stomach with peanuts; at night, he hopped from one hashish den to another, smoking for free, then spent the night at a friend's house or in one of the cubicles at Fishawi café. His appearance deteriorated, his health grew feeble, his clothes threadbare, and he resembled a tramp, but his pride expanded into insolence and impudence.

We were sitting together at Fishawi's when he suddenly had a fit of laughter.

"Imagine if I died before the old dog?"

"It's possible and quite expected," I said with a smile.

He cursed me. "I'm prepared to worship God if He takes his soul . . .In any case, I can't complain as long as I find some hashish at the end of the day!"

He was crouched at Fishawi's in 1947 or 1948 when a messenger from his brother arrived with word that his father had died and inviting him to the palace. He was stoned and didn't understand at first. When reality struck and roused him, he stood up reeling, and stared at the arabesque wall, lost in some unknown emptiness, then left without a word.

His brother, a judge, met him and took him inside. "What happened, happened. This is a hallowed moment when hatred is forgotten." He led him to the pasha's bedroom. "Go in, say farewell to your father so God may forgive him, you, and all of us."

Adli went in—as he told us later—and stood alone by the head of the shrouded corpse. He uncovered the face slightly, stared at him, then muttered, "To hell, swine!"

"Impossible . . . impossible!" voices called.

He looked at them contemptuously. "I'd love to mutilate his corpse," he growled.

Some of us did not believe a word, others believed every letter and surmised he may have done even more. At any rate, fortune smiled after a long frown.

The pasha left land, buildings, and cash. Adli's share was two buildings with a net income of one thousand pounds a month, and forty thousand pounds.

"The years of vagrancy were a lesson, so he could learn the value of a piaster and treat it well," many friends said. They gathered around him after the funeral to plan a happy future.

"Lucky your needs are reasonable, you can live like a king for the rest of your life."

"Make yourself a beautiful home, see a good doctor, thank your God you didn't get hooked to gambling, food is simple, your taste in women is modest, and we never heard of hashish destroying anyone's home. So congratulations on your legitimate wealth!"

"Enough advice, damn you," he yelled at them.

He hated advice and considered it despicable arrogance; yet he seemed drunk with joy. He spent the night at the Semiramis hotel, then stayed there until he settled his affairs. Unusually energetic, he rented an apartment on the Nile for fifty pounds a month, decorating it lavishly—we simple folks were shocked to learn this had cost twenty thousand pounds and were awed by an oriental room with an American bar and hashish den, whose tools were plated in gold and silver. He also bought a Cadillac. Including clothes, he spent thirty thousand. It was an extraordinary amount of money, but his friends excused it by his long deprivation; they also said getting started usually cost much more than daily expenses.

The oriental room witnessed evenings which gathered friends, parasites, night-club girls, and stars. Liquor flowed and blue smoke curled, tables of food were brought in from the Automobile Club, and he strutted among the guests, dressed in silk, revered and venerated.

The remaining ten thousand pounds soon flew away and only the revenue from the two buildings remained. Optimists said the time had come for discipline, then life would follow its balanced, reasonable path. But he had become accustomed to squandering and incarnating the spirit of *A Thousand and One Nights*. Although he spent lavishly on club girls, he made love only to modest prostitutes and a peasant girl who sold peanuts at Fishawi's. So he never found equilibrium, and he had to sell one of the two buildings despite his friends' pleas. Then he followed with the other one, deliriously happy, beyond caution, past or future.

By 1950 he had sold his apartment and returned to the Semiramis. Then he sold the car. The future appeared clear. I remember discussing it with Reda Hamada.

"Is he mad?" I asked.

"He's not without madness."

"He doesn't feel tomorrow."

"Or he's entirely engrossed in the moment."

"With all the worries that burden us, I almost envy him."

He laughed. "Life must be serious or it can go to the devil," he replied.

When his account ran out, he left the Semiramis, facing life once again without a penny or the hope of someone dying. But he was not without a plan. He downed two bottles of whisky, swallowed a quarter of an ounce of hashish, and wandered off. He was found the next morning a lifeless corpse on the banks of the Nile.

Azmi Shakir

We met at the salon of Doctor Mahir Abd al-Karim in 1960.

I immediately said, "I saw you at Abbas Fawzi's during the Second World War."

"We haven't met in a long time," he replied. "Incidentally, how do you explain his switch to writing religious books? Is it really from faith?"

"You know he's always been interested in heritage," I replied cautiously.

Azmi Shakir was forty when I met him. His intelligence, culture, and frankness drew me; I felt he took matters seriously, searching for paths to hope. He had a doctorate in history from France and was married to a professor of science.

"He was a wafdist student. From the outset he was interested in social issues," Salim Gabr, who knew him, told me. "And he acknowledges that my writings were a primary influence."

When I questioned Azmi Shakir, he said, "My wafdism wasn't as strong as it was with your generation. I had completely abandoned it before the revolution, but remained close to the Wafd's left wing. Since then, I've been considered a communist. I greeted the July revolution with enthusiasm and caution. I admired its abolition of the monarchy and evacuation of the British, but I wasn't pleased with the agricultural reform. Soon, I saw it as a coup d' état aimed at reform to avoid a real revolution."

Because of his views, he was fired from the university, then interned for several years; after his release, he worked in the press, writing what allowed him sincere expression—foreign affairs and occasionally history. After the July 1961 socialist laws, his position changed radically. He had joined our friends who met at Salim Gabr's office and the salon of Mahir Abd al-Karim.

"The revolution is the most suitable historical movement for our country in its present stage," he told me one day.

"So you've changed your mind?" I asked.

"Yes, we must put our ideologies between parentheses and support it," he replied.

I saw no reason to doubt him, I believed in his sincerity. Since then, he has supported the revolution with heart and pen, in private and in public. But his position was not understood among his friends.

"He's a bastard, not more, not less, even if he's dressed as a saint," said Aglan Thabit.

"I believe he's sincere, and have no doubts about it," I replied.

"His words justify your hesitation, that's all there is," he scoffed.

He had an opportunity to return to the university, but preferred to continue in the press. It's important to note that he was not a blind supporter and was aware of mistakes.

"It's unfortunate the revolution did not rely on the real revolutionaries, making enemies of

Azmi Shakir

them or placing them under surveillance," he often said. "Corruption is spreading like a plague. We can only warn, and even that is rarely possible."

He was a regenerative communist, always aspiring to freedom, believing that freedom was enduring a bitter tragedy, but he never belittled the historic leap the country had made, and clung to the bright future when the pitfalls of the present plagued him. When I introduced him to Doctor Sadiq Abd al-Hamid, he sensed a closeness in views and they became friends.

He grieved when communists were arrested, besieged by guilty doubt—"It's fanaticism, belief in books more than reality," he said—and was delighted when they were released, and more so when they disowned the Communist Party and cooperated with the revolution.

"There, they're taking the position they'd accused me of!"

"But in very different circumstances," Doctor Sadiq Abd al-Hamid commented.

They took senior positions in the government and press, leaving him, relatively speaking, in the abyss, and not without bitterness. This phrase escaped him: "I fear that one day writers will discover that the absurd is also suitable for dealing with ideologies!"

He no longer found in the press the psychological comfort he had enjoyed, and requested a return to teaching at the university, which was quickly granted. When the June 1967 defeat struck, like everyone else his essence quaked. The violent torrent of criticism pulled him, he plunged in, and surfaced, but he did not write a word although he had a weekly column in a political magazine. He was among the first to regain equilibrium, perhaps the first. In October that year, he published his famous article that analyzed the defeat and considered it a lesson; he warned of surrender to the tyranny of self-criticism and losing confidence. In the end, he asserted that the revolution was the real disputed ground, not Sinai or Jerusalem, and that was what had to survive and continue.

During the years that followed, he wrote his magnificent book, *From Defeat We Begin*, a charter for a new life forging its way, dusting itself off. I saw him work at his unit of the Socialist Union with bewildering zeal, and often listened to him on television—one of the few who did not suffer schizophrenia, the same person whether he talked in public or in private.

Praising him angered many who were defeated by the events, like Aglan Thabit and Salim Gabr. I can't forget Salim Gabr's anger when I commended *From Defeat We Begin*.

"I always respected him, but he's become an objective civil equalizer," he said coldly.

Aglan Thabit called the book *From Opportunism We Begin* and laughed. "It's enough to have writers like Gad Abu al-Ela and Azmi Shakir in the country who still celebrate the Prophet's night journey and ascension when men are landing on the moon!"

But Professor Azmi Shaker is still steadfast in his belief, sincerity, and effort.

Aziza Abduh

When Zuhayr Kamil introduced us, it was not the first time I had heard her name: maybe I'd seen it in a newspaper or magazine. She was with her husband. Dark-skinned, fine features, light-spirited—I guessed she was thirty. Gad Abu al-Ela said she was forty. It was 1960. She and her husband, who was in his fifties, were artists. They invited me to their home in Madinet al-Awqaf where I inspected their work. I was surprised, moving among realist paintings at a time when realism was rare and the abstract overwhelming—it was a realism with clear goals.

Aziza Abduh

"At last I get some reactionary art," I joked.

"You're looking at progressive art ... the only progressive art," she protested sweetly.

A deep affection developed between us, and as she had convinced me of her art, she convinced me of a genuine motherhood for two boys. She was more capable of friendship than her husband, who refused attachments—present in body, his spirit was absent from time and place. She was cultured, both were leftists, but she always made me aware of her strength, unlike her gentle husband, a piece of straw pulled by the lightest breeze.

At her suggestion, I brought Ustaz Yusef Badran, the editor of an art paper, to her house. I saw a rapid spiritual understanding and an exchange of respect and affection.

I was visiting Yusef Badran at his apartment in Qasr an-Nil Street. We sat chatting, his breath impregnated with alcohol. Then the bedroom door opened and Aziza Abduh appeared in his pajamas. I was stunned and non-plussed, but faced the situation with the appropriate language and nonchalance; she encouraged me with her sweet laughter and natural conversation. Her breath exuded alcohol as well. We discussed many things, but her presence in the apartment in that condition passed without light or explanation, as an axiomatic fact.

Yusef Badran told me later, "Love fell on us from the sky!"

"You love to flirt," I replied.

"But she started."

I gave him a dubious look.

"Believe me," he said, "and her grasp is stronger than her beauty."

"Do you love her?"

"She loves me, that's enough."

"And you?"

"She's not a small treasure, but she's not the type I love."

"And her husband?"

"He has nothing to do with it."

I met her at Gad Abu al-Ela's salon. She was alone, her husband was in Alexandria, and she asked me to take her home.

As we were walking, she said suddenly, "I value your friendship."

"And I value yours," I replied sincerely.

"There is no friendship without respect."

"And I respect you."

"I can almost read the questions inside you."

"I'm not quite as naive as you might think."

"Perhaps you find a couple odd because of their differing view of life and freedom?"

"I don't think so."

"I have not and never will practice infidelity!"

"Don't mistake my understanding, my dear."

She told me about her past. She'd gone to secondary school, armed with her kind mother's directives, chorusing the voice of the past generation; but she gave herself to the first boy who loved her back, thinking he would keep his promise, then repeated it many times, sometimes in rebellion, sometimes for fun, occasionally out of love.

"Sometimes I was afraid, but I never had regrets."

She stopped walking. "I've become my own mistress. I've challenged the whole world and all its values that I no longer believe in. I've always believed that I'm as pure as oxygen."

When we parted, she clung to my hand. "We're the real hope for the future!" she said.

Some years after we met, her husband was imprisoned with the communists. Her sorrow was profound. She shouldered the family although she was expecting another child, and disappeared from salons and exhibitions—the phone was our only connection.

I asked Yusef Badran about her.

"You know as much as I do."

"Aren't you seeing each other as usual?" I asked in amazement.

"She ended the affair when her husband was imprisoned."

"Really?"

"She's a strange woman, but I'm not sorry."

I lost contact, rarely remembering her, then visited her years later—when her husband was released—to offer my congratulations. Her two sons were university students, and her daughter was in sixth grade. Activity returned to her life, but she did not reconnect with Yusef Badran, who had married an intellectual Palestinian exile.

On a group visit to the Eastern Front, Yusef asked me, "Have you seen her little girl?"

"Yes," I replied. "She's very pretty."

"She's my daughter," he quietly whispered in my ear.

"No!" I said in amazement.

"It's true," he replied. "I tried to convince Aziza to have an abortion, but she refused."

"When was that?"

"A few days before her husband was imprisoned."

"Why did she refuse?"

"She said 'I've loved you as I've never loved before and will keep the fruit.'"

"Although she shut the world out when he was imprisoned?"

"She refuses to indulge in deceit."

"Does he know?"

"I don't know."

I thought for a while. "The girl does look like you," I said.

"Yes. That's why I avoid seeing her!"

In 1970, Aziza had the first real success of her artistic career when her exhibition was a triumph and she was acknowledged as an original Egyptian artist.

Ashmawi Galal

His house stood at the east end of our street where it connected to Abbasiya Street. It was gray, with two stories and a semi-neglected garden where only a jasmine, two palms, and a haughty mango tree still grew. Whenever I walked by, I glanced at it with curiosity and disgust, as did all the inhabitants of our street.

When I was new to the neighborhood, during the reconnaissance period, a friend—it may have been Reda Hamada—pointed to the house and asked, "Do you know whose house this is?"

Of course, I replied that I didn't.

Ashmawi Galal

"The house of Ashmawi Bey Galal!"

I was dazed for a moment, then I yelped, "Ashmawi Bey Galal?!"

"Himself."

"The student murderer?"

"The student murderer."

"Do you see him?"

"Nobody knows where he is, neither him nor his family. They're scared of the Black Hand Society. But that's his house."

"Did they live here?"

"Yes."

"When did they leave?"

"When the devil became notorious for killing demonstrators."

The name Ashmawi Galal was linked to terror in my consciousness since childhood. He was a senior cavalry officer in the Egyptian army, rightfully earning his epitaph: the 1919 revolution's Enemy Number One. News of him ran like tales of horror: that he killed with no mercy, that he tortured his victims, tying students to his horse and galloping away, his victim dragged behind, mangled by stones and asphalt until dead. When Saad Zaghloul became prime minister in 1924, he retired him. He slunk back to his deserted house on our street and locked himself inside, as if it were a prison.

I often wished I could see him, if only once, and gazed at the windows, balconies, and garden; I caught a glimpse of his wife and two daughters, but never him. His disappearance was a subject of conversation; he never left the house, appeared in a window, or walked in the garden. When occasions were held on the street, he neither visited nor showed courtesy. How did he spend his time, and how did he bear his prison?

"He stays alone because he has no friend," said Gaafar Khalil.

"He fears the people's revenge," said Reda Hamada.

"It's said he lost his sight and can't move, but hides it so people don't gloat," said Surour Abd al-Baqi.

He had a son and two daughters. He sent his son to school in England, fearing the students' revenge in Cairo. We heard he studied medicine in London, started a practice, married, and became a British citizen. The two daughters played in the garden. They were handsome and attractive, and I was amazed that the beast could produce them. When they reached youth and were veiled inside the house, the music from their piano descended on us in the street. Again I wondered how the beast could live with music.

Around 1935 they were married to unknown husbands. Only the man and his wife were left in the house. Then it was rumored in the neighborhood that he had deserted the house, leaving his wife alone. It was said—and his wife confirmed—he had moved to the family mausoleum and lived in the reception room for visitors on festival days, and that he had willed to be buried with no funeral or celebration.

His wife was beautiful and kind. After his departure to the tomb, she emerged from her seclusion, visited her neighbors, easily won their affection, and gained a distinguished position in the neighborhood.

Henceforth, all that was known about the man-beast came from the men of the previous generation, the old residents of the neighborhood. They said he had been a reclusive child, but polite. Despite his efforts, he failed at school. His father, overseer of a small endowment, enrolled him in the Military College through his friendship with Herbert Pasha, the school principle. When he graduated, he worked in Sudan. His efficiency earned him the admiration the English, and served their shrewd policy of collecting taxes viciously to make the Sudanese hate Egyptian officers. A bond of friendship developed between him and the British officers. Ashmawi Galal's admiration for the English knew no bounds: he was proud of their friendship and regarded it as his first honor in life. He spent his vacations in England and believed the English were the masters of mankind, sent by divine providence to civilize humanity, especially backward people like the Egyptians. Reda Hamada told me that because of his views, the debate one day between Ashmawi and Reda's father reached vile words that severed the relations of affection and neighborliness.

During the 1919 revolution, the Egyptian army was summoned to assist the army of occupation in quelling the rebellion and crush the revolutionaries. Its sympathy for the revolution and loyalty to its leader were discovered, even defending him openly when enemies conspired to betray him. Ashmawi Galal was the exception, insanely attacking the revolutionaries, betraying them, and torturing their student leaders, outdoing the English in brutality and viciousness. He occupied in their hearts a position no Egyptian had ever held. His countrymen detested him. The sultan gave him no sympathy because he knew his loyalty was to his British lords, not to him. Unsuccessful attempts were made to assassinate him, although a splinter from a nationalist bomb caused a surface wound on his leg. The man ignored the people's attitude toward him, persisting in his folly as though he were performing a religious obligation. His wife, chatting with her neighbors, said her father had once asked him to be moderate. "Do your duty without extremism," he had told him.

"I'm not just doing my duty as an officer, I'm defending a principle. I believe that Egypt's independence from England will lead to its decline and corruption. If we leave the Empire, we abandon civilization!" he had replied.

His wife died of a heart attack before the Second World War and was buried yards from the lonely man living in the reception room of the tomb. He joined her in the first year of the war when his liver gave out. Incredibly, his name has not been erased from our generation's memory until today, and many still remember the popular song composed to denounce him.

Isam al-Hamalawi

The Hamalawi house looked onto our street and onto Bayn al-Ganayin on the other side—the biggest house on the street, surrounded by a large garden; over its high walls the tops of palm and mango trees could be seen in profusion.

The landlord was Isam Bey, a notable and stock exchange speculator. His family was composed of a wife and three daughters. A carriage carried him back and forth, its clinking bell announcing his movements. His family did not belong to our time, its brilliant colors foreign to our race. A self-subsisting entity with no connection to the neighbors, it neither visited nor was visited, observed no tradition nor honored any festival. When mother and daughters left the house, riding or walking, they appeared unveiled, enchanting onlookers with their ivory complexion, golden hair, and colorful eyes.

Isam Bey broke custom when he invited a famous actress to his home. When she visited regularly on specific days, it became clear she was his mistress. *Art* magazine said he had given her a necklace worth ten thousand pounds. We gathered on the street to watch her arrival and reception, and thoroughly enjoyed it.

"We see her for free, but the rest of the play, we can't imagine," said Gaafar Khalil.

"How does the pimp bey behave in front of his wife and daughters?" Khalil Zaki asked.

"He behaves with them as they do with him," replied Sayyid Shouayr.

Sayyid Shouayr's house was the closest to theirs, and the Hamalawis excited his interest. He came one day saying, "The lid's off."

We clustered around him eagerly.

"The hanem is in love with Muhammad, the pressing man."

We knew him well: he owned the pressing shop on the street, a one-eyed thug. How could the beautiful hanem whom we compared with Mae Murray love this one-eyed thug with a flabby belly, bulging neck, and flat face?

"She goes to his house wrapped in a chador, I saw her myself," said Sayyid Shouayr.

The woman dispensed with subterfuge. The presser now carried the clothes to the house and stayed for an hour or two. When Isam Bey took the actress on a trip abroad, he visited without reason, spending the night openly. Meanwhile, the three girls met their admirers at the edge of East Abbasiya or received them at night in the garden. Among the admirers, I saw Eid Mansour, Shaarawi al-Fahham, my relative Ahmad Qadri, the police officer from al-Wayli, the neighborhood dentist, and a French teacher! We thought manly duty required we picket the house and its visitors, even if youth and weakness permitted only throwing stones from a distance, but a policeman came to protect the house, perhaps sent by the loving police officer.

Drowning in my love for Safaa, I was infuriated by the behavior of Isam's daughters, seeing a distortion of life's loftiest emotion. But from 1930, the neighborhood's calculations were thwarted. The three girls, one after the other, made excellent matches. The eldest married an engineer, the middle one a cabinet minister's secretary, and the youngest a successful lawyer. Astonishingly, they completely renounced their old lifestyle and formed families that were examples of rectitude. In the fifties and thereafter, I came across some of their children, successful and prosperous youth, some known for progressive political awareness.

Isam Bey died during the Second World War, the same week Shaarawi al-Fahham was killed. The estate was divided, and the hanem inherited a large income. She was fifty, but her vitality exceeded her age, and she retained much of her old beauty.

She lived alone in the house, rarely visited by her daughters, which we interpreted maliciously. The fact is, her affair with the presser continued, but it seems the man wished to be rid of her. He even slapped her once in his store in front of servants, as she argued with him.

Within weeks, she had started an affair with the butcher.

"The lady is an aristocrat, but she has popular tastes," laughed Gaafar Khalil.

At the end of the war, she sold the house and left the neighborhood. But she didn't leave my sight for long, and was always seen in al-Liwa café, Groppi's, or Argentin with a drink, leaving when she had snared a young man, until she became famous downtown. I saw her at the Atheneos in Alexandria playing the same game. She would disappear for a while, then return to the same haunts, in the same role, while age crept, wilting persisted, and elegance decreased, confirming that her money, like her days, was running out. Every time I saw her, I realized she was deteriorating and approaching the inevitable end—she'd become nothing but a destitute old woman. She stopped going to exclusive places, or was forced to, content to wander the streets in tattered clothes, then in a gallabiya and slippers, finally reduced to begging or close. I never saw her stretch out her hand, but owners of small cafés, who knew her famous story, offered her a sandwich or a little money.

Whenever I catch a glimpse of her, melancholy returns as memories come back of the old street at the time of lanterns dangling from gates, open fields, and absolute quiet. This woman, victim of insatiable lust for life, has her successful grandchildren living nearby, completely ignorant of her distress and loneliness.

Eid Mansour

Of our old group. He befriended it and it befriended him, connected for life, but he was and remains a friend with no friendship, he was and remains with no heart: even Khalil Zaki had a heart, Sayyid Shouayr had a heart, but Eid Mansour has no heart.

He lived with his father and an old servant; his mother died right after his birth. His father was a real estate merchant who had worked with the Jews a long time, acquiring their style and skillfulness. He was old, already fifty when Eid was born, and never remarried. Eid was his only child. He was a miser, finicky, crude, and emotionless, raising his son strictly, with no mercy or compromise, determined to fashion him in his own image—our friend never knew emotions, or tasted affection or compassion, as if he was being raised in a terrorist camp. His talents manifested themselves early: he was practical, strict, opportunistic, and heartless—thus he remains, today and tomorrow. Since childhood, he took the piaster for his idol and gauge of masculinity and superiority—his heart never had room for other than that one god.

As I said, he is the friend without friendship, a friend by virtue of neighborhood, school, play, and a lifetime, but with no passion, affection, or real love. He laughs at a misfortune as you'd laugh at a good joke. He did not show a trace of emotion over the deaths of Shaarawi al-Fahham or Gaafar Khalil, and when Badr al-Ziyadi was killed during the strike, he didn't conceal his delight at losing his rival for the captaincy of the soccer team. When he sensed my eyes burning him that day, he grit his teeth to suppress one of his cruel laughs.

"You're a devil," I said.

"May God hear you," he whispered in my ear, then with more scorn, "There's no difference between you and me except that I'm honest and not a hypocrite."

He was accustomed, by virtue of his upbringing and temperament, to living outside our traditions, religion, and aspirations, not because of reflection or philosophy, nor motivated by corruption or devilishness like Khalil Zaki and Sayyid Shouayr—his energy was deployed for work and profit alone. Even sex, his only entertainment, occupied a margin of his leisure time.

When he received his high school diploma in 1930, his father took him into the business, training him until he died in 1935, and leaving him a considerable fortune. And despite his adventures in the Hamalawi garden, I think he was never more attached to a woman than to Soraya Raafat. He saw her while working for his father and rushed to seduce her.

"I was under her spell. If she'd continued rejecting me, I might have ..."

"Married her?" I asked.

"At least thought about it."

"Weren't you sorry or ashamed about deceiving her?"

"I don't think so," he laughed.

He never knew love, desired marriage, or yearned for fatherhood. Even today, at sixty or slightly older, he still works with the same energy, collecting money voraciously, with no other goal in life.

He angered me when he scoffed at our nationalistic passions and at my tears the day Saad Zaghloul died. He discounted all that and would say, "But for the English, but for the Jews, this country would have no life!" He repeated this until the last day the English were in Egypt.

Although he was a miser like his father, he developed a novel tradition in miserliness. He never spent an unnecessary millieme unless to provide himself with a comfortable existence.

"I'm a bachelor, and I'll stay a bachelor with no heirs. So I must enjoy my life."

He despised marriage, and considered it weakness and stupidity. He never regretted a decision he had taken, and as he got older, enjoyed satisfaction with himself and his decisions. In 1936, he left our neighborhood after selling the house, and moved to the Mena House Hotel permanently, preferring the convenience of hotel life that relieved him of domestic issues. At the same time, he rented a country house near the Pyramids for his periodic female affairs—he didn't like long affairs and was partial to foreign cabaret girls. He pampered himself with fine food and drink, was moderate in alcohol, and had a natural aversion to drugs. He spent his evenings in business entertainment with real estate colleagues, but always attended our weekly evening gatherings. It was important for him to compare his success with that of our friends like Doctor Surour Abd al-Baqi and Ustaz Reda Hamada, never concealing his superiority in fortune, his first and last value in life.

I teased him once. "Look, Khalil Zaki competes with you in wealth and success."

"He's a dirty pig," he protested.

"You consider your financial activities honorable?" I asked.

"The meaning of honor changes from one environment to another, I could make a deal you would consider extortion but we would call experience and intelligence. But I despise Khalil Zaki's methods, the experience of poor people," he replied.

A European cabaret girl fell in love with him and wrote him letters. He read us the correspondence mockingly. "Here's how a woman imagines herself in love if she wants to grab a man and possess him!"

His civic feelings were ugliest the day war broke out with the Jews in 1948. It seemed he hated his country for reasons I didn't know, or else his commercial interests had ruined sentiments we considered instinctive. This was repeated in 1951: with the treaty abrogated and the struggle of the Canal, he hated the Wafd, despite his general political disinterest. But his life continued along its secure path until the July 1952 revolution. Although he was not touched, the revolution disrupted his assurance and threatened his confidence. Anxieties followed: the abolition of the monarchy, agricultural reform, and the evacuation of British troops. His instincts for self-defense were alerted, as he realized that although he was not a direct target he was on a frontline and might sooner or later be uprooted. The Suez invasion in

Eid Mansour

1956 gave him a transfusion, but the spark of hope was soon snuffed out. Many of his Jewish friends left.

"I'd love to smuggle my money out and emigrate," he told me.

When he saw my indignation, he said, "Egypt's not a place for smart people any more!" He cracked his cruel laugh. "If I weren't Egyptian, I'd wish to be Egyptian."

He continued working with the same zeal despite his fears, recovering his breath in June 1967. Although he observed the events following the defeat in stunned amazement, he did not lose hope this time.

"No escape!" he told me maliciously. "Of course you've heard of awakening after death."

Months went by, a year, two, three years, matters improved, resolve hardened, and hopes for struggle were renewed, but that never defeated him, although it worried him occasionally. He held to his fixed idea and nourished it by listening to hostile broadcasts and seditious rumors.

When Reda Hamada and I questioned his loyalty, he said, "There is no homeland today except the homeland of interests. You're either American or Soviet, you can choose freedom, creative will, and humanity, or order, blind justice, and mechanical will."

He lost hope in the English. His golden dream was for America to control the Middle East and assign it an axis in its vital sphere where Arabs and Jews played complementary roles.

Self-interest had taught him to talk politics. He's still at work, putting up buildings and selling them, living at the Mena House, enjoying his life as a bachelor with no family, having sex once a month. He visits us at specific times, a token of half a century of association, a friendship with no real love or respect. We see him a misfit hewn from rock, and he sees us a group of frivolous fools, with no real value.

Ghanem Hafiz

He was the math teacher in secondary school. At the time, he was young and known for politeness, dignity, and good demeanor—no student ever exceeded the limits of propriety, not even devils like Gaafar Khalil, Badr al-Ziyadi, and Eid Mansour. Eid Mansour asked him for private tutoring after he persuaded his father it would be cheaper than a repeated year's fees. Ghanem Effendi Hafiz met with Eid's father who asked him what he would charge. He asked for a riyal an hour; the man was horrified and said he would pay no more than a shilling. Ghanem Effendi smiled modestly and suggested giving the lesson free on condition Eid attended it with another student from the same neighborhood. For two months, Eid Mansour received private lessons in math for free.

I saw him weep the day Badr al-Ziyadi was killed; we recompensed him with love and respect. After I went to university, I knew him well at the neighborhood café: the pupil became friend. He had a gentle disposition, a quiet temperament, and was smartly dressed. He sat with us once a week—especially during the summer vacation—smoking the narghile, listening politely, and rarely speaking. He treated all topics within his gentle disposition; however violent and burning the subject, his tongue transformed it to a dulcet whisper in a smiling halo. He was never seen to be angry, sharp, or loud, and politics was translated into an attractive, gentle conversation, even if his beloved Wafd was attacked. If he spoke in their defense, he'd say, "They're good people," or "Mustafa al-Nahhas? He's a good and blessed man."

Ghanem Hafiz

The furthest he went was, "God forgive you!"

That—and casting his vote for the wafdist candidate on election day, if the elections were free—was the limit of his political activity. Only in the 1919 revolution did he participate with his heart. He was extremely humble and not ashamed of his origins, unlike many of his class.

He told me of his background. "My father was a policeman, keen on making me one too, but a neighbor advised him to send me to primary school. My success earned me free tuition until I got the diploma. The only school possible was the teachers' college, so I joined it."

He married the Arabic teacher's daughter, who had the primary certificate. "My wife's family's position, although modest, was still higher than mine. I faced unfortunate difficulties." With a touch of sadness and sincerity, he added, "The situation required someone stronger than me, but my wife has given me three sons."

He had one day of leisure, which he spent at the café, otherwise not leaving his family except to go to work. Historic years went by as he remained tucked in his nest, watching events from afar, discussing quietly and making gentle comments, focused on raising his three sons, until the eldest graduated a cavalry officer, the middle one an engineer who joined the army, and the youngest a vet.

His two older sons miraculously escaped the 1956 war. He praised God, gave thanks, and continued his work until he retired in 1960 in good health to a happy family life. When our troops in Sinai went to arms in mid-1967, his heart beat violently after a long quiet, and he asked all and sundry, "Is it war or not?"

Disaster struck, although darkness allowed a speck of light: the middle son returned wounded, but the eldest was listed missing. He was devastated. His habitual serenity dissolved and his collapse invited pity—he loved his boys like a mother and refused to believe his son was dead, dreaming a miracle would bring him back. The middle son recovered and returned to the front. He was torn between his dream for the lost son and his fear for the soldier, following news from the front hour by hour, day by day; trembling at word of a raid, let down by faith, shaken by love for his sons.

I see him occasionally, an old man, slightly bent and white-haired. He sits with a lost gaze, contemplating the unknown, his appearance showing no ability to confront life's savage demands. I waver between blame and pity, then I join him in sympathy, and we exchange guesses about the unknown.

Fayza Nassar

We met at Aglan Thabit's house in Giza around 1960. She was thirty, her face had a calm, peasant character despite her modern elegance. Moderately beautiful, she possessed strong sexual appeal. Her husband—Abduh Ibrahim—a garage owner in his fifties, flabby and sluggish, participated in the conversation with a glance, a stupid smile, hardly speaking.

"She's our neighbor in the building and my wife's friend," Aglan told me.

"I'm not convinced by her husband," I commented.

"But he has a respectable income. They have two children, and she's not a bad mother, even though she's illiterate."

"She seems intelligent."

"She's the daughter of a cheese and butter vendor, but she has aptitude, making progress through radio, television, and girlfriends."

On another visit to Aglan Thabit, I met Fayza Nassar in the company of a fortyish man with a keen gaze and a strong build. I learned he was Galal Mursi, owner of the Pyramids Casino.

"Last time you met Fayza's husband, now you meet her lover!" said Aglan.

The room burst into laughter—Aglan's wife, Fayza, and Galal, the casino owner.

"Don't believe it," said Galal.

"Are you disowning me?" Fayza asked threateningly.

"Believe it," he told me, lowering his head submissively.

"And he's a friend of her husband!" added Aglan.

Fayza invited me to her home, and I became friends with both her and her husband. We went several times to the casino, where Galal Mursi joined us at our table. I noticed the deep relationship between him and the couple, but couldn't ascertain how much the husband knew about the affair between his wife and her lover. Even Aglan Thabit knew no more.

"Get used to these relationships and be cured of your bourgeois slavery," he told me.

One time we were at his house, Aglan, his wife, Fayza and myself. With no preliminaries or occasion, Aglan pointed in my direction. "He's suffering from his love for you!" he told Fayza.

She moved lightly to my side and put her soft brown arm round my neck. "Show me!"

"Slowly, so he doesn't get scared," laughed Aglan.

"On one condition," she said.

"What?" he asked.

"One night..." she replied. She looked me in the eyes. "The virtuous woman can have only a husband and one lover!"

That's how she joked; but she really loved Galal, and at the same time was keen on her household's purity and her children's upbringing.

"What really tires her is her ambition. Despite her illiteracy, she dreams of being something big," Aglan told me.

"Maybe it's money?" I asked.

"She has an affluent life, but she loves money, and something even more..."

"What?"

"Art, if my hunch is right. And I've been asked to invite you to their house with me."

I questioned the motive.

"Apparently something important, we'll soon find out."

We found Fayza, her husband, and her lover. We greeted them and sat down, aware of the tension that electrified the atmosphere and their expressions.

Immediately Fayza said, "The problem is, a film director has offered me an important part in his next film!" She looked at us. "What do you think?"

When I saw her eyes chasing me, I said, "That involves you and your husband, first and last."

Abduh Ibrahim raised his head to find a passage for the words through his chin.

"Ladies of good families act these days," he said.

"I'd like to know how and when this producer saw you," Galal Mursi asked.

"He saw us when we were with you at the casino," the husband replied.

"And her talents were manifest from the first glance?"

"That's his business, not ours."

"As your loyal friend, I don't approve of her entering that field," Galal said.

"Why?" asked Fayza, who looked happy despite the general tension.

"You've never shown any interest in art before."

"There was no opportunity."

"It isn't born suddenly, even if a director suggests it."

"That's exactly how it is born."

"I think so," the husband said.

"They don't offer parts for nothing," Galal said sharply.

"For art," said Aglan Thabit.

"And not for art's sake either!" retorted Galal.

"I'm not a minor!" said Fayza.

"She deserves our confidence," said her husband.

"As your loyal friend, I don't approve," Galal repeated.

"It's a chance that shouldn't be ignored," said the husband.

Aglan concurred and so did I, as if it were an impromptu conspiracy. Galal Mursi rose, and as he took his leave, he said, "I've said my opinion and I insist on it."

"You should meet the director as soon as possible," Aglan said cunningly.

"Abduh Ibrahim knows everything!" I told Aglan when we had left.

"He seized the opportunity and gave his rival a good blow," he replied with a loud laugh.

"What do you think she'll do?"

After a moment, he said, "If my guess is right, her ambition is stronger than her love!"

He was right. She played the part and was an unexpected success. She was offered two new roles. Galal left her and she made no attempt to get him back. Soon afterward her husband divorced her, claiming he was protecting his home and children from the atmosphere that was invading it, proving that his inertia was merely a veneer concealing a long bitterness. Fayza moved to a small, elegant apartment in Zamalek. I visited her with Aglan and found Doctor Sadiq Abd al-Hamid there with his mistress, the journalist Nimat Arif, Zuhayr Kamil's wife, who had become an art critic. Fayza was cheerful as usual, happy with success.

"She might long at times for her children," Aglan said on our way home, "but she won't fall apart over it. I must admit I'm happy with the success of any peasant man or woman, whatever the price."

Fathi Anis

He caught my eye the first time I set foot in the office. I took him for a senior bureaucrat or the son of a noble family, then was surprised to discover he was the secretariat's filing clerk. He was in his thirties, with a primary education and a salary of eight pounds. Tall and elegant, with handsome features, he was married and a father of five.

"Look at nature's folly, it gave him the looks of a chamberlain at the foreign ministry, but withheld any benefits," said Ustaz Abbas Fawzi. "He's alive but isn't provided for."

Fathi Anis

He was responsible for his mother and two divorced sisters, and thus he faced the war days and the rise in the cost of living. He often sidled up to Abbas Fawzi or Abd al-Rahman Shaaban and simply asked, "Who will give me a piaster to buy a *foul* sandwich and be rewarded on the Day of Resurrection?"

If he spotted a member of the public in the corridor, he'd ask him if he needed any help and in the end unabashedly ask for a cigarette.

Abd al-Rahman Shaaban took pity on him and said to Abbas Fawzi. "Fathi's situation deserves consideration."

He agreed.

"Put him in a post where he can earn bribes!" Abd al-Rahman suggested.

Abbas Fawzi smiled. "There are opportunities in Personnel, Accounts, Warehousing, and Purchasing, but he doesn't have qualifications."

"There are directors with the primary certificate," Abd al-Rahman retorted in anger.

"I mean connections. The most important person he knows is Amm Saqr, the messenger!"

He discovered a way of exploiting his looks to fight hunger. He'd present himself to a family as a suitor and was welcomed until inquiries were made; meanwhile, he would visit, staying until it was lunch or dinner time. When invited to the table, he would say, "Only a scoundrel refuses generosity." He would eat like a savage, as though conserving food for the rest of his life. Results of the inquiries would of course prove unsatisfactory, and they would apologize for not accepting him. He would leave, having won several unbelievable meals, and continue his forays in other parts of the city, until word reached the employees, who made a joke of it.

One day he appeared in the office in a gallabiya. Ustaz Tantawi Ismail, still chief of the secretariat, summoned him and asked, "What's the meaning of this, Fathi Effendi?"

"My suit's worn out. I turned it three years ago, it's on its last legs and I can't buy a button!"

"But it's against regulations!"

"There's nothing mentioned in the regulations about it," he replied confidently.

We discussed it inconclusively. Embarrassment worsened when we received an unexpected inspection from the new wafdist minister. When the minister saw him, he thought him a messenger. "Haven't they issued you a messenger's uniform?" he asked.

"I'm a civil servant, your excellency, but I can't afford a new suit," he replied.

The minister was surprised and asked him about his position, his certificate, his salary, and the number of his children, who were nine by then. Then he asked him laughingly, "Is procreation your only hobby?"

"I support the Wafd, I won't be humiliated while you're in power," he replied.

The minister gave him two raises, followed by a cost of living increase, authorized for the first time. He bought a new suit, but his situation only improved a little. One morning, Amm Saqr whispered as he poured my coffee, "The son of a beggar succeeded at last!"

"Fathi Anis?"

"Yes."

"How?"

"He's going to marry a very rich widow."

"Really? Is she beautiful?"

"She's sixty, and looks like a mummy."

It was true, as with all Amm Saqr's news. Fathi married an old Turkish widow, beneficiary of a large endowment. People said he had married with his first wife's consent, who chose her children's happiness over her own. His circumstances changed noticeably. His clothes, health, and appearance showed prosperity. Despite all he had been through, it caused envy.

"How can you make love to a mummy?" Abbas Fawzi asked with a scoff.

"When a man has filled his belly with four kinds of meat and five glasses of whisky, he can make love to the angel of death himself," he replied.

His new wife died after the Palestine War in 1948 and left him a large fortune. He could not conceal his delight, even during the first days. He resigned and thought of starting a business. He decided to open a large café in Tawfiqiya, and endured losses for a year or two until he had mastered his new profession, but then the project was a great success.

I lost touch with him until Amm Saqr came out of prison. He told me of his wealth and buildings, living in a mansion by the Pyramids, his sons' success in school and college—they now numbered twelve. He had kept his first wife, but had taken an Italian dancer as mistress.

"He's sixty-six now," Amm Saqr continued, "but he's strong and imposing, like someone in his prime going out with an Italian dancer. Have you heard of a lover at that age? It's all luck, everything else is false."

Qadri Rizq

A frequent visitor at Adli Barakat's luxurious flat at the beginning of 1948. Thirty or slightly less, in a cavalry officer's uniform, he brought the assembly his jovial lightness. He did not seem interested in politics, and but for an assassination attempt on Mustafa al-Nahhas I would not have guessed his wafdist sympathies, probably inherited from his father, a member of the Wafd caucus.

He was slender and dark, with pronounced, attractive features and a thick moustache he always flirted with admiringly. At the famous hedonistic soirees in Adli Barakat's flat, I witnessed his successful conquests with many artistes.

Following the 1948 war, his joie de vivre abandoned him, and his general appearance betrayed anger and disgust. Reda Hamada and I, deeply distressed, flooded him with questions, hoping he could dispel some gloom or ease our wrath.

He would not go into details. "The army was sacrificed in a despicable attempt to destroy its honor and the lives of its men," he said tersely. He shook his head in frustration. "This will not pass without a price!"

"But we weren't defeated," I said innocently. "Al-Faluga was a clear victory."

"We were defeated, caught between two enemies, one outside, the other inside," he replied.

My soul responded to his anger.

"It's a result of rule by minority parties that allow the king's despotism," said Reda Hamada.

"And the Wafd's weakness, impotent to carry out the people's will," replied Qadri Rizq.

Reda Hamada was not pleased. "The Wafd always relied on the people's revolutionary spirit, but the people have given up."

"The Wafd is to blame," Qadri Rizq retorted, whom I'd never seen this angry, "for the people

Qadri Rizq

abandoning their revolutionary spirit!"

Our relationship grew closer, as we met regularly in the flat of Adli Barakat, whom we watched disintegrate until his suicide. Qadri continued to see us, either at Reda Hamada's house or at al-Fishawi café, back to his old nature, disinterested in politics, a promiscuous womanizer.

With the July 1952 revolution, we discovered he was one of the Free Officers, and were amazed at his incredible ability to conceal. On the night of the revolution, he was with us at Fishawi's, his usual joking, chatty self. Before midnight, we walked together to Abbasiya by the mountain road. I turned off to West Abbasiya, and he—I had assumed—continued north to his home on Ahmad Mahir Street. Actually he never went home that night, but to Manshiyat al-Bakri, where he commanded a small platoon that held a crossroad.

Events kept him away for a considerable time; meanwhile, the king was banished. He reappeared, promoted to a new rank. Developments followed—agricultural reform, the evacuation of British forces—as we met regularly every week in Reda Hamada's house until his arrest, and thereafter at my house, his, or at Fishawi's. Politics was our only conversation,. We had no serious disagreements—the revolution had won our hearts and hopes in a historic, legendary moment.

"The satanic forces that impeded the people's advance have been crushed, the King, the British, the corrupt rulers. Control has returned to the real people: it's the people ruling the people, for the good of the people. Corruption and decadence are finished, reform and progress will continue for ever," said Qadri Rizq.

We said it was time the dream came true for this people—suffering injustice, enslavement, poverty, and alienation for thousands of years—to enjoy freedom, progress, and justice. Yes, we were apprehensive at the readiness to destroy the Wafd.

"Wouldn't it be better if you made the Wafd your popular base?" Reda Hamada asked him more than once before his arrest.

We were also fearful of America, that it might replace Britain in one way or another, when we saw its support for the new regime.

"The Americans are of great use, we have nothing to fear because of the patriotism of our new leaders," Qadri Rizq told us.

Political parties were dissolved, the Muslim Brothers and communists were interned, Qadri's enthusiastic support was unconditional and unrestrained.

Eventually I asked him, "But who are you people?"

He laughed. "We are the friends of nationalism, Arabism, and revolution, and the enemies of corruption, fanaticism, and heresy. Our goal is the people's liberation from whatever enslaves them, whether it's a person or a class, poverty or disease, then pushing them to their rightful place under the sun."

Our joy was disrupted by our friend Reda Hamada's affliction with his wife and his son. Qadri Rizq was deeply moved. But the tragedy was made more tolerable by the strength of our steadfast, patient friend. Qadri admired him and said few men were his peers, wondering how two men like Reda Hamada and Zuhayr Kamil could grow from the same soil.

Great events continued—turning to the Eastern bloc for arms and nationalizing the Suez Canal—and our enthusiasm soared, intoxicating Qadri, intoxicating us all.

"Do you see? We're Egyptians first and last, not Americans or Russians!" he told us.

Qadri married the daughter of a large feudal family who had been subjected to agricultural reform. This was a point of divergence that required notice and interpretation, although it could be considered normal if viewed from the innocent, emotional aspect. It did not escape me that my friend was proud of marrying into that family despite his revolutionary fervor, loyalty, and kindness, but Reda Hamada said, "It's one class aspiring to replace another."

Then came the Suez war and its turnabout against the aggressors. Our friend Qadri Rizq was wounded in the leg and lost his left eye and had to leave the army. He had been on his honeymoon when the fighting broke out, and was summoned from the arms of his bride to his military duty. He was appointed to a senior cultural position in the Ministry of Guidance, and commenced his interest in culture for the first time in his life. He worked by day and studied at night, proving his capacity for learning and management. Later when the socialist laws were announced, he studied socialism with as much intent as culture.

He was always ready to believe in whatever the revolution said should be believed in: his real belief was only the revolution. He was and still is bourgeois in ethics, dreams, aspirations, and customs—a bourgeois with a socialist tongue, not from hypocrisy or fear, but from a genuine loyalty to the revolution. I consider him the sincerest of men, the purest, and most upright, also the most indignant with exploiters and abusers who betrayed the revolution.

When we were struck by the 1967 defeat, his existence was shattered, I thought he was dying alive. "Was all this history for nothing?" he asked in a frenzy. His pale face peered into ours. "Must we bow again at the feet of reactionaries and colonialists?"

He fought to recover his breath, to create new hope in the loss, to turn defeat into a lesson. Every day that passed without surrender restored some of his well-being. His nails dug into the solid earth of reality, searching for drops of hope, like Azmi Shakir and Sadiq Abd al-Hamid.

"The modern history of the Arabs is a chain of defeats by reactionaries and colonialists. Whenever despair sets in, a new light emerges from its darkness: the Mongols, the Crusaders, and the British left, and the Arabs remained," he said.

He wishes the revolution to endure, to be victorious, whatever the price, so the renaissance may not be hindered, in an age that does not permit delay. He follows news of the fighting, regretting he can no longer participate, sad if we receive a blow without returning it, as he waits impatiently for the day we are prepared to fight. He lives day by day, or rather hour by hour, following, anxious, hopeful, relentlessly holding himself to account.

Regardless of Salim Gabr's contradictory opinions, Aglan Thabit's sarcasms, and Reda Hamada's bitter criticism, Qadri Rizq is an honorable man and a sincere member of the July revolution. He may be difficult to define in terms of world principles, but he can be defined with precision by the National Charter—he believes in social justice as he believes in private ownership and incentives, in scientific socialism as in religion, in the homeland and Arab unity, in heritage and science, in the popular base, and in absolute rule. When he approaches me, limping, looking at me with his one remaining eye, my heart pounds with affection and esteem.

Kamil Ramzi

We met at Azmi Shakir's house in 1965. He was new to freedom after five years in jail. Tall, thin, dark-skinned, bald, with a large head and small bright eyes, fifty years old, he held a doctorate in economics and, until his arrest, was a professor at the College of Commerce.

"I read your book on economic schools, it gave me pleasure and benefit," I told him.

He thanked me. "University life suited me very well."

"He was wrongly accused of political action," Azmi Shakir told me. "The truth is he's a thinker, his activities never went beyond ideas and writing."

The week we met, he was appointed to an important position. Azmi Shakir said he was a model of learning, resolution, and integrity. He was friends with Salim Gabr and Zuhayr Kamil, and I introduced him to Reda Hamada, Qadri Rizq, and Sadiq Abd al-Hamid. He earned their respect but no one was overfond of him. His conversation was sincere and knowledgeable. He had completed his education in England; well-read in sociology and politics, he was a superb debater. When he spoke, he was confident, direct, and assertive. He didn't believe in halfway measures, in courtesy or toleration, only in his own opinion to the point of fanaticism: opposition aroused him out of the proper equilibrium expected from a person in his position, as he erupted furiously with arguments and proofs, as though fighting a bloody battle. He resembled Abd al-Wahab Ismail in his fanaticism, despite the contradiction in their styles.

"He's a scholar with a religious mentality," I once said to Azmi Shakir.

"He's undoubtedly fanatic and fiery in his debates, but his nerves have only been this edgy since prison," he replied.

As I knew him better, I met his wife, also a doctor in economics and teacher at the College of Commerce, a model Egyptian woman. And I learned of his way of life, peculiar in our age— he was spartan in his clothes, his food resembled a diet, and he did not smoke or touch liquor.

"I didn't touch a woman before my marriage, and resisted temptation when I was studying abroad," he told me once.

It surprised me to see him fast in Ramadan despite his total belief in dialectic materialism.

"What's the meaning of this?" I asked.

"My father was a simple worker," he replied with a laugh. "He was devout and raised us in religion. I grew up amid Islamic ethics that I couldn't discard, except what contradicted my new creed. I retained fasting because it's an exercise that completely suits my way of life."

He thought a while. "Religion's greatness is only clear when it's not considered a religion."

I was reminded of Zahran Hassouna, astounded at the difference, a devil and an angel.

"Our life cannot be free of contradictions," I said.

"The important thing is to work for the future."

"You believe in communism, of course?"

"That's true."

"Do you consider yourself loyal to the revolution you're serving?" I asked him with a smile.

"I was born to worship work and be loyal to it," he replied with clarity and force.

"I'm asking about your loyalty to the revolution."

He took a deep breath, as if it were a bodily translation of his thought.

"I've never been two-faced. As I've agreed to work in its service, I'm loyal to it."

"That's the answer I was asking about, but something is missing."

"I'm loyal to it, but I don't believe in it, not entirely. For now, it's enough for me that it's paving the way for a real revolution!"

I pointed to Azmi Shakir. "Your position is like the one he adopted since the beginning."

He laughed. "He surrendered before the battle; we resigned when the battle was futile."

"Maybe he was more far-sighted!"

"In that case, allow me to damn far-sight!"

Azmi Shakir admired him, as did Reda Hamada in spite of their difference in principle. Kamil Ramzi's personality tempted analysis and evaluation.

"I pleaded with him to transfer an employee," Reda Hamada told us, "and he lectured me on the corruption of connections. Although I was hurt, my admiration for him grew."

"His minister recommended an employee to him," said Azmi Shakir. "He declined, in order to preserve the principles of justice,"

"His own minister?" I asked.

"Yes. He was made in steel, impossible to bend. I doubt very much he'll keep his position."

"Can they fire an employee for his integrity?" asked Reda Hamada.

"There are more reasons to fire an employee for integrity than for corruption."

Kamil Ramzi himself admitted that no one in his department liked him, from the janitor to the minister. "I can't mind both people's emotions and public interest—my position requires a snake, not an honest civil servant. We're a nation of courtesies and deals. We worshiped Mustafa al-Nahhas because he was upright and unyielding, qualities every ordinary citizen should have. For their rarity, we made them the principal qualifications for popular leadership!"

"Did you once worship Mustafa al-Nahhas?" I asked.

"I was a wafdist," he replied with his usual candor. "My sympathy lasted a long time, even after my belief dried up. Say what you like about the Wafd, but never forget it was a popular party in the precise meaning of the word. Sometimes it altered its policy in response to the wishes of secondary school students!"

He told me of the events of 1935: how he and a group of students had debated with Mustafa al-Nahhas, how the discussion became heated, how the Wafd withdrew its support for Tawfiq Nasim's cabinet and declared revolt, and how blood had been shed less than an hour later.

As Azmi Shakir had predicted, Kamil Ramzi did not last long in his position. He held it for a year until people groaned under his firmness and integrity, then the morning papers announced his transfer to a newspaper organization. A malicious glee prevailed. I wasn't too surprised, recalling Ustaz Tantawi Ismail's tragedy, and Doctor Surour Abd al-Baqi. The power of their integrity exposes weak people to themselves, filling them with envy. I heard no regrets except from his closest friends.

He was angry and overwhelmed with bitterness, imagining that the laws of nature had been disrupted and thrown off course. But it did not stop him applying himself to his new work with the same energy, integrity, and strength. He even found some spare time and resumed academic activity, compiling his political dictionary. He remains a flame of continuous energy, a light that pursues the darkness of despair.

Kamil Ramzi

Camelia Zahran

The day she arrived in the secretariat, with her elegant dress and bonnet-cut black hair, I remembered Abda Sulayman, but what a distance between 1944 and 1965. The old faces—Tantawi Ismail, Abbas Fawzi, Adli al-Muadhin, Abd al-Rahman Shaaban, and Amm Saqr—had disappeared; the secretariat had been stormed by youth, half of them of the fairer sex, and here was Camelia Zahran joining us as the latest pick of these flowers. We had become used to their presence, accustomed to rumors hounding them during the crucial period preceding marriage. Most married outside our ministry, except one who married a colleague in the legal department; none gave up work because of marriage.

Camelia Zahran was a twenty-three-year-old law graduate. She received her clerical position grudgingly, feeling her legal studies were going to waste. I saw in her eyes a forthright, daring expression beyond the submissive, languid, harem look, and I felt her experience in life was hardly different in worldliness from her male colleagues. She was soon informal, but never overstepped the bounds of traditional etiquette, as one looking wisely to the future, taking into account the oriental complexes males carried from their ancestors at home.

After the summer vacation, a comparatively old colleague told me, "Perhaps you didn't know that Camelia Zahran was a skilled dancer?"

"Dancer?" I asked in amazement.

"I saw her at Hannoville dancing with a young man. She was so involved in dancing, like she was a melody herself."

I leapt to her defense. "What was unacceptable in our day is no longer wrong."

He scratched his head. "I'd love to imagine what life would be like with a wife like her!"

"The divorce rate is lower now than it was in our day," I said, "and polygamy as well."

"It seems you're a modern man despite your old age," he replied with a laugh.

"I wish I were part of this generation," I replied. "Not to belittle its problems, but because it has unburdened itself of many complexes that sullied our lives."

I repeated my words to Reda Hamada, the most conservative of my old friends. He asked what I meant.

"Exchanging love in an atmosphere of healthy frankness is better than suppression and traveling from the arms of one prostitute to another," I explained.

"It seems to me that love, like democracy, is now regarded as another antiquated travesty," he replied dubiously.

I strained to listen to conversations among the young people of our department, learning from the scattered words, particularly about Camelia, who gripped my attention because of her novelty. Her family was average, she was the first of five children to be employed; it's not hard to imagine difficulties a family of that kind and class face, or those challenging the girl, an independent person responsible for herself, and perhaps partially for her family, the expenses of modern life, or the demands of a future for a girl hoping for a respectable husband. Thus her interest in public affairs was superficial, and her acceptance of matters like religion and the revolution realistic. Her primary concern was her private life, love, marriage, and the fruits of modern civilization.

We rarely encountered a woman with a real interest in religion, philosophy, or politics—perhaps we had only average ones as colleagues and the exceptions found their way to

Camelia Zahran

universities or public life. Doctor Zuhayr Kamil had an opinion on the matter: "Women's lack of interest in ideology or philosophy proves that ideology and philosophy hinder real, vital activity. A woman is only concerned with creation and all things connected, she is a beautiful creator, and creation is the center of her life. All other activities are of man's making, and are necessary for domination, not creation! The world is a woman's goal and idol—in a another sense, it's the goal of creation; this proves that we were created to care for the world. All else is false. Eternity must be achieved in it. If religions had pictured God as a woman, they would have given us a new wisdom that is genuine happiness."

It may be difficult to interpret these views in the light of our knowledge of Zuhayr Kamil's mentality, but they could be understood from his life—he missed his wife and daughter who had left the country, and was opening up to a new love for Nimat Arif.

A sullen, grim cloud hovered over our heads in the wake of the June 1967 disaster when my old colleague said, "There are strange events, unrelated to the battle ..."

I asked him what he meant.

"Camelia Zahran is playing that old game with the director-general!"

Directors, unlike in the old days, were young; our director-general was in his forties, but he was married and a father, and, on that score at least, had a good reputation.

"Maybe it's a rumor," I said.

"And maybe it's true!"

"How do you explain it?" I asked.

"It could be love," he replied. "If it is, one home will be destroyed and a new one built."

After a long silence, he added, "And maybe it's the old Sharara al-Nahhal game."

"Has our generation's opportunism crept up on the fresh generation?"

"Temptations today are stronger and more violent."

"Opportunism may be recognized as a new morality or new skills, like technology."

I discussed it with my friend Azmi Shakir.

"You're an excellent thinker," I said. "Why don't you study the new morals? I mean those suited to the modern age, that must be derived from the new society, not from old values."

"What drove you to such an idea?" he asked.

"Look at what happened to our friend Kamil Ramzi," I replied. "And I've known many like him in the course of my life, people we consider fine human beings. Could it be that their morals no longer fit the modern world?"

"You're venting your bitterness," he said with a smile.

"The truth is I'm perplexed and sad."

Rumors spread about Camelia Zahran and the director, and suspicions became certain when she was finally transferred to the legal department, but no home was destroyed. When Sabri Gad was appointed to our department, love grew between him and Camelia. At first he seemed rebellious and reckless, but he loved her and she loved him, and although he was more than two years younger, they officially announced their engagement.

I was delighted with the happy ending—it had attracted them to a steadfast life and the responsibility of procreating and bringing the new human being to a solemn path. Day after day, my faith confirms that man's purity is as much from outside as it is from inside, and that we must provide light and clean air if we want beautiful flowers.

Mahir Abd al-Karim

He was an associate professor in his mid-forties when I went to college in 1930; his academic, moral, and humane reputation was like the scent of musk—no professor bewitched his students with his spiritual nature and the munificence of his face as much as he did.

Descended from an old family known for its wealth and, in modern history, its loyalty to the Nationalist Party, he was counted by extension a party supporter—but it did not touch our love for him. He never revealed a political leaning, nor fell victim to fanaticism, and never uttered a word of caprice, prejudice, or envy, giving himself to scholarship and good works.

"If all the rich were like Mahir Abd al-Karim," Doctor Ibrahim Aql once told us, "I would have said the highest ideal for man was to be rich."

His generosity ate up his wealth. He never refused the needy, charitably donating in secret as if hiding a fault. He was a model of magnanimity in his scholarly and public debates—even political ones, if he was ever dragged into them—as if his facial muscles were made only to express contemplation, welcome, and smiles, unable to reveal exasperation or anger.

His old mansion in Munira was the meeting-place for scholars, litterateurs, and thinkers, with room for his students, whom he introduced to the elders and treated as equals—these were the many thinkers I met in his salon. The dominant current of conversation was cultural, with politics mixed in only rarely. But Ustaz Salim Gabr did not hesitate to discuss class differences one day in 1931 when he had just returned from a trip to France.

"In some circles," he said, "they despise us because of our people's bad condition."

Doctor Mahir Abd al-Karim smiled and said, "I believe it's a bad situation."

Doctor Ibrahim Aql said to Salim Gabr, "In France you mingle with extremists who may despise France as much. Man's civilization is not determined by what he owns, but by the pulse of his thought and heart. Personally I consider an Indian fakir a nobler human being than Ford or Rockefeller."

Salim Gabr was enraged and accused him of the reactionary idealism and sufism he considered responsible for the East's backwardness. Mahir Abd al-Karim did not think like Salim Gabr; he always believed Islam ensured complete social justice, and that education achieved the same result in a different way.

One day after a lecture, he invited Gaafar Khalil and me to his mansion in al-Munira. We found him alone in the reception hall. He welcomed us, then said, "An American girl has asked to see me, and I've chosen you to translate."

He did not know any English, and perhaps he preferred us to one of his older friends to understand the reason for this strange visit. At sunset a beautiful blonde girl in her twenties arrived. She greeted us and sat down, apologizing for her intrusion. We were offered tea and cakes, as she started her story. She was visiting Egypt with a group of young people, and her mother had asked her to find someone in Egypt called Mahir Abd al-Karim who had studied at the Sorbonne after the Great War. The hotel manager had located him and telephoned his mansion. It was clear her mother had been our professor's classmate in Paris and his girlfriend as well, and was taking advantage of her daughter's trip to Egypt to send greetings. Throughout the visit, talk revolved around old, happy memories and the two old friends today.

When we left, I said to Gaafar Khalil, "It seems our professor's effect on those around him goes way back to his youth."

Gaafar winked. "But affecting women is a different matter," he said with a laugh. "His good looks are enough to make him the romantic lead in our films!"

I recited the words of al-Farazdaq that always reminded me of our professor's face:

He averts in modesty and averts his dignity/he never speaks but that he smiles.

"I can't imagine him without his dignified manner," I told Gaafar. "If dignity for others is a dress, for him it's flesh and blood."

There was never a blemish to his reputation or conduct. At this point, it's my duty to report a rumor that attacked him during the period of turbulence and political assassinations after the Second World War. It is said he wrote a secret letter to King Farouk, warning of the rebelliousness sweeping the younger generation, explaining its causes and suggesting a remedy. It was a café rumor, and until today I have not ascertained its truth. All was guesswork inspired by conflicting political passions. The wafdists said he had recommended dissolving political parties and establishing a beneficent dictatorship to speed up reforms and provide young people with a scholarly, religious education. The extremist Salim Gabr's disciples said it was an invitation for a counter-revolution to avert the real revolution. I was insulted by the letter—whatever its contents—as a violation of constitutional freedom and a disdain of the people's authority. I was at odds between respect for my professor and my clear political position; I was embarrassed to broach it with him, but Gaafar Khalil found the courage. It happened when we visited the professor so that Gaafar could say farewell before his trip to the United States. My late friend told him of the rumors. He listened, silent and smiling.

"Do you believe the rumors?" he asked Gaafar.

"No," Gaafar replied in retreat.

"Fine!" was all the professor said in response.

This reminds me of two men's opinions. One his old friend Ustaz Salim Gabr, the other his disciple Ustaz Abbas Fawzi. Salim Gabr loved and admired him, but thought he was an aristocrat who had never known poverty and regarded people from above, with a personal vision attractive and pure, but alien, like the language of another planet.

Abbas Fawzi—the lexicon of biting satire—expressed his opinion but with caution and slowly, drop by drop, careful not to pour himself out in one draft. "He's a noble prince, a mamluke from the line of mamlukes," he said one day. I pondered this, knowing his spite, and wondered what the devil meant. Another time, listening to me praising the professor, he said, "These are the virtues of rich noblemen, virtues that have not endured bitter experiences!" On a third occasion, he said, "In Egypt, nobility, wealth, and learning don't meet. The rich nobleman pretends to be learned and exploits the intelligence of the poor; they research for him and suggest ideas, he listens with dignity and seals with his signature!"

"Your professor is a gourmet." he said another time. "In a single day he eats enough to feed an army brigade. When he's finished digesting, can he find time for thinking and research?"

But we were in direct contact with the professor's mind and knew his precision, his clarity, and the abundance of his knowledge. Events passed him by, and he was steadfast in his dignity. But I detected an anxiety in his soul during unforgettable events in our lives—the political assassinations, the burning of Cairo, the July revolution, the socialist laws—but nothing beyond that. I don't believe a feudalist received that historic blow with his equanimity, wrenching from his hand ten thousand feddans. He sold his old mansion in al-Munira and

Mahir Abd al-Karim

bought a beautiful villa in Heliopolis that continues to receive people of thought. He taught at the university with the same zeal until his retirement in 1954, and then as a visiting professor. He was appointed a member of the Higher Council for Literature, received the State Achievement Award in social sciences and the Decoration of Merit, First Class. Thus the revolution recognized his academic position, fine reputation, and general uprightness that kept him above suspicion.

He never publicly declared allegiance to the revolution, remaining distant from the media and refusing to impose himself in a dishonorable fashion, yet he did not hesitate in private.

"I believe in what's happening," he said one day. "It's the least to be done for the homeland, for life to thrive in it."

There was no bitterness in his words or behavior—and there was no point probing further, expecting more than that he face with wisdom a historic revolution dedicated to uprooting his class, and convince himself intellectually that it was an inevitable, historic movement.

In 1969, he celebrated his seventy-fifth birthday. The salon crowded with the old professors who were still living and friends like Salim Gabr, Reda Hamada, Azmi Shakir, Kamil Ramzi, Qadri Rizq, Gad Abu al-Ela, Abbas Fawzi, Sadiq Abd al-Hamid, and Nimat Arif on behalf of her husband, Zuhayr Kamil. Memories of Ibrahim Aql and Gaafar Khalil flooded back. There were a few young people, like Sabri Gad and his wife Camelia Zahran, but white hair, wrinkles, abstract gazes, and walking sticks prevailed. Until that day, I had never quite felt the passage of time, its weight, majesty, treason, eternity, effect, arrogance, modesty, wisdom, and impetuosity; as if I had dozed on the diesel train to Alexandria and woken up in Sidi Gaber Station.

Yet Mahir Abd al-Karim still had his blue eyes, his conquering smile, and his sweet dignity. Our professor said, "This is not a celebration in the real sense of the word, we cannot celebrate when we're at war, but it's a good opportunity to get together."

The conversation went east and west, but always reverted to the Middle East conflict, from political, economic, philosophical, and religious aspects, branching out to the global situation, scientific discoveries, general human problems, dangerous disturbances in the East and West, the decay of values—and the future: with what face would it greet us? A wave of pessimism came sweeping in, repeated like a jangling melody among the old, a stone hurled at the world gone by. Our professor joined the chorus, but with a different tune.

"God have mercy on Ibrahim Aql," he said suddenly.

What made him remember him? He was his dearest friend. I saw his tears only at his funeral in 1957; I recalled Aql's words to us before graduation.

"He acknowledged faith as he acknowledged death and facts like the rising of the sun . . ." He smiled. "Say what you will about the world, there's nothing new in pessimism. Life is for the benefit of the human being, otherwise his numbers wouldn't increase, or his control over his life."

Mahmoud Darwish

He attracted attention in college with his tall, lean frame and was soon singled out by his intelligence and incredible industry, earning a position of respect among fellow students and professors, Egyptian and foreign. He was handsome with delicate features, but gruff and introverted, a colleague or companion but not a friend. Books were his real friends. His father was imam of a mosque in Giza, with a large family and meager income. Mahmoud Darwish led a very sparse life.

From the first day, he and Aglan Thabit fell out. Aglan laughed when Mahmoud said his father was imam of a mosque.

"What are you laughing at?" Mahmoud asked.

"Doesn't it make you laugh that the imamate is a job?" Aglan replied.

"You have no manners," Mahmoud replied in anger.

"Shut up!" Aglan yelled back.

We separated them, but they insisted on enmity to the very end. When Aglan was accused of stealing the tarboush, Mahmoud testified against him, and this was one of the reasons that led to his expulsion from college. We reprimanded Mahmoud, but he said, "There's no good in offering society an educated thief."

Frustration and deprivation appeared in his eyes every time they fell on a girl. Suad Wahbi almost caused him insanity, but instead of flirting with her or at least trying, he campaigned against her impropriety almost publicly. He was the first to inform the dean of her indecent attire and the riot she caused in the lecture hall.

It seems he suffered violent crises, conflict between vitality and compulsory deprivation. His father—with a provincial, religious mentality—found no other solution but to marry him to an orphaned niece in his care. He returned to college the following academic year, married to an illiterate peasant wife, but she gave him a peace of mind that directed his energy to studying with no distractions. Now his only interest was scholarship and excelling.

When he worked on a research paper, he wrote with skill and ability a coverage that asserted his breadth of reading and familiarity with the references. He would sometimes follow our torrent of politics like a sane man listening to madmen.

"How do you find time to study after this?" he asked.

"As if the English are occupying a country that is not yours, and as if the king's tyrannizing a people that are not your own," replied a student in amazement.

He made no distinction between Mustafa al-Nahhas and Ismail Sidqi; sometimes he forget the name of the pasha heading the government. When the strikes broke out at university, he faced them with impotent fury. He would sneak to the library and read alone until it closed. One day he leapt to the dais after the student leader's revolutionary speech; with insane daring, he asked students to return to their work and concentrate on studies. There was an uproar, and students demanded he be brought down; but for the respect he had earned with his excellence, they would have certainly attacked him. The university was closed down for a month; during that time all the student leaders were arrested. When we returned, I heard whispers.

"They say Mahmoud Darwish is connected to General Security," Gaafar Khalil said.

I refused to believe him.

"They say his father, a Security spy, recommended him."

"But he's a straight young man," I replied.

"They also say he's the one who informed on the student leaders," he added sadly.

It was a strong rumor, with no way of proving it. Some tried to provoke him over his role in the conspiracy, but Doctor Ibrahim Aql summoned them and threatened that if they did it

Mahmoud Darwish

again, he would notify the authorities. The rumor lingered long with me—I was disgusted by him, I never liked him—almost believing it when after graduation he was selected for a scholarship in France when scholarships had been suspended.

I lost track of him for many years until I saw him in Ustaz Adli al-Muadhin's office at the ministry. We shook hands and chatted. He had a new look, full of health and energy, and his eyes peered at me through elegant spectacles that gave him a scholarly air.

"I'm a teacher at the college," he told me.

"And he's publishing a series on Sufi philosophy," added Adli al-Muadhin.

"The war caught me in France before my thesis was finished, so I went to Switzerland and received my doctorate there," Mahmoud Darwish continued.

After he left, Adli al-Muadhin said with a laugh, "As you can see, he's returned a foreigner to find an illiterate peasant wife waiting for him."

I asked him about the old rumors of Mahmoud's links to General Security, as Adli al-Muadhin was employed in the university administration at that time.

"Rubbish," Adli replied tersely.

When I recounted the incident to Ustaz Abbas Fawzi, he had a good laugh.

"What a naive person you are! Don't you know Adli al-Muadhin himself was connected to General Security at that time?"

I met Doctor Mahmoud years later at Doctor Mahir Abd al-Karim's salon in al-Munira. His foot was firm in the world of books: he had published more than three books regarded as important references in the modern study of Sufism, and I had heard nothing but praise for them from our professor Mahir Abd al-Karim. I asked about his life.

"I have four sons in engineering, commerce, law, and literature. My daughter is married to an air force pilot," he replied.

"Do you practice sufism?" I asked with interest.

"No," he replied with a laugh. "But there's no denying that one specializes in a field embedded inside himself."

I thought of his wife—primitive in every sense—whom fate had made mistress of a household of educated people. I wished to delve into that recess of his life, but he appeared glowing with happiness and success.

"You heard about Doctor Ibrahim Aql's tragedy, of course?" he asked me.

"Of course," I replied. "A real disaster. But I didn't see you at his sons' funeral."

"I was out of Cairo. Have you kept in touch with him since you left college?"

"No."

"He's a teacher with no students or disciples."

I met him once more at the Munira salon, then he was invited to teach at an Arab university and traveled abroad. That was the last I heard of him.

Magida Abd al-Raziq

On a visit to Salim Gabr's office at *al-Masri* in 1950, he introduced me to a beautiful woman. "Magida Abd al-Raziq, editor of the women's section," was thirty, her black eyes intelligent and attractive, and her strong personality imposed itself from first contact.

Magida Abd al-Raziq

The second time we met was at an election campaign party for Zuhayr Kamil.

"So you're a wafdist?" I asked.

"I'm a student of Doctor Zuhayr Kamil," she replied smiling.

"In literature?"

"Journalism."

"And a wafdist?"

"Far beyond!"

"What do you mean?" I wondered, looking at her beautiful eyes. She smiled but didn't reply.

When I met her for the third time at Zuhayr Kamil's house, we were moving from cordial acquaintance to genuine friendship. After she left, Zuhayr Kamil said, "She is cultured and worthy of respect."

"I think so," I said enthusiastically.

"And she's also a communist," he continued with a smile.

"A communist?"

"A tormented Egyptian woman, victim of the transition."

A strong friendship and mutual respect brought us together. We met intermittently at Groppi's with a group of friends. She ignored flirtations as minor trivia, refusing old feminine tricks, and had no respect for bourgeois values. She always sought a sincere, genuine passion.

"Don't think me frigid," she told me one day.

"What made you think of that?" I asked.

"I worship love," she said fervently, then correcting herself, "Love and ideology."

When her confidence in me was secure, she told me her story at al-Fishawi café.

"I was born into a small bourgeois family, its head an obscure civil servant, and I the only girl among four brothers."

"So you were a spoiled jewel," I said with a smile.

"Quite the contrary, I was persecuted by all, and it got worse as I got older. But I forced their respect with my excellence in school."

I announced my admiration with a smile.

"A man proposed marriage when I passed the secondary certificate. Although everyone approved, I stipulated that he allow me to complete my university education. He asked why, I told him I wanted to work. He did not agree, and my family took his side. I insisted, so he left."

"And you realized your plan in full!"

"Yes. But at college I met a professor who had a major impact on my life. You've heard of Ustaz Muhammad Arif, of course?"

"Yes."

"He taught me knowledge, and what's more dangerous..."

"Communism?"

"Yes. We fell deeply in love and got married as soon as I had graduated."

"I thought you weren't married!" I said in amazement.

"I lived happy times and bore twins, a boy and a girl."

"How wonderful!"

"His mother ran the house, and when she died, we had problems. I was torn between my job at the newspaper and household duties. My husband loved order and being the object of attention. He suggested I devote myself to the home."

"A sound idea."

"No!" she retorted angrily. "I had my own aspirations, I refused. I got no sympathy or respect from him."

I said nothing.

"I discovered his selfishness and bad manners, and his deep-seated desire to dominate. Our home was ablaze with violence and enmity, then it ended in divorce."

"When was that?"

"During the cholera."

"And how are things now?" I asked sympathetically.

"As you can see," she replied proudly, "I'm doing well at my work, a good woman is helping me with the children, and he pays me the legal support."

The July revolution sowed the seeds of a stubborn disagreement for the first time in our quiet friendship. She said it was reactionary, a new brand of fascism, or a petit bourgeois coup to satisfy the ambitions of petit bourgeois like me! She persisted until the revolutionary regime turned to the Eastern bloc, then her views changed and her stubbornness softened.

Her loneliness distressed me. I felt it must cause her sharp bitterness, but she always rejected the frivolous advances of her male colleagues, anticipating the true love that she worshiped, as she had told me long before.

"I was betrayed once," she told me with her sweet candor.

"I don't believe it," I replied.

"My pediatrician, damn him!"

"But how?"

"He was married!"

"A married man!"

"Truly a mistake, but it was love. He told me he wasn't happy and was getting a divorce for reasons that had nothing to do with me."

"And you believed him?"

"Deceit is disgusting, worse than murder. I submitted with no restraint."

"How awful!"

"Damn him! His days were black, like his deceit. We met at his clinic during the air raids of the Suez invasion."

After that experience, suspicion settled in, reinforcing her loneliness and longing for true love. Time invaded. She is fifty now; her daughter is married and her son works for Kuwait radio. She has drowned in lonely old age, yet she keeps a slender figure and a touch of beauty. When she appears on television, she captivates eyes and ears with her personality, flexible logic, and wealth of information; alone, I almost hear moaning rise from deep inside her.

She still visits her old teacher, Zuhayr Kamil, and a close friendship has grown with his new young wife, Nimat Arif. She undoubtedly knows of her affair with Sadiq Abd al-Hamid, but ignores it completely, hoping the truth will never be disclosed to her teacher. I learned recently—to my great delight—that she is going on a journalistic tour of the Mediterranean. I hope it offers some relief for her loneliness, renewal for her life, and material for her pen.

Nagi Morcos

A name I will never forget, as if it belonged to a great person—yet we were classmates in secondary school for only three years, between 1925 and 1928. He had gone to primary school in Sudan, where his father worked. When he returned to Egypt, they lived in Abbasiya and sent the son to our school.

"We were four brothers, three died and I lived," he told me one day.

He also told me, "My mother is sad, she never laughs."

He was tall, slim, and handsome, polite and grave beyond his age, the only one in first year to wear long trousers, and probably the most brilliant student I ever met. Every student excelled in some field, one at languages, another in mathematics, but Nagi Morcos was excellent at everything: Arabic, English, French, arithmetic, algebra, geometry, physics, chemistry, history, and geography. The top student with no rival, he was respected by teachers of different nationalities—Egyptian, English, and French— and treated as a man not a pupil. Badr al-Ziyadi called him Abd al-Halim al-Misri, likening his brilliance to the famous wrestler's strength.

"How do you excel at everything?" I asked him.

"I pay attention in class, and study from the first day of the school year," he replied with his extreme politeness.

"Don't you go to the cinema every Thursday?" Gaafar Khalil asked.

"Only on festivals and holidays," he replied.

"Don't you play soccer?" Eid Mansour asked.

"No."

"Do you have a hobby?" Reda Hamada asked.

"I play the piano in my spare time," he replied.

"You never take part in strikes," Reda Hamada said. "Aren't you interested in nationalism?"

"Of course, but . . ." He hesitated. "My elder brother was killed in a demonstration."

He did well in the qualifying exams, placed among the top ten in the country. When we returned to school at the beginning of the new academic year, Nagi Morcos was not to be found. He lived far away, at the edge of Abbasiya near Manshiyat al-Bakri. We went to his home and learned he had contracted tuberculosis and had been sent to his grandmother in the south to recuperate for at least a year. We were saddened by the news, as were all his classmates and teachers; we sent him a group letter with our best wishes for a speedy recovery.

At the time, Mustafa al-Nahhas was taken to court in the case of Sayf al-Din, but the Supreme Court acquitted him. Delegations of people descended on Bait al-Umma with congratulations; one among the many was our friend's father, an employee at the Ministry of War. Unfortunately, he appeared in a photograph among the well-wishers, and the ministry decided to fire him. He took it hard: poor and with a bad heart, he became paralyzed and died.

Nagi recovered his health, but could not continue his education. Some good people seized the opportunity of the Wafd's return to government to employ him in a minor position at the Ministry of War. Thus circumstances destroyed the most brilliant student of our generation.

I often remembered him and regretted his end; whenever some success came my way in my academic or professional life, he'd return to my mind with a pang of sorrow for the glories buried alive by a blind stroke of the absurd.

Nagi Morcos

Years passed without seeing him or hearing about him, until a chance meeting in 1960 at the casino in the Azbakiya gardens. I walked past him without recognizing him, my eye catching his white beard, and assumed he was an artist. Then his voice called me. When I turned around, I knew him at once. We shook hands warmly and sat down. His face had hardly changed except for the beard and gray hair; he radiated an aura of translucence, like sweet perfume or an embracing tranquility. We reminisced about the past and old friends— those who passed on like Badr al-Ziyadi and Gaafar Khalil, and those who had excelled like Reda Hamada, Surour Abd al-Baqi, and the others.

Then it was his turn. "I'm still at the Ministry of War and reached the third grade. I'm married and a father to a twenty-year old girl, a student at the College of Sciences." After a short silence, he continued. "For a long time I've been studying spirituality from books and correspondence."

"I've read some books about it," I said.

He smiled. "I study it and practice it."

"Really?"

"The world of the spirit is incredible, more than the material world," he said with emotion.

I was following with interest and respect. "It's man's hope for true salvation," he continued.

"Man needs salvation," I replied, civil and sincere at the same time.

"Our civilization is materialistic. Through science, it achieves unbelievable triumphs every day and lays the ground for man to dominate his world. But what's the use of owning the world and losing your self?"

"Humanity should control both," I replied cautiously.

He smiled sweetly. "Perhaps you don't believe what I say, or you're not entirely convinced. But the spiritual world harbors as many unknowns as the world of matter. Mining it promises mankind great victories no less staggering than those of space travel. We only need to believe in a spiritual process as we do in the scientific process, and believe the complete truth is the meeting of two roads and not the end of one road."

"That's plausible."

He looked at me affectionately with his black eyes—and I saw their color for the first time. "How faint the sound of the truth amid the grinding machines," he said with grief. "And how needful humanity is today for a savior."

"How do you envisage the savior?" I asked curiously.

"I see it as a man, or an idea, or an expensive lesson!"

"Like an atomic war?"

"Perhaps. I feel a veil separates us, but it's subtle, with weak roots, and that your aptitude for the love of truth is great. I practice spiritualism at home—maybe you'll visit me one day?"

He gave me his card with his address on Deir al-Malak Street. I had listened with love not conviction. He had appeared in my hellish existence like the scent of orange blossom. That evening, I saw Salim Gabr at his office in the newspaper. I told him about Nagi Morcos and his invitation; as a goad and challenge, I suggested we visit him together. But he scoffed at the idea and reminded me there was no longer a divide between the worlds of matter and spirit. My friend was inviting me to magical rites in the space age. I have not seen Nagi Morcos since, but occasionally he hovers as a childhood memory, and I realize that he lives in a corner of my self.

Nadir Burhan

Nadir Burhan

He was one of the heroes of our young lives in primary school between 1921 and 1925. He was years older, tall, and strong. On our first day in school, we were told he was the student leader. We gathered around him in the school yard, following his words attentively.

"Never think yourselves small, you are Saad's soldiers, soldiers of the homeland … We must inure ourselves to accept beatings, prison, even hanging. Life with no freedom has no value, and there is no freedom without sacrifice. God sent us Saad Zaghloul a leader and we must be worthy of his leadership."

I respected and admired him, Reda Hamada worshiped him, Sayyid Shouayr and Khalil Zaki did not dare sneer at him. If he talked about his visits to Bait al-Umma and his debates with the leader, we were in awe to the point of madness. My patience expired, and I went up to him and asked, "I want to see Saad with my own eyes, will you take us to Bait al-Umma?"

He gave me a sympathetic look. "You're still young and in short trousers. Visiting Bait al-Umma is a dangerous adventure, not a safe journey."

If a strike or a demonstration were called, Nadir Burhan waited until the morning lines were drawn up, then stepped forward and clapped loudly. Soon the lines reverberated with clapping. Then, school monitors went over to the lines of younger pupils and, with the consent of the striking students, led them to their classrooms. We left off shouting for the life of Saad, while the rest went on a demonstration with Nadir Burhan at their head in the street, where they joined with pupils from other schools. In one demonstration, he was shot in the leg and spent two months in hospital. A slight limp stayed with him for the rest of his life.

Under his leadership I attended my first demonstration in 1924. He called us to strike. In a speech he said that King Fuad was trying to manipulate the constitution, that Saad Zaghloul, who was Prime Minister, was resolutely defending the people's rights, and that we had to go to Abdin Square to support the leader. As it was a popular government for the first time, and its head was also Minister of the Interior, we were allowed to participate in the demonstration, since it was to be a peaceful one. We walked with huge crowds of schoolchildren, students, and townsfolk until we filled Abdin Square to the edges, and we pounded on the palace gate with our hands, shouting, "Saad or revolution." In the distance, waves of shouting rolled our way, announcing the approach of the leader on his way to meet the king. Pressure increased on a narrow path the police had forced for the leader's car to pass.

I told Reda Hamada with immense pleasure, "We're going to see Saad Zaghloul!"

"Yes, even if just for a few seconds!"

With stubborn deftness, we edged to the path; the car approached slowly, people surrounding it, clinging to its sides, standing on the hood. We peered with anxious, ravenous eyes, but saw only human bodies, not a glimpse of the leader. Our disappointment lasted a long time.

When we moved to secondary school I lost contact with Nadir Burhan, and neither heard nor saw more of him. Forty years passed before I ran into him again at the Astra café in 1965. I was on my way back from a daytime rendezvous with Amani Muhammad and stopped for a cup of coffee. I spotted him sitting by himself, a portly giant, his coat folded over the back of a chair next to him. I recognized him at once. He hadn't changed much, although he was sixty; except for his sideburns, even his hair had stayed black. I walked up to him with a smile. He gave a look as though he didn't know me but shook my hand nevertheless. When I reminded him of primary school and leadership, his face broadened and he invited me to sit down.

"You haven't changed," I said.

He laughed. "I'm from a family known for longevity. They only die in accidents."

I reminded him of friends and told him of destinies. He knew only of Reda Hamada. When I asked about his life, he welcomed the opportunity to talk, as though he was searching for relief.

"After primary school, my father moved to Asyut, where I went to secondary school. I was expelled during Muhammad Mahmoud's regime, then returned in al-Nahhas's regime. I was expelled again during Sidqi's regime, then accused in the plot to assassinate him and received a ten-year sentence. I was released with a pardon during the al-Nahhas government that negotiated the treaty. I saw no sense in trying to complete my secondary education. The Wafd appointed me agent for *al-Jihad* newspaper in Alexandria."

He paused, his faced dark with memories unknown to me. "Nothing distressed me more than the disagreement between Mustafa al-Nahhas and al-Nuqrashi. Al-Nahhas was my leader, al-Nuqrashi my spiritual father. I couldn't see a livable world with enmity between the two men. Events took their course and my disgust reached its limit. As the treaty had sealed the 1919 revolution, and we had gained independence, albeit some time later, I decided to retire from politics. It coincided with my father's death and my inheritance of a decent fortune. I opened a fish restaurant in Sidi Gaber, and God has been generous to me."

"So you retired from politics?"

"Since 1937. Of course I follow events. I may be the only fish merchant who scours the newspaper every day before he opens his place." He shook his head sadly. "I watched things fall apart with distress. Whenever weakness crept into the Wafd or a generation of youth abandoned it, my heart was torn. But there's nothing to be done."

"Everything has youth and old age, it's the law of life," I said.

"But the Wafd in our life personified the era of youthful vigor and rebirth. Show me another historical period, from pre-dynastic times until today, when the people were masters and giants as they were under the Wafd!" He continued with a laugh, "With the July revolution, I thanked God for the decision I'd made freely before being forced to it or worse."

"But surely you give the revolution credit for its great deeds?"

"Admitting the truth is a virtue, but I can't forgive trying to discredit Saad Zaghloul."

"Politics has its exigencies. Don't forget Mustafa Kamel's attitude toward Ahmad Urabi."

"Did you watch Mustafa al-Nahhas's funeral?" he asked me with interest. "There was a popular rehabilitation of Saad, the Wafd, and the greatest popular revolution of our lifetime."

He told me he had visited Cairo from time to time over the past two years, because his daughter had married and moved to the capital. He talked about his family. "My eldest son's a fishmonger like me, the middle one's an engineer, and the youngest an air force pilot."

Since then, every summer I eat dinner—at least once— at my old friend's restaurant in Alexandria. In the summer of 1969, I found him unusually sad.

"At the end of last year, my engineer son emigrated to Canada." He continued, his voice cracking, "And this winter, my pilot son was killed for the homeland!"

Haggar al-Minyawi

Shaykh Haggar al-Minyawi was the Arabic teacher at our primary school and moved up with us to secondary school. He was from Upper Egypt and spoke its dialect. He was strongly built, tall, and dark-skinned, and he gave little care to his appearance—a turban too small and ill-matching colors in his jubbah and caftan. But he forced respect with a strong personality, command of his subject, and tremendous courage. He was not narrow-minded and loved a joke, and he recited beautiful poetry to us. Once he had a quarterstaff-fencing contest with the sports teacher in the schoolyard; swinging dexterously, he beat his opponent amid loud applause.

Gaafar Khalil came late to class after we had taken our seats. As he loved to joke, imitating our teacher, he said 'Good morning' to him in classical Arabic: "*Im sabahan.*"

The class laughed, Gaafar was pleased with himself.

The shaykh waited until he sat down, then called. "Gaafar Khalil."

He stood up.

"Conjugate '*im sabahan.*"

Gaafar failed, and the shaykh opened his grade-book and gave him a zero.

"But it's difficult!" Gaafar protested.

"Then why do you use what you don't understand?" the shaykh asked quietly.

In primary school—age of the revolution—he taught Arabic and nationalism. He seized any opportunity to talk nationalism, recall glorious memories, and eulogize the heroes; we followed with tears in our eyes. He talked of Saad Zaghloul as a saint or thaumaturge, considering his leadership a heavenly mission, a miracle of history. We learned about Saad's upbringing, his skill as a lawyer, his positions as Minister of Education and Minister of Justice, his leadership, his challenge of British might, his magic and eloquence, and what he held for the country's future.

"His eloquence stirred emotions, and in his name the revolution started," he told us.

He defined the perfect student. "He who acquires knowledge and revolts against tyrants."

We loved him as much as we respected him, receiving from him nationalism and a purity of identity. Because of him we loved Arabic and adored its poetry.

In secondary school, the flavor of struggle changed. English faces receded, and those of their Egyptian allies appeared. Partisan politics occupied first place in the struggle, and the shaykh fought the new battle with the same force and steadfastness.

"The battle is the same, but the enemies have increased: we must double our efforts."

The day of our strike during Muhammad Mahmoud's regime, the day Badr al-Ziyadi was killed, the headmaster demanded he ask the students to return to their classrooms. He was irascible by nature, flaring when challenged in blind fury; he mounted the dais in front of the headmaster's office and cried in a terrible voice, "Learning demands order, the homeland demands struggle. You only have your conscience, so use it ..."

The headmaster sent a report to the Minister of Education, and he was soon fired. The day he was absent from school and the word spread, students stormed the headmaster's office; he was forced to flee the school, and the Ministry transferred him for fear of his life. The shaykh returned to the school during the Wafd government, but he was fired again in Sidqi's regime and moved to Bayn al-Ganayin, to a private school owned by a known wafdist. During the

Haggar al-Minyawi

treaty government, he was appointed inspector in the Ministry of Education, and received a just settlement. In the 1942 elections, he ran on the Wafd platform and won, and again in 1950. I met him several times at Reda Hamada's house, and met some of his sons. When political parties were dissolved after the July revolution, he returned to his village in Upper Egypt and never left it again. I don't know if he's still alive or if he has passed on.

In September of either 1952 or 1953, walking in front of the old army club in Shatbi, I saw members of the Wafd in the club yard ringed by soldiers. I gathered from passers-by that they had been arrested and were being taken to Cairo. I spotted, among the officers supervising the operation, Muhammad Haggar, son of our old shaykh Haggar al-Minyawi. I contemplated the situation, looked long at the son, remembered the father, then imagined I was hearing the roaring of time, carrying its conflicting contradictions.

Widad Rushdi

I saw Widad Rushdi when she came to visit Camelia Zahran in the secretarial department one day in 1965. She was a giant, tall and wide, but graceful for her size. Her features were large but acceptable, beautiful in their position on the sprawling figure. She conveyed strength, beauty, and ease, like a statue. Her honey-colored eyes impressed with their unusual boldness. And she possessed an irresistible sexuality that penetrated like fragrant perfume. Every time I stole a glance, I found her looking at me, and my curiosity was aroused. I guessed she was thirty, her left hand told me she was married, and I wondered why she followed me with her eyes. My relationship with Amani Muhammad was at its prime, and I thought I knew the reason when she and Camelia walked over to my desk.

"Excuse us, Ustaz," Camelia said, "we'd like your opinion about a problem."

"At your service," I replied.

"My friend Widad Rushdi will tell you herself."

In a clear, loud voice that matched her size, Widad said, "Five years ago I earned my degree in Law, then I got married and didn't look for a job. Now my husband is in Kuwait for a year, and I'm thinking of employment. Can it be done through the Workforce department?"

"No," I replied, "but try your luck with a special request or reply to an announcement."

"Obviously, there's not much hope."

"I wouldn't say it's strong, but you should try."

"She has two children, and she still wants a job," Camelia said.

"All my friends are married and have jobs," Widad said.

"What about the children?" I asked.

"That won't be a problem," she replied.

"And your husband?"

"He agrees."

"Please help her in any way you can," Camelia said.

Widad put in her own recommendation. "We are neighbors from the old times!"

"Really?" I asked in amazement.

"You don't remember because I was little. That was twenty years ago, I was ten, then we left your neighborhood fifteen years ago when I was fifteen."

Widad Rushdi

"That's old history, but not that old. How is it that I don't remember you?"

"I remember you, Reda Hamada, Surour Abd al-Baqi, and Gaafar Khalil, may he rest in peace. Surour Abd al-Baqi is our favorite doctor. I still remember Gaafar Khalil's strange death."

"What memories!" I said affectionately.

"Do you see?" Camelia asked cunningly.

A week later, she phoned about the job, but I felt it was an excuse to talk. I wondered what this giant, beautiful, married woman wanted. I compared her with Amani Muhammad, and with Durriya. Passion flared, and from the dungeons of the past, invited Hanan Mustafa and Safaa al-Katib.

"Won't you be visiting Camelia again?" I asked.

"Would you like to see me?" she asked.

There was no escape but to say, "I'd be delighted."

"Why?" she asked in challenge.

"Seeing you is a pleasure," I stumbled.

She laughed. "Your department is crowded and stinks of paper."

I accepted the maneuver and forgot the consequences. "Then somewhere quiet."

"Do you like quiet places?"

"Very much."

"On one condition."

"Yes?"

"That you come with good intentions."

"Of course."

"Remember that."

"It's a promise."

"What's the quietest place for you?"

"The Fish Garden."

I found her waiting with no anxiety or shyness, as though she were waiting for her husband or brother. We strolled in the semi-wilderness, then sat at the foot of the hill.

"You must wonder about the brash woman who threw herself in your path with no finesse."

"Why wonder if I'm happy," I said, dancing with desire.

"Don't forget my condition!"

"I remember."

Seriously, she said, "You must understand that I'm a respectable woman and a faithful wife."

A little worried, I said, "No question about it, I can see that, and my reckless days were over before you left our neighborhood!"

"Please talk about that time with respect and affection."

"It has my love and respect forever."

She smiled with more daring than I'd seen. "I didn't meet you by accident."

"Really?"

"Camelia told me about her colleagues. When I heard your name . . . what shall I say? I decided to meet you."

"But you want a job!"

"It's not important."

"Don't leave me in the dark."

"I've known you for twenty years," she said, laughing with happiness.

"Yes…"

"I lived in the green building. Do you remember it?"

"In front of the fountain, on the main street!"

"But I was only ten, and you didn't notice me," she said reproachfully.

"We walked by, but we never stopped there, and the age of ten…"

"The age of ten is not noticed. Then I was thirteen, fourteen, and fifteen, and still you didn't notice…"

"Bad luck when it persists…"

"At the time, I thought the bad luck was mine."

I looked at her, embarrassed; she gazed back with a laughing, unrestrained, daring look.

"I tried the impossible to attract your attention, but never succeeded."

"What memories like fairy tales!"

"But they're real, and they live inside me, a disappointment with no remedy."

"You exaggerate," I said in confusion.

"Never! Every word in the world is nothing compared with the truth of that past."

I listened, satisfied and captivated but with no passion. With her incredible candor, she asked, "Is it true that first love never perishes?"

I thought of Hanan, and Safaa, and returned to my extinct heart. "A popular saying is never without an enduring truth," I said.

"It's a magical emotion, never to be repeated, and never be forgotten," she said passionately.

"What's the use?"

"None."

"But you're happily married."

"Yes," she replied sadly, "I won't deny that. But the eye wants what it lacks."

"Thus happiness is difficult wisdom."

"My husband is a perfect man, a model any woman would want, but he doesn't share my imagination. Sometimes I feel lonely, and my old failure bites me!" She laughed. "I have indigestion from happiness, but my soul is thirsty."

"How old's your husband?" I asked.

"Forty."

"You're in paradise! You've no right to dream!"

She frowned a little. "You're getting old. I bet you've never known love."

Where was Safaa? Was she still alive? If we met, could we have a conversation like this?

"Forgive me," she said, retreating a little. "Sometimes my frankness takes me beyond the bounds of decorum. But I expected you would respect my feelings."

"I do," I replied warmly, "from the bottom of my heart."

"Thank you," she said with emotion and gratitude. "I hope our contact continues. Would that bother you?"

"It would make me happier than you can imagine!"

"A spiritual contact that will not affect our respect for ourselves."

"A pure, charming suggestion that I accept happily."

"We'll meet on the phone, so we're not victims of something we don't deserve."

"As you wish."

"If longing overcomes me, we'll meet briefly."

"How wonderful to meet, even briefly."

Since that meeting, a new life opened its doors, and I entered, driven by affection, attachment to memories, and curiosity. I've lived her family ties and daily problems, her capacity for fatherhood, motherhood, and childhood, emotional and even sexual relationships, arguments, pleasures, diseases, dreams, and desires of every shape and color.

Widad is a dimension of my life no one knows about, an indivisible part of my being.

Yusriya Bashir

Return to childhood, to Bait al-Qadi Square and walnut trees with sparrows' nests. From a side window, as a little boy, I looked out on Qurmuz alley, a narrow, paved street that sloped downhill. On one corner stood the Bashir house. I was seven or eight, and I liked the sight of Shaykh Bashir, sitting in front of his house every afternoon with his prayer beads, his white skin, gray beard, and the bright colors of his turban, jubbah, and caftan illuminating the place.

When he walked toward Bait al-Qadi Square on his way to the Egyptian Club, Yusriya would appear in the window. She might have been sixteen, her face like the moon—white, cheerful, comfortable, and shining—crowned with black hair. She'd call my name in a soft voice and joke with me. I stared at her, happy, satisfied, amorous—if a boy of seven can be amorous. My attachment can only be love: she was neither a relative nor my age, and she never gave me a toy or a piece of candy, or extolled her beautiful face.

She sometimes tempted me to go to her. I'd sneak from the house into the alley, but the servant always caught me just at the right moment and carried me back inside, as I kicked and screamed to no avail. One day it rained. I stood by the window, watching the rain pour down the alley and flow like a river into the old drain. Soon the water level rose, and the street was awash. Qurmuz became a stagnant pond impossible to traverse except by porters or a cart. Through the pouring rain I saw Yusriya in the window beckoning me. I had an idea and decided to try it out immediately. I secretly climbed to the roof and carried a copper washing basin and a broom with a long wooden handle down to the street. I set the basin on the water, jumped in, and started punting with the broom toward the Bashir house. The servant realized, but it was too late: this time she couldn't brave the water, and she stood at the corner yelling but getting no reply. I disembarked from the basin at the door of the Bashir house (a stuffed crocodile hung over it) and went inside barefoot, my gallabiya soaking wet.

Yusriya met me at the top of the stairs. She led me into the room and sat me on a Turkish sofa in front of her, then played gently with my hair, as I glued my eyes to her luminous face. Despite the effort and wetness, I felt accomplishment and exultation in her hands.

She wanted to entertain me, so she took my palm and spread it.

"I'll read your fortune," she said.

She followed the lines on my palm and read the unknown, but I was absorbed in her beautiful face.

Yusriya Bashir